'A fascinating, dark and witty look at a world gone wrong.'

—Lou Sanders, comedian

'Bloody (and) brilliant. Prepare to be pulled into a world where dark comedy and high tension collide, driven by characters alive with hope and desire, greed and violence.'

—Phil Davies, playwright and screenwriter

'Michael Millar's writing is original, accomplished and entertaining. His characters are unique and memorable, and he's established a not-too-distant and credible dystopia with terrifying ease.'

—Bryony Sutherland, author of *Being Biracial: Where Our Secret Worlds Collide*

'Taut writing and sharp-edged tension. Millar is like a darkly humorous Kafka.'

—Jack Hayes, author of *When Eagles Burn*

TO THE DEAD ALREADY

ALSO BY MICHAEL MILLAR

TO THE DEAD ALREADY

Part Two of the Revenge of Jimmy Mac

MICHAEL MILLAR

First published in 2021 by whitefox

ISBN 978-1-913532-84-0

Also available as an ebook

ISBN 978-1-913532-85-7

Typeset by Jill Sawyer Phypers
Cover design by Jack Smyth
Project management by whitefox

Second time lucky, for those who danced with the General at dawn, dined at the end of the universe, found something nasty in the woodshed, and through it all cried 'What ho!'

I am not a man. I am more than a man. I must be. Man is subject to misfortune and the greater the man, the greater the misfortune. Even the masters, for all their genius, could not rise above this simple truth and it was their ruin. I know now that I cannot simply seek to emulate their work, I must elevate it. I must be more than a man.

And so we begin again.

For all its failings, the specimen's story thus far makes clear that I must find a way to overcome the paradox of discipline. The people still need oppression if they are to rejoice in being Good Citizens. And yet, the very requirement of discipline presupposes criticism and dissension. This must change. It renders the whole system unstable. It makes me a man. And so we begin again.

Over these weeks I have noticed a change in the specimen. There is a new eagerness to its activity. The sound of the typewriter carries clearly to me both day and night from the cell. Does this denote an acceptance of the inevitability of my victory? Of the futility of its struggle? Or is it simply a desire to finish the story and be spared the daily horror of the African sun and the heavy breath of the beasts as they circle in the freezing night?

I still believe that this specimen is special and that somewhere in these pages lies the key to my victory. The people have always bowed to something – something upon which they can bestow their reverence. First it was fire, and then it was religion, then technology. Now they will bow to me. They will bow with love in their hearts and their would-be saviour is the one who will hand me that victory. It is James Macfarlane, the Wolf of Badenoch, who will give me their minds.

CHAPTER 1

Oh Sweet, Oh Lovely Wall!

The number of people who wanted me dead was greater than normal and that went a long way to explaining why I was awake at such a despicable hour of the morning. In those days I had a rule that I should not be roused before the break of midday. If there were serious matters to attend to I would – under duress and with dark mutterings – emerge at the crack of ten. It was a mark then of how terribly out of hand everything had got that I found myself overseeing the packing of my suitcase at an hour that I will not dignify by naming.

I stood in the pre-dawn gloom, pondering my predicament and coveting a strong drink. On the face of it I was going on a business trip. Nothing special there, just part and parcel of being a world-renowned whisky distiller, dontcha know. But if you're familiar with my, ahem, situation, you'll know there was rather more to it than that. Firstly, I was very suspicious of the man I was going to meet, fellow distiller Hildebrand Blunt. This was partly due to him being English (how many of them do you see about these days?) but mainly because he had recently blasted me in the face with a 12-bore shotgun. Blunt had assured me it was an accident, and I hadn't been in a fit state to argue.

At that same event, a pheasant shoot held by the illustrious Lord and Lady Farquharson, I had been shanghaied into helping an obnoxious dissident, Professor Randolph Spring, escape my despotic homeland of Caledon. That whole exercise had only finished the previous evening and I was still periodically retching, partly due to all the seawater I'd swallowed and partly due to the creeping fear that the Mallice, our appalling (but admirably capable) secret police, were on my tail. Much to my surprise, they were yet to come knocking on the front door, bearing gifts of electric shock batons and screams in the dark. As such, common sense dictated they – and their ghastly leader Thomas 'the Headhunter' Loker – had yet to connect me with my insurgent alter ego, the Wolf of Badenoch. But I wasn't keen to hang around and find out. The last thing you want is a man who collects human skulls as a hobby on your tail. I had to get away. I needed time to think; time to restore order to my plans for chaos.

My sole comfort in the wee hours was the reassuringly large figure of Archie, my butler and Olympic-grade ruffian, who was agonising over my sartorial options. I didn't interrupt as, for a giant, scar-encrusted man who loves nothing more than beating people to a pulp, he takes his domestic duties very seriously.

As he finished up, I ventured to ask a favour.

'Archie?'

'Aye?'

'After a very trying night and this terribly early start, you don't think you—'

'Over oan the table,' he replied without even looking up.

I turned and saw the silver platter placed by the bed. Lord knows when he'd put it there. Resplendent upon it was one of Archie's signature pick-me-ups, 'The No. 2'. I've set down the ingredients elsewhere and shan't torture you by listing them again when you might lack ready access to brandy, milk, sugar, and all the rest (and, perhaps, the requisite antique soda syphon). Discreetly tucked out of the way behind the platter was a bottle of whisky with my *other* alter ego (how many is too many, you have to ask yourself). Jimmy Mac smiled laconically from the label, resplendent in full Highland soldier rig. I ignored Jimmy, who, for all his success at catapulting me to international stardom, could take a back seat for now. No, this wasn't the kind of easy-going morning that called for whisky. It called for something special if I was to make it to elevenses intact.

I marched over to the table and mixed up my breakfast. The idea of asking (yet again) what 'The No.1' might be didn't even occur to me and Archie's answer would have been the same anyway: 'Jist pray yeh never need it.'

I raised the mixture and offered the soldier's lament. 'A cup to the dead already.'

'And hooray fer the next tae die,' Archie replied, bobbing his head in respect.

The concoction burned its way through my digestive system and gave me the courage to deliver bad news. Archie was very upset to learn he wasn't joining the trip to London. (Not because he was scared for himself – he fears nothing – he just didn't trust me to look after myself.)

'D'ye think ah'm buttoned up the back?' he demanded, which was his colourful way of asking if I was treating him like a fool.

'Look,' I said, 'if something goes wrong then there's a strong chance it'll happen at The Wall. If that's the case, then you know there's no fighting our way out of it. All that will happen is we'll both be up the Swanee.'

'Up the whit?'

'Never mind. Look, as I was saying, if they make a move on me, I'm going to need you on the outside to tidy up any mess and then have a bloody good go at rescuing me.' I paused. 'In fact, rescue first, worry about the mess later.'

Archie nodded at me, accepting the logic. But he remained grumpy throughout the short time until we set off. I could tell this by the way he brought my snack of smoked salmon on triangles rather than squares of bread. It was white bread too, the animal. He truly is a man of violence.

Before we left Glenlairig (that's my home), I called on Archie and Wally to join me in the loo (and before your mind goes to naughty places, you animal, I had a secret lair under the floor). My distillery's head of security came shambling in, looking nothing like the terrifyingly dangerous hacker he was. They stood next to each other and, for once, didn't instantly begin their good-natured bickering. Normally such behaviour would prompt me to demand what was going on and threaten them with early bedtime, but looking at them there – Archie ramrod straight and Wally looking as if he'd arrived via a peat bog – made me as proud of them as I'd been when we'd served together and done all that silly stuff, running around, kicking in doors and hiding in dark places.

Their combined talents meant I could worry about myself in peace, since the chance of Loker's goons catching the two of them was almost zero. My boys would know the Mallice were coming before they knew it themselves.

'Wally, how are we looking?' I asked, kicking off our subterranean council of war.

'You're all good to go,' he replied, bright eyes moving rapidly from me to Archie and back again. 'Your Citizen Credit Score is intact so there's no barriers to travel or anything like that.'

'And the, err, other business?' Even in our pit, dug deep under the house, I hesitated to utter the name of the Wolf, lest the walls have ears.

'It's all kicking off, no doubt,' he said, the look of childish glee I knew so well spreading across his face.

'What does that mean?'

'The regime is going gangbusters trying to control the narrative and shut down chat about the Wolf of Badenoch saving Professor Spring.'

It had been impossible for anyone to miss this, what with Wally plastering our logo – a laughing wolf's head in a buckled circle like

4

the crest of a Highland clan – all over CaledoNet (only people like Wally had access to the complete, World Wide version of the internet nowadays).

'Anything we need to worry about?'

'Nothing I'm picking up at the moment. Lizzy Burke is doing quite a job leading the anti-Wolf brigade.'

The mention of Lizzy's name made my heart beat a bit faster. Caledon's legendary Confluencer – sitting at the intersection of media, politics, and every other area of influence you could think of – was a key intelligence asset for the Wolf of Badenoch. Why she took the risk continued to baffle me, but I suspected she did it simply because she could. On the flip side, she was the obvious pick to lead the regime's media blitz against the Wolf. Also helpful.

'They're calling you a straight-up terrorist now, no mincing their words anymore,' said Wally. 'What d'you think about that?'

'If I'm honest, Wally, it doesn't sit that easily,' I replied. 'Then again, I haven't been a terrorist for long and I suppose it might grow on me.'

'So we don't need to say anything to Miss Burke?'

'Oh God, no. Leave her to it. But do keep channels open with her in case she hears of any developments. Anything else?'

'No, sir.'

'Don't call me that, Wally, we're not in the army anymore, for Christ's sake.'

'Sorry, Mr Mac.'

'Alright, lads, it's that time again. Go silent.'

'Leave no shadow,' they answered in unison, completing our mantra.

I gave each a small nod.

'Aye?' rumbled Archie.

'Aye,' murmured Wally.

'Time to hunt,' I replied quietly.

Wally was still standing in the doorway of the house as we pulled away. His face was studied and grim, like a child watching its parents leave and wondering if they will ever come back. Archie guided the car over the gravel of the drive and down towards the road. We were on our way. Towards the border. Towards The Wall.

The Wall is the ultimate expression of the Marischal's iron grip on our lives. It was built at a time when erecting such edifices was all the rage. Got a troublesome neighbour? Build a wall. Want to keep unwanted immigrants out? Build a wall. Want to keep an uncooperative population *in*? Build. A. Wall.

I turned the gold bracelet nervously on my wrist. On it were the names of family members I held responsible for asset stripping my dear granny and sending her to an early grave. I thought happy thoughts of taking my revenge on them when I wasn't quite so busy toppling a despotic government. But no matter how many times I turned the bracelet, The Wall and its horrors kept returning.

The physical and metaphorical value that a great big bloody wall offers a despot should not be underestimated. It is different to, say, countries throwing up the firewalls that divided the once ubiquitous internet into rigid national territories. Giving us CaledoNet changed our lives and controlled what we could see and learn and buy. For them it was – and remains – a powerful but practical tool to measure, monitor, and shape behaviour. But for us it quickly became a part of day-to-day life. The Wall is different. There is no subtlety to it. No sense of integration. It is a visceral scar on the landscape. A constant reminder of the obstacles you face if you want to mess with the regime. It is not just tyranny being done; it is tyranny being seen to be done.

Our wall (for there are of course many like it elsewhere in the world) runs coast to coast, a few miles north of the border. It doesn't match the border exactly, due to arguments with England about its construction. They didn't want this monstrosity hard against their land, understandably. A compromise was reached when the Caledon government realised that pulling The Wall back would mean it could locate its air and rail transport hubs in the strip of land left between wall and border, ensuring rigorous vetting of people before they came into or left the country.

That land, once called the Borders, is now known as the Newmarch. Outside of the airport and central train station it is a lawless place: a demilitarised zone where criminal gangs known as Reivers rule the roost. They are smugglers and bandits, and England is always complaining that the Caledon government is complicit in their forays south of the border. Of course, the Marischal denies this, but either way, it costs England considerable time, effort, and cash to keep an eye on the place.

I've always wondered if the designers and architects of The Wall had intended it to be in such violent contrast to the land around it. Did they want to lull you into a false sense of security as you wound your way south, enjoying the greens and browns and yellows of the Lowland fields, the undulating hills and the deep green woodlands, before this fearsome beast reared up in front of you? Because that's what happens and it gets you every time.

As our car pulled up in front of the departure checkpoint, I stared up at the towering behemoth and felt very small. The gargantuan dark grey wall towered over us. Watching us. Judging us. Over a hundred and thirty feet of huge concrete slabs rose up and cast a cold, malevolent shadow over everyone who approached. It stretched as far as the eye could see to both east and west, dominating the landscape like a giant tsunami waiting to crash down and wipe us away in its fury.

Hundreds of eyes stared down from the unforgiving grey face as cameras swivelled in perpetual surveillance. Keepers – the guards patrolling the walkways that criss-crossed the structure – kept watch to make sure the animals stayed in the zoo.

Far off to the right I saw a black cloud of birds rise from the top of The Wall and wing their way south, raising the question that bothered me every time I arrived there: how do they keep it clean of bird shit? Just one of life's many mysteries.

'Remember: rescue first, tidy up second,' I said quietly, keen to ensure Archie had his priorities straight.

'Guid luck, sir.'

'For the umpteenth time, Archie, enough of the *sir*.' These old titles bothered me, partly because they belonged to the old days, but mainly because Archie and Wally only tended to call me 'sir' when they were worried about me.

'Aye, sorry, Mr Mac. See yeh when yeh get back. Bring me a present, eh?'

'Look after Wally, will you? Try to stop him getting into trouble.'

'Aye, ah will. Go silent, eh?'

'Leave no shadow,' I replied, gripping the arm he had extended.

We shook hands and kept eye contact just a little too long, confirming Archie's suspicions that I was not safe in my own hands. I desperately wanted to look back as I made the short walk to the departure terminal. But I knew I mustn't.

Processing began immediately. I was funnelled into one of many thin white corridors, lit by harsh strip lights embedded in the ceiling. The path was barely wide enough for two people to walk abreast, and curved so you couldn't see more than a few metres ahead. Silver mirrored windows interrupted the sterile whiteness at regular intervals. Whether anyone was actually behind them made no difference; the glass was enough. It showed you the reflection of a guilty person. The whole set-up works a treat, I can tell you. You can enter those corridors with a head stuffed with naught but unicorns and rainbows, and still reach the control desks a guilt-ridden wreck. Which is entirely the point.

I fell back on the 'positive visualisation' skills I'd been taught in army leadership seminars. Like almost all psychological techniques and theories, this suffers from sounding like pretentious toss, but at that moment it really worked. Breathing slowly, I made a clear and powerful picture in my mind of what I wanted to achieve (in this case, breezing through security without being murdered), and then replayed it over and over. The idea is that what you 'see' yourself as on the inside is what you will *be* on the outside. As they say, 'perception is reality'. Give it a go the next time you're marching towards possible arrest and appalling suffering under The Question (that quaint term Loker and the Mallice had adopted for torture). It'll make all the difference, I assure you.

Unfortunately, this trick is much more difficult to perform if the people in front of you are doing exactly the opposite. A young woman and a little boy, perhaps six years old, were shuffling forwards in the queue, which was snaking through the thin white corridors at an excruciatingly slow pace. The kid was immaculate in his jumper and trousers, hair parted fastidiously to one side. He was fidgeting, complaining about the wait, asking for food, then demanding to play games. For her part, his mother was sweating and glancing nervously from side to side, only stopping to stare dead ahead when we passed one of the mirrored observation windows. Eventually his needling made her snap.

'Blair, please, just stand still and be quiet,' said the mother in a desperate whisper. 'It's really important, darling.'

'But I'm bored. And I'm hot, and—'

'Don't worry, wee one, we'll be out of here soon.'

The mother was already speaking too loudly. Already giving herself away.

'But I don't want to go. Ow, you're hurting my arm!'

'I'm sorry, darling. I didn't mean it. But Grandpa's very ill and we need to visit him. We'll only be gone a couple of days.'

'So why was Grandma so sad when we—'

'She was just sorry to see us go. She's always like that when we go . . . go on holiday.'

'No she isn't.'

'Yes, she *is*, darling.' The mother's breathing was fast and shallow now. 'Please, just stand quietly with Mummy and everything will be fine, I promise. But it's really super-important that we just . . . that we just wait quietly. Our turn is coming. We'll be through soon. We'll be out . . . outside . . . in the terminal, and then we can get awa— get on the plane.' She hugged the child to her side and kissed his head, before starting forward once again. 'It'll all be over soon. I promise.'

I found myself shuffling almost to a standstill, letting a gap open up between the mother, child, and myself. I was nervously turning the golden bracelet again. I wanted to scream at her *Play it cool, for God's sake! You're burying yourself!* She turned and caught my eye and what she saw there scared her even more. Her face was frozen in mute appeal; pleading silently for salvation. I had none to offer. This was no place for heroes. All I could do to try and save her from herself was to look at the floor, where my feet were now planted, leaving her and the wee son alone and exposed in front of me.

They let the charade play out for a short time longer. Just to be sure, I suppose. Then they appeared. Doors on either side of the curving corridor opened silently. I marvelled at how well hidden they were, and at the pure black of the rectangles of darkness that stood behind them, contrasting violently with the white of the walls. From each of these voids two Keepers in their grey uniforms and caps emerged to stand in front and behind the woman and her child.

'Madam, please come with us,' said the one now stood at her elbow.

'I d-don't understand?' the mother stammered. 'W-what do you want? We haven't done anything.'

'Please come with us,' the Keeper said, repeating his quiet command.

'But we have all the d-documentation and visas. We are cleared for travel. We are visiting a sick relative—' She was babbling; panicking now.

'We will establish all of that. Now, please come with us; you are inconveniencing the other travellers.'

She looked in desperation at those around her, as if they would somehow offer help, support, or perhaps some kind of affirmation of her circumstances. She caught my eye again. I looked away. We all do it.

'Madam, come *now*, please, and we can clear this up.'

The mother's shoulders slumped as the desperate hope that they would somehow be swayed by her explanation was extinguished. She was putting all her faith – betting her future – on the Keeper's promise that it would all be 'cleared up'. The Keeper had offered her hope and she had to cling to that and not make things worse, just as he had intended.

The mother turned and put a hand out to take the child's hand.

'OK, Blair, we need to go with this gentleman,' she began. 'Don't worry, everything—'

Then she stopped, because his hand wasn't there to take. The boy was now stood between two Keepers who had appeared from the wall on the other side of the corridor.

'What's going on? Blair, come to Mummy . . .'

The child tried to move but the Keepers held him tight and pulled him back towards the darkness of the doorway. One looked my way as he took the boy, challenging me to step in.

'Mummy, I can't. Mummy, I'm scared,' Blair said in a small voice.

'Oh God,' the mother said. 'Please don't take him away from me.'

'Madam—'

'Don't take him away! Oh God. Blair, it's OK, don't be scared. Please, sir—'

'Mummy!' the boy screamed as he was lifted up and back into the black doorway.

'Blair! Oh God, please, no!' the mother shrieked as she was carried into the opposite void.

I heard their cries and pleas in stereo, loud in the darkness before the doors slid shut and extinguished them. The only evidence they had ever been there was the white space mother and son had occupied seconds earlier. I stepped into it fearfully, waiting for the doors to open again to swallow me. They didn't.

The next set did, though.

Suddenly, Keepers were either side of me and politely requesting that 'Sir comes with us'. It was the same men who just moments previously had taken the mother and child. Already back in their posts. Already the victims had been handed on, down the chain, deeper into the dark.

I had barely even considered arguing when I stepped with them into the twilight. Then all was black as the doors sealed us off from the light. How they saw their way down the cloying darkness of that pitch-black corridor is beyond me. I guess some kind of night-vision lenses, but I don't know. Aside from our light footsteps and the rustling of their uniforms, it was almost totally silent. I tried to gauge the width of the tunnel but it was impossible. The bracelet moved faster and faster around my wrist as I turned it with mounting alarm. The walls could have been inches away or metres. The longer we were in there, the more I began to fear someone turning on a torch or striking a match to reveal some nameless horror leaping out at us from the darkness. Unholy visions filled my head of what lay just out of view, behind the impenetrable black curtain.

With firm hands at my elbows we walked straight and wordlessly, before turning right, then left, then right again. I forced myself to breathe slowly and deeply to calm my brain and flood it with oxygen, so I would be ready for whatever came next. Ready to fight.

A door in front of us slid open and the corridor erupted into light. Dazzled, I covered my eyes with a hand. There was noise, too – lots of noise – which assailed my ears after the stillness of the tunnel. My heart banged hard against my chest and sweat broke out on my forehead. My cheek started to twitch as adrenaline rushed through my body, preparing me for whatever terror was to be unleashed. I lowered my hand and squinted into the light. Then I un-balled my fists. We were in the terminal. All around us people were bustling around, endeavouring to be busy and unobtrusive, shopping at tax-free outlets, and trying to relax after enduring Processing.

'There you are, sir,' said the Keeper on my right arm. 'Thought I'd recognised you, Mr Macfarlane. Couldn't have you waiting in the queue with everyone else, could we?'

He was smiling now, this man who had just meted out terror to a mother and her small child. He extended a hand for me to shake. I stared at it in confusion, slowly raising mine to take it.

'Captain Gillain,' he said, pumping my hand hard in his. 'I'll take you straight to the executive lounge, but before, do you think I . . .' Then he stammered and, God have mercy, went red in the cheeks. 'Could I, you know . . . Could I get an autograph? All the others in the division would be so jealous.'

I looked at this purveyor of panic in disbelief. I wanted to ask how he could disassociate himself so quickly from what he'd just done. How could he go from separating a screaming, begging child from his mother, to being coy about asking for my autograph? As he stood there, I made a note of his face. I promised myself that one day, somehow, I would repay this man's cruelty and callousness.

As I stared at him, Gillain held out a tablet and stylo. Then anger began pulsing through me. Screw him and his autograph! Different versions of what I would say before I jammed the stylo into his eye coursed through my mind. With one deep breath, I made my decision.

'Of course you can have my autograph,' I said.

Then I posed for a selfie.

I imagine you would have done things differently. But there we are.

CHAPTER 2

Flights and Fancy

My flight was ruined before we'd even got into the air when I accidentally fell into conversation with the man next to me. It was my own fault. I normally shun all contact with fellow travellers. I'm not a backpacker, for Christ's sake. But, having had quite the scare during Processing, I was thirstier than a camel in a sweater. Once ensconced in the executive lounge by Captain Gillain – who kindly took time out of his busy schedule of Imposing the Unforgiving Will of a Brutal Regime on Innocents to make me comfortable – I proceeded to remedy the situation.

I settled on the prescription offered by Scottish doctors throughout the ages, whenever confronted by a patient with a case of Unwanted Memories. This miracle cure is known as the 'hauf an' a hauf'. It is simply a glass of whisky followed by a half-pint of beer as a chaser. It's a virtuous circle in which the whisky prepares the palate for the beer, after which the latter then kindly prepares the palate for the former. Did I say virtuous circle? I meant vicious.

The whisky was out of one of my bottles, The Rare Reserve, from a line we created for airport travellers who didn't know what was good for them or how much they should be paying (*Colour:* light amber. *Flavour:* rich, honeyed. *Finish:* balanced). Jimmy Mac smiled at me from the bottle with all the bravado for which he (and hence I) was so well known. It's funny how easy it is to sell a lie.

With Jimmy's help I was soon well on my way to being cured of any pesky recollections of terror, claustrophobia, and the appalling nature of the human condition. By the time I settled into my seat on the plane and we'd begun the short hop to London (where I had decided I would steal Hildebrand Blunt's business ideas), I was comfortable and snug. Yes, Blunt had shot me in the face, but (I reasoned drunkenly) this time *I* was hurtling towards *him* at several hundred miles an hour and would do as much damage as I possibly could – if not more. The shoe was on the other foot. The cartridge was in the other barrel. The snail was upon the thorn. I felt safe for the first time in weeks. I was drunk and I was feeling chatty, fool that I was.

I got talking to an overweight and half-shaven sales manager. His name was Tony, but given his strange patois, which I correctly guessed hailed from Yorkshire, it might just as easily have been 'Terneh'. He wasn't keen to talk to start with, but my incessant charm and unwillingness to stop asking questions won him over. It turned out he had been up doing a deal in Caledon for a speciality drill bit for the oil industry.

'Aye,' Terneh affirmed. 'It's great you guys are still so into your black stuff.'

At least, I think that's what he said – I'm translating here. I quizzed him energetically, nodding vigorously or solemnly as we went, based largely on his intonation. He went on to talk about the evil plague that was electric cars and the horror of wind, wave, or any other power Mother Nature had a hand in.

'Yes, all these do-gooders have no idea about the importance of energy security,' he moaned. The longer he went on, the more predictable he became and the more predictable he became, the more worried I became. Was it just drunken paranoia? Or was there something slightly wrong about Terneh? It was time to test a theory.

'What's taking you to London, Terneh? Sorry, I mean Tony.'

'More meetings. Boring stuff.'

'Boring stoof? Oh, I see, stuff. Gotcha. Do you like it there?'

'Aye, ah do.'

'Not a patch on Yorkshire though, I expect?'

'Oh, I wouldn't say that.'

I sat back, a feeling of despair settling over me. I had no more questions. I closed my eyes and wondered who Terneh really worked for. It hadn't been a great performance, really. But then I am a judgemental drunk. I'd been on to him almost from the start. His answers had been too staged, too obvious. As if he was reading from a script. The answer about London had sealed the deal, as I had hoped and dreaded it would.

If you have ever had the good fortune of spending time with a Yorkshireman – which I had on a number of sales conferences that I won't bore you with and which I certainly never expected to teach me lessons in spycraft – you will know there isn't a single one who doesn't think of his corner of England as God's own county. They'll tell you the tea tastes superior, the roses smell sweeter (well, the white ones, anyway), and a pint of their ale is better preparation for a fight – the hallmark of any successful English night out – than any other. But you will never, *ever* find one who will make favourable comparisons between London and Yorkshire.

Terneh wasn't who he said he was, that much seemed clear. The question was, who *did* he work for? The Mallice? The English government? Was it Hildy's people spying on me as I tried to spy on them? Surely the Farquharsons and their goddamned Underground Railroad weren't planning to ensnare me in another crackpot scheme, were they? My ungovernable imagination was, yet again, running amok, taking me down all sorts of rabbit holes, each of which ended in visions of my own horrible demise. Through the haze, Common Sense, who had been absent for some time, reminded me there was still a chance I was just being a paranoid drunk. It was impossible to tell, so I drank some more and left Terneh to his own thoughts, which that other villain Pride said were probably about me.

When we landed, barely an hour later, Terneh did his best to ignore me, playing the grumpy Northerner card. Perhaps I had done him a disservice. Maybe he was from Yorkshire after all.

My fears were temporarily forgotten as I went through customs, an experience that was deliriously exciting by virtue of its monotony. I revelled in the long queues of different nationalities, the cornucopia of people in this wide, well-lit room. No one threatened to assault or kill me. Not even once.

It reminded me what a big world there was beyond The Wall. It's so easy to forget. You could spot the other travelling Caledonians in the crowd, who were staring around in something of a daze, just as I was. They were also suffering that curious fear – akin to agoraphobia, I suppose – the fear of having the space and freedom to move. When a nation hugs you so close to its bony bosom – when it marshals your daily life so attentively – suddenly being set adrift feels uncomfortable, like a battery chicken being promoted to free range. I looked around hopefully for the mother and child. They weren't there.

I followed instructions sent to me by Blunt's people, all too late realising that they required taking the Underground rail line. (Public transport, *moi*?) The note apologised for the lack of ceremony and stressed that discretion was the order of the day, lest rival businesses got wind of my presence.

Garish yellow signs led me to the Tube – the sprawling underground network that serves London. It was hellish. Every stop we passed more people got on and fewer people got off. I had never seen, felt – or indeed smelled – anything like it.

When I finally emerged from the subterranean journey, I was pretty much sick of the city already. Even the imposing Georgian architecture of the St James's district, looking down on us with a paternal air, failed to move my stony heart. Christmas decorations hung across the street, as cars, taxis, and red buses shunted past, caught in the massive web of traffic. The air was cold and crisp.

As a rule, I steered clear of cities. More than anywhere, cities made me feel caged. The air felt to me thick with an invisible fog of data. In cities I could almost feel the billions of ones and zeros that watched, categorised, and judged as they wrapped themselves round and flowed through me. I shuddered, involuntarily rubbing a hand across my chest in a bid to cleanse myself of the miasma. In the countryside I could pretend I wasn't drenched in data; that I was alone. Visions of one of Wally's lectures on data security filled my mind. He talked about little else.

A strong hand gripped my shoulder and I spun on my heel. Hildebrand Blunt was lucky not to get his nose broken.

'Goddammit it, Blunt.'

'Oh, no need to be so formal. Look, I know what you're thinking: this is London, right?' he said brightly, an arm gesturing towards the vehicular mire that covered the road. 'One of the great cities of the world. What a bloody mess, eh? Well, you're right, but being a great city means a *lot* of people – we're over eleven million now, you know – and the roads haven't been upgraded in forty years. And that means jams today and jams tomorrow, eh?'

Whatever this meant, it was lost on me.

'They're always trying to sort it out,' he said apologetically, eyeing the dawdling vehicles. 'But you know what it's like: death by committee.'

'Yes, we have that too,' I answered, my heart still racing. 'It just means something a little different.'

'Yes, I imagine it does,' he said sympathetically. 'Anyway, welcome nonetheless. Let's make time, shall we? I've got a surprise for you.' He marched off into the heavy pedestrian flow, winding his way through the crowds with practised ease.

But I wasn't going anywhere. I was staring across the road to where I could swear I had just seen a man I knew. A man who bore a striking resemblance to an overweight salesman by the name of

Terneh. Was it my mind playing tricks? I stared some more. The crowds parted and there he stood. Our eyes met and a look of shock crossed his face. With huge willpower I didn't look away, instead pretending to admire the Georgian splendour of the hotel behind him, trying to sow doubt in his mind about whether I'd seen him or not.

Hildy was still marching away when I called after him. 'Mr Blunt!'

'Please call me Hildebrand, or Hildy; that's what my friends call me,' he said, as he strode back to my side.

'OK, Hildebrand. Just one question for you: have you visited Yorkshire before?'

'Excuse me?'

'I have recently made a friend from Yorkshire; his name is Tony. Well, *Terneh*, if you're going to be a purist about it. Just wondered if you knew him.'

There was the briefest of pauses.

'Aha!' His eyes lit up. 'Is this like when I ask you if you know Jock McTavish, because we presume you all know each other in Caledon?'

'What? Er, yes, sorry, I suppose so,' I replied weakly, no wiser as to any relationship between them. 'Forget I said anything. It's been a long day.'

'It's 11 a.m.'

'Oh God, is it? I shouldn't even be up yet, you know.'

'Totally understand, old boy,' he said, although the look on his face made it clear he did not. I got the feeling Blunt was an early riser. 'Anyway, look, I promised you a treat, didn't I?'

I didn't want a treat. I wanted to be rid of Terneh. I wanted to lie down somewhere dark. The sunlight was playing havoc with my burgeoning hangover.

'I'm quite tired, actually, Hildy. Can we go to my hotel, please?'

'Oh, no!' he replied. 'Don't you worry, this won't take long.'

'Let me rephrase it for you, Hildy. I *am* going to my hotel. Where I will freshen up – and by that, I mean fill a large glass with whatever passes for strong drink down here. Then I may venture forth. Indeed, I may even venture forth with you in tow. But right now, I want to go to my hotel.'

Blunt stared at me. After a few seconds he spread his arms in supplication, a look of worry crossing his face. 'Look, James, I've got you an appointment with a very important person and if we miss it, I don't know when we'll get another. It will reflect badly on me if we don't go.'

'I meet very important people all the time, Hildy, what's another to me? If he or she wants to meet me, he or she can bloody well wait.'

Hildy's eyes narrowed. 'OK. Understood. My fault, of course. Wrong of me to be so presumptive. Let's go to your hotel. I'll hail a cab.'

This sudden volte-face made me uncomfortable. If he wanted us to get a cab, then that was the last thing we were going to do. Terneh would probably be bloody driving it.

'Oh, Christ no, look at the traffic. Can we walk?' I didn't give him time to answer.

My main objective right now, aside from finding ways to tame my hangover, was to disrupt other people's best-laid plans as much as possible. I went into counter-surveillance mode. Hildy gave directions but I never took the road turnings he said, urging him on to different landmarks in which I feigned interest. I took us on diversions into wide-open areas with little cover so I could draw any pursuers out, followed by sudden detours into busy areas so I might lose any unwanted shadows. And, because I'm a philanthropist, I thought the walk would do Terneh some good. Or give him a heart attack. Either would do.

During that short but circuitous journey, Hildy seemed to take my erratic rambling in his stride. Perhaps it was his lack of concern, or the seeming absence of Terneh; perhaps it was the concerted efforts not to bring up either half of my hauf an' a hauf; whatever it was, I found myself lulled into a false sense of security. On top of it all, London exuded a tremendous energy that was intoxicating. It was so different to the air of sombre mystery that hung over my home cities in those days. People were scurrying here and there, with places to go and momentous things to achieve, all lost in their own worlds. I peered at them as they passed, wondering if they had the retinal implants that I knew had long since supplanted our own medieval aug-specs. No one even noticed.

Many were speaking, as if to no one. Then they would touch a spot beneath their ear to switch off the cochlear implant, hurrying on their way as they dipped in and out of the digital world. (Old hat no doubt to you, wherever you are, but subdermal GPS trackers never really took off in Caledon, what with its unrepentant surveillance state and all that.) I noticed the smallest things as we walked, such as the way the windows were thrown open: casements staring out and welcoming the world, so unlike the streets of closed curtains at home, which were more like narrowed eyelids suspiciously surveying those on all sides. Yes, London was a place of wonders, to be sure.

Coming out of my reverie, I realised Hildy himself was talking, as if to no one.

'Well, use a van,' I heard him say in an agitated tone. 'What do you mean there aren't any? Oh, for God's sake, send a car then. And hurry up about it.' He saw me looking at him and tapped that spot under his ear. 'Sorry, old boy. Delivery problems at the distillery. I'm sure you know how it goes?'

'Indeed, I do.'

On we walked, with me continuing to lead us left and right like a wide-eyed tourist through a warren of streets until I was sure we were walking alone. I sensed Hildy becoming increasingly tense as we walked along. He clenched and unclenched his jaw. His fingers danced by his side, as if miming playing a piano on his hip. His eyes were darting about, rarely resting on any one thing for more than a second. My unease about his identity and what he really wanted grew stronger. I found myself clenching and unclenching my fists involuntarily. Then Hildy stopped and turned to face me, a look of concern on his face.

'It's a bit awkward, James, but I was wondering. Well, you see . . . Oh God, how to . . .'

'Spit it out,' I said warily, wondering what would be the latest line spun in the growing web of deceit. Whatever I'd have guessed, I would have been wrong.

'Lizzy. It's about Lizzy,' he stammered. I could swear he was panting.

'Lizzy?' I managed, eyebrows arched in surprise.

'Yes, yes, Lizzy Burke. Have you talked to her since Invereiton?'

Well, this was a development I hadn't expected. What could Blunt want with Lizzy? I knew she had been his chaperone – and God knows what else – at the Farquharsons' shoot. In truth, I hadn't talked to her and, truth be told, was still furious about the role she'd played in forcing me into rescuing Professor Spring. I had no plans to make contact whatsoever – at least until my vile libido got the better of me. So, another day or two, at least.

'Yes,' I lied, 'spoke to her yesterday.'

'Did she, er, well, what I mean is . . . um, did she mention me?'

Well, well, well. What have we here?

Before he said another word, I knew what was on the cards. This always happened with Lizzy, particularly when she encountered fine, upstanding lads like Hildebrand Blunt who got up too early in the morning. Men who had been raised on a diet of fresh air, cold baths, and 'God Save the Queen'. She had a special talent for turning such men – brave as they no doubt were in the face of all sorts of dangers – into quivering wrecks.

'Oh yes, she's quite the fan of yours,' I lied again, pulling Blunt into my own personal web. 'Told me to send you her love when I saw you.'

A smile spread across Hildebrand's face and he nodded, full of all sorts of innocent joys that a scoundrel like me can't fathom. We walked on in silence and, while my hangover grew ever stronger, Hildy had a new-found spring in his step. A grin played around the edges of his mouth and it wouldn't go away. This much was clear: Hildebrand Blunt was in love. The stupid bloody fool. But it was hardly surprising. Lizzy Burke's charms were stealthy, subtle, invisible, and overpowering. Just like bubonic plague.

We turned down a quiet side street, moving further away from the crowds, and I started plotting how to use his boyish crush to my advantage, whether it be for business, espionage, or whatever the hell Hildebrand Blunt was mixed up in. But I didn't have time to develop these plans further, did I? Of course I bloody didn't. No one gave me enough time to plot and scheme properly anymore. At that moment a large dark car pulled up sharply next to us. I spun to face it as the doors flew open and men in black combat gear and balaclavas spilled out. In seconds they were on me, pinioning my arms behind my back and driving me towards the rear. I turned my imploring face to Hildy's.

'I'm so sorry about this, old boy,' was all he said.

They pulled open the boot and tumbled me inside, where my spine crashed against some unknown detritus that left me gasping. Then the boot slammed shut and the car moved on, back into a disinterested sea of humanity.

CHAPTER 3

Tired of London, Tiring of Life

And so I missed out on many of the things that make London great – the ancient landmarks, the green parks, the crowds of excited tourists, the angry taxi drivers – as I lay alone and in the dark, with an ache in my back and bile creeping up my throat, threatening to turn the boot into a charnel house.

It wasn't long until I felt the car mount the kerb with a bump and come to a stop. I cursed my captors for the umpteenth time and made ready to explode out of the boot with maximum prejudice, as my training dictated. From outside I could hear a muffled noise. It sounded like chanting.

The boot was wrenched open and I was bathed in bright light. I leapt up in an explosive and prejudicial sort of way, caught my leg on some detritus and fell out onto the road. I lay there groaning and swallowing hard to keep the vomit down, all the while making silent promises about abstinence that I would surely not keep.

Waves of noise crashed over me. Yells, chants, and even songs. There were colourful placards and banners. All the focus seemed to be on a large black gate. The pounding in my head grew stronger.

'Quickly, old boy!' Hildy yelled over the din, grasping my arm in a friendly but insistent way and yanking me upwards. My assailants were now dressed as civilians and had formed a ring, screening my untidy exit from the car.

'What the hell's going on?' I gasped, blinded by the light, nauseous, and now half-deafened by the rabble.

'A demonstration. Not sure what about,' Hildy said. 'Quick, let's get you inside.'

'A demonstration? What are you talking about?'

'You know, against something the government has done. They're protesting.'

'They're protesting against the government?' I was amazed. 'Why aren't the police wading in?'

'What do you mean?' he said, puzzled, still pulling at my forearm.

'You mean they're *allowed* to do this?' I burbled in astonishment. 'And no one is going to, you know, drag them away, subject them to The Question, and pack them off for reconditioning?'

'Of course not!' He looked horrified, and then his look softened. 'It's all a bit different down here.'

I marvelled at this strange practice of 'demonstrating'. In so doing, I clean forgot about the golden rule of any kidnapping – don't let them get you to the first stop – as Hildy and his henchmen bustled me off the road and through a doorway.

Inside it was quiet and cool. We were in a long corridor, full of ornate stonework and large worn flagstones. I gathered my battered senses and rounded on Blunt.

'Right, you bastard, what the bloody hell is going on? If you don't explain yourself right now, I will strangle you with your tie – or at the very least be violently sick on your nice shiny shoes.'

He eyed me placidly. 'I am sorry about your treatment, I truly am. But, as I said, there is a meeting that we simply can't miss. Oh, and one more thing – and I can't stress this enough – please don't try anything, as it will be pointless and it will end badly for you.'

His level gaze was convincing. So were the men with big muscles and sensible haircuts who were guarding the door we'd just clattered through. My head was pounding. I had no idea what to do, no idea where I was, and even less of a sense of who or what Hildebrand Blunt was.

'After you, please,' Hildy said, extending an arm down the corridor. I scowled in return but, shorn of any other viable options, started walking. Our steps echoed on the flagstones, the noise bouncing off the thick stone walls. It felt like being in a castle. I looked round apprehensively. Lead-cased windows were set into the ornate stonework. The place looked ancient, but as I cast my eyes to the ceiling, I spotted a host of tiny black glass domes placed at regular intervals along the vaulted grey stone. They looked like an infestation of well-ordered arachnids and betrayed the bevy of security cameras that was watching our every move.

We approached an imposing oak door and I automatically focused on the entry procedure. What kind of entry pass would be used? Could I somehow steal it? What kind of keypad? What was the code? Synapses in the Macfarlane brain fired with an incendiary fervour.

The door swung open automatically, revealing a plush and important-looking corridor. I sagged slightly. Being outfoxed by a door felt like a new low. Hildy clocked my confusion at the lack of security straight away. He was sharp, that one; I'll say that for him. Granted, he can roast in hell for everything he did, but credit where credit's due.

'Retinal scanners – the key is not to look down when you're approaching, otherwise they'll not register who you are,' he said jauntily. 'I'd pay a pretty penny to sit in the control room and watch as all those civil servants, their noses stuck in old files, walk headfirst into the door. Happens all the time.'

'But, but,' I stammered, 'I could have a gun to your back and you've just let me in.'

'Lord, no,' he replied with a laugh. 'Firstly, they knew you were coming, and secondly, the body scanners haven't picked anything up or you'd know about it by now. Oh, and we've got your retinas on file, naturally.'

'I'm sorry, what? How?' I was feeling very far out of my depth.

'Never you mind,' he replied. And that was that, it seemed. We stepped forward and the door shut behind us.

'Welcome to Downing Street,' said Hildebrand Blunt.

'Pfff,' I replied. 'Say that again?'

'I'm pleased I can still surprise you, James. You might call this the business end of Downing Street. This is the way people with serious matters to attend to come into Downing Street. Only journalists, people with petitions, foreign delegations, and ministers who are about to be fired actually come through the front door.'

He led me through a network of corridors where people scurried about, faces glued to screens. The carpets were deep and the portraits looked expensive. It was as if the great affair of government business were being conducted in the home of a rich octogenarian spinster, all hidden in plain sight from the populace.

'It never occurred to me to ask who lived at numbers one to nine Downing Street,' I wondered aloud.

'Nobody ever does,' Hildy replied. 'That's the way we like it.'

We came to a dark wooden door and Hildy placed his open palm on a small metal disk on the wall. It glowed blue and I heard the lock open.

'Shall we?' he asked, one hand grasping the door handle as if ready to make some great reveal.

'No, we shan't,' I replied. 'I'm not going another foot or stepping through another door until you tell me how you got my retinal scan.'

'Oh, that's from all the audio and visual bugs at your distillery,' he replied matter-of-factly.

'You bugged my distillery? How?'

'No, of course we didn't. The Marischal's people bugged your distillery. We bugged their bugs. Much cheaper and quicker than doing all that dirty work oneself.'

I gritted my teeth and pictured the arse-kicking I would give

Wally when I got back. (Of course, Archie would never let me harm a hair on his head, but the idea of it helped fortify me – as violence against weaker people always bolsters a coward.)

'When you're quite ready, please do hurry up and come in,' called a voice from the other side of the door.

Hildy pushed the door open and, with a hand on the small of my back, ushered me across the threshold. We entered the large square room where the strangest of smells hit me. The air was musty and thick. It smelled like . . . like . . . the past. To my left and right were giant bookcases, straining with old volumes, beautifully leather bound. I couldn't remember the last time I'd seen so many books. Such a collection surely didn't exist in Caledon. This was a place of imparted knowledge and learning, so different from our books – those that were permitted at any rate – which were carefully digitised, ordered, categorised and tagged so that while they imparted information, they were sure to take a little piece of you in return. It was intoxicating.

Straight ahead was a great mahogany desk with a leather top. (It's impossible to conduct affairs of state or make decisions of great import without a good-sized desk, you know.) Behind that were tall windows, reaching almost from floor to ceiling. They gave a magnificent view of a garden and trees. Beyond them, through the skeletal, leafless branches, I could see a dusty, open area.

'As a military man, you'll be familiar with Horse Guards Parade,' announced the voice that had called us in. I started, and turned to meet it.

Standing just by the doorframe was a short, portly man, whose frame was partly disguised by a beautifully cut double-breasted suit. He had a high forehead with thin, curly hair on top of it. His face radiated a simple charm and I'd have been fooled if I hadn't registered the eyes, which were sharp and bright behind small round glasses.

'Hello, Chief,' said Hildy.

'Ah, yes, young Blunt,' the man exclaimed enthusiastically. 'Thank you for escorting our guest to my humble abode. Won't you both take a seat? Just time for a quick chinwag, eh? A spot of gossip.'

He beamed at me, but said no more.

After a few seconds, Hildy broke the silence. 'Chief, allow me to introduce Mr Macfarlane. He is—'

'Oh, I know all about Mr Macfarlane,' the Chief said genially. 'OK, OK! You've got me there. I don't know anything of the sort, but I know all about men *like* him. The cut of their jibs. Or was that their cloth? Oh, never mind. Now, young Blunt, enough of your prevaricating. Are we ready to crack on? To get stuck in? Well, man?'

'Chief, Mr Macfarlane has yet to be apprised of the, er, objective. I thought it best if you . . .'

'Of course you did, young Blunt. Wouldn't want poor Mr Macfarlane to get all tied up in your convoluted verbosity.'

'No, sir.'

'Well then, Mr Macfarlane, now Mr Blunt has finally handed over the conch, let me reveal the lie of the land, and no doubt you will be raring to go in two shakes of a lamb's tail.'

'Chief, if I may, I think Mr Macfarlane might need some persuading as to the *necessity* of our plans.'

'Well, that's always a good sign.'

'Chief?'

'We don't *want* him to want the job, do we?'

'Chief?'

'We want rebuff, rejection, and refusal!'

'Sir?'

'It shows steel, Blunt, steel! Grit and determination! Good for you, Macfarlane. Not wanting to do the job clearly makes you the best man for it.'

I stared in amazement. He blundered on.

'Browsed your file, of course, but details are for the foot soldiers, don't you agree? As I say, much more important is that I understand men of your ilk. Know your type, Macfarlane, eh? Now let me look at you.' He scuttled over and clamped his little hands on my arms so he could inspect me. 'Ah yes, I know you. Merchant adventurer. A self-made man of means. A realist and a dreamer, eh? Means and dreams. Just what we want.' He slapped me on the arm and turned to look wistfully out the window, thumbs now hooked in the pockets of his suit. 'I can see you now in your office in the Highlands, Mr Macfarlane. Sitting at your antique desk – handles missing from some of the drawers, I'll bet. You're a grafter and a romantic, aren't you? Still, I'll bet there's a neck of brass hidden under all that, eh? No doubt you know all about looking after the pennies and what to do with the pounds. Am I right, Blunt?'

'Up to a point, Chief.'

'Up with the lark every day, no doubt, to steer the good ship commerce. A few hard hours' graft before you call upon your pretty assistant to bring you tea, which of course she does, as she has done for twenty years, for you and your family before you. You look surprised. Pretty close to the mark, eh?'

'I was just thinking you're the first person to call Archie pretty.' It was the first thing I'd said since the conversation began.

'Archie?' The Chief looked confused. 'Funny names you have for the ladies up there. But one never ceases to learn. I once knew a Chinese chap who adopted an English name that the dictionary told him showed strength and steadfastness. Called himself "Concrete", don't-ye-know? So, who am I to judge your darling little Archie? Each to their own, eh?' Another hearty smack on the arm. 'Yes, I can see you all together, artisans one and all: wedded to the job and to posterity. Returning to your Highland bothies and a roaring fire at the end of a hard day, replete in your simplicity. And I'm willing to bet your success hasn't changed you. Mr Blunt, is Mr Macfarlane an understated and self-effacing man?'

'Again, Chief, up to a point—'

'I knew it! And I am willing to put a year's salary on the line to say he is of the mould of those who can walk with kings and keep the common touch, is he not?'

'I suppose . . .'

Amid this extraordinary exchange I found myself smiling; found myself beginning to like this funny little man.

'And that is why, unlike the cynical young Blunt here . . .' He paused and a conspiratorial note crept into his voice. 'That is why I am sure you will help us in our time of need.'

I eyed him cagily. Suddenly, he didn't seem so funny.

'Just what do you need, Mr . . .? I'm sorry, I don't know your name.'

'Oh, my apologies! How could I be so rude? It's Smith,' he said, beaming.

'Smith?'

'Yes. Smith.'

'I imagine I'd meet a lot of Smiths if I walked around this building,' I replied slowly.

'Oh yes, positively dozens of us,' he said without blinking. 'Something of a family business.'

'What do you want, Mr *Smith*?'

'Aha! Quite right. You see, young Blunt? Mr Macfarlane just wanted to get to the point, like I knew he would. Now, do you think you might quieten down for a moment and give him time to speak?'

'Of course, Chief.'

'About time. You must excuse Blunt, Mr Macfarlane, just the enthusiasm of youth. Now, before he gets going again, I should explain, I work for a government department that exists to promote the reunification of the United Kingdom.'

He waited for a response, but I did not have one.

'I believe you are in a unique position to aid us in this project,' Smith continued, stabbing an over-optimistic finger in my direction.

'And why would you believe that?'

'Because you have achieved a nexus that no one else has come close to: you are a cornerstone of the Scot . . . Apologies . . . of the *Caledon* economy. A key figure in its social fabric. A clarion call to the Marischal's vision of what it means to be Scot . . . sorry, Caledonian.'

'Wait. Hang on. You're accusing me of propping up the regime?'

'Accusing? Lord no! Just stating facts, Mr Macfarlane. But you are missing my point, I fear. I'm not interested in you propping it *up*. Quite the opposite. My point is you have the means and desire to bring it *down*.'

'Er, you what now?' I replied incisively.

'Oh, come, come, Mr Macfarlane,' he said in that happy, disarming voice. 'Let's not beat about the proverbial. Perhaps you would prefer it if I called you by your more colourful moniker, the Wolf of Badenoch?'

Oh bugger. Buggery, buggery, bugger.

I was reeling. I had to play for time. *Think Mac, think!*

'Hold your horses.' I adopted the voice of command to disguise my lack of authority. This was no time for that quaking coward James Macfarlane. Jimmy Mac stepped onto the stage. 'You've got the wrong end of the stick. In fact, you've got the wrong stick entirely.' I contrived a laugh. 'To think I'm the Wolf of Badenoch is nonsense.'

'Well, of course it is.'

'You think I did all those things?' Jimmy boomed heartily, all honest, bluff, and courageous. 'You think I blew up the railway, the water supply, the dam? Well, I'm sorry: you've got the wrong man. I wouldn't even know where to start.' I crossed my arms. That was that. Discussion over.

'My mistake, surely,' Smith replied, turning to Hildy. 'Young Blunt must do his homework better, mustn't you, Mr Blunt?'

'Yes, Chief.'

'Although I confess it seems a waste of so many years of special-forces training if you couldn't manage those things. Nonetheless, indulge me a moment, please.' He wiggled his fingers in the air like a magician casting a spell. 'Let's just pretend you *did* do all those things. No one could say you haven't done exceptionally well to evade the attentions of your government – in particular, those vile Mallice fellows. Am I right, Mr Blunt?'

'Yes, sir. Vile people.'

'Quite. But you see, while they are vile, we understand they are also extremely capable, and you can't just hide up the mountains and sally forth on guerrilla missions for ever and a day, can you? That plan has a very short shelf life, don't you think, young Blunt?'

'Like fresh vegetables, Chief.'

'What? Why the devil are you talking about vegetables, Blunt? We're discussing life and death here!'

'Sorry, Chief.'

Smith stroked his chin. 'William Wallace was a sally-er, was he not? Crikey, remember what they did when they caught him? Hung, drawn, *and* quartered, was he not?'

I was about to step forward and declare that sallying hither and thither, as and when the opportunity arose, was *exactly* what I planned to do. And, if he wanted to get all historical about it, Robert the Bruce had done the same thing and they made him *king*. Then I remembered I hadn't yet admitted my guilt, so kept schtum.

'So, I have one question for you, Mr Macfarlane, and please don't take it the wrong way.' He looked quizzical. 'Do you have any idea what you are doing? Any idea at all?'

He let the words hang in the air. Out of nowhere I felt horribly exposed, as if he had stripped back my armour and revealed the squishy frailty beneath. Jimmy Mac started inching back towards the side of the stage, to be replaced with another voice.

He's right! yelled Common Sense, once again in good voice. *We've got no strategy and our tactics aren't much better. We're doomed, I tell you. Doomed!*

Smith was smiling again, damn him. 'You see, I like you, Mr Macfarlane. I like your simple honesty. I see nobility in it, and in your actions. Oh, I can't abide the thought of your assistant coming to any harm, as oddly named as she might be. I certainly wouldn't want to see you parted. I can picture it now: the heartbroken Archie, tears streaming down her face, arms outstretched, perhaps even declaring a long-held secret love as she tries to steal a single kiss as they drag you away . . .' Smith paused and I could swear there was a tear in his eye. 'Poor, darling Archie,' he muttered, shaking his head ruefully. 'And you must know that scenario is bound to unfold eventually, because the regime *will* catch up with you and, when it does, everything you have done will be for nothing.'

The emotional rollercoaster dipped and I found myself furious at his easy dismissal of all my work. Jimmy Mac stuck out a righteous finger, ready to ask what the bloody hell did Smith know? I was fomenting a popular uprising, I was . . .

He stopped me with a placating hand before I could utter a word. 'Please don't start telling me you are fomenting a popular uprising or some such romance. It's a non-starter, I'm afraid. Revolutions very rarely happen without foreign state intervention. Take my word for it. Or if not mine, then Mr Blunt's. What do popular uprisings need, young Blunt?'

'Foreign state intervention, Chief.'

'Well done, Blunt! He's really coming along, Mr Macfarlane. I'm quite proud, you know. Anyway, here's the good news. You may be having a kick-about in the lower leagues right now, but I'm offering you a chance at the cup final! You see, luckily for you, we are offering the support you need.'

I abandoned all pretence. 'Go on.'

'Our resources and capabilities are far superior to those of the Marischal. We know more than he does about a great many things. We know *far* more than you do. We can help you achieve a great deal more, and do it a great deal faster. I simply ask that you accept our help. The alternative is to carry on as you are. In which instance, we both know it is only a matter of time before they find you.'

'They might never find me,' I shot back.

Smith didn't bat an eyelid at this admission that I was the Wolf. 'Oh, Mr Macfarlane, they will find you, I can promise you that.' The smile faded from his face and a note of genuine sadness entered his voice. 'We'd have to make sure of it.'

So that was it. It's always the same with these geopolitical types. They can dress it up as much as they like, but at the end of the day you're either with them, or for the mincer. I didn't want the mincer but I also wasn't about to roll over.

'I'll consider whatever it is you want,' I said, 'if *you* do what *I* ask.'

With that, the smile was back on his face, masking his whimsical brutality. The man who had just threatened to have me killed positively radiated charm. 'But of course! What can we do for you, Mr Macfarlane?'

'I want a drink. Whisky. Good whisky – and I can tell the difference, so don't try anything – and a little jug of water on the side.'

'Mr Blunt, would you do the honours?' Smith didn't miss a beat.

'Of course, Chief,' replied Hildebrand, a note of relief in his voice. He turned and left the room.

'A good man, that,' said Smith, staring after him. 'Absolutely dedicated to the whole reunification effort, you know. Once upon a time, he would have been one of those zealous, stout young builders of Empire. All moustaches and self-righteousness. Putting an end to suttee,* tracking down slave ships, and so on. And, like those explorers, he is also extremely brave and resourceful. I wouldn't have sent anyone else behind The Wall to assess you.'

'Ah.' Another piece of the jigsaw fell into place. 'And that assessment included trying to kill me, did it?'

'No, no.' Smith was clearly aggrieved at the accusation. 'An unfortunate error in an otherwise impeccable mission, carried out far behind enemy lines. You were supposed to make friends and I hope you still can, because Mr Blunt is going to play a key role in your ongoing success.'

'Doing what exactly?'

'Assassinating the Marischal, of course.'

Oh, sweet Jesus. Not for the first time, I was lost for words. Looking out of the tall windows, I watched the trees swaying in the winter breeze. It's funny how quickly one's perception – and so, of course, one's reality – can be changed. With those few words Smith had transformed the trees, with their spindly arms and weathered trunks, into demon guardsmen who had me surrounded. I stared at them, then past them. Trying to think of my best escape route. The trees eyed me malevolently, their skeletal branches declaring that none should pass.

Once again, it seemed the only thing to do was to act bluff and manly, and convince Smith I was on board with his obnoxious plan. Afterwards I could begin feverishly extricating myself from the cock-a-leekie.**

'Why do you want me to assassinate the Marischal?' I asked, keen to get as much intel out of him as I could.

'It's a complex picture,' Smith began. 'I hardly understand it myself.'

---

* A Hindu custom whereby widows threw themselves or were thrown onto the funeral pyres of their dead husbands.

** A soup traditionally made with chicken and leeks.

'I don't believe that. Try me.'

'Oh, you're too kind, Mr Macfarlane. We are getting on tremendously well, are we not?'

'You just threatened to have me killed.'

'Water under the bridge! Best of pals now, eh? Anyway, here's where we stand: you may not know it, but England has suffered considerably over the last few years. All sorts of problems, driven by all sorts of things. I won't bore you, but let's see . . . There's the weak currency; tax issues; the plunge in foreign investment; the loss of reserve currency status; the whole vaccine debacle, and all the rest. Anyway, the list goes on.'

He lifted himself off his perch on the desk and paced the room, counting off national crises on his fingers.

'We've got much higher unemployment than we'd like, social inequality that's at its worst since records began. And, to top it off, the whole climate-change thing has meant three years of drought. The country's restless. It's a tinderbox waiting for someone to light a match. We can no longer suffer an unstable tin-pot dictator sitting on our doorstep making things worse. The usual intrigues – you know, spying and so on – we take for granted from other nations. But it's the unpredictability that's the real problem, you see? Did you know that during the last drought your Marischal doubled the cost of the emergency water supply?'

From the offhand way he said it, it sounded as if Smith found this terribly unsporting more than anything else.

'We had to pay, of course, but it was an object lesson to us. We simply can't afford, with things the way they are, to leave him there. Then some clever chap realised that we could kill two birds with one stone: remove that unpredictability and help unite the populace too – give us a cause for the nation to unite behind. A new leader would mean greater stability for us, a more tolerant regime for you, and could be a major step towards reunification.'

Out of nowhere, I was angry. Angry at this manipulative little man, safe in his little office, hundreds of miles from the fury of the Marischal. Who was he to decide what was right or wrong for us in Caledon? Years of conditioning threatened to burst out of me.

Caledon! roared Pride, who had appeared from wherever he'd been hiding and was somewhat confused at having to defend the regime. *Where you leave your doors unlocked at night. Caledon! Where the streets are clean and drugs are no longer peddled on corners. Caledon! Where everyone has a job and a purpose. Caledon! Where morality is restored and people respect their elders. Caledon! Where the benevolent eyes of the Marischal watch over a people reborn, driven by a national unity and purpose that is the envy of the world.*

But now there was a new voice in my head, dragging a different reality to the fore. It was Common Sense, raring to take the fight to his old adversary, Pride. I unleashed him and a battle raged inside my head as Smith waited patiently for my response.

Caledon! Common Sense railed mockingly. *Where tawdry licks of propaganda gloss over a reality that is cheap and violent and nasty, giving everyone on the outside a reason to look the other way. Caledon: where you never bother to lock your door because the Mallice will just kick it in anyway. Caledon: where crime is down because arresting the criminals is the least the state can do while it is abusing and locking up so many innocents. Caledon: where morality and unity and purpose are just euphemisms for forced obedience. Caledon: in whose end lies our salvation. Or doom, of course.* Bloody Common Sense.

It was almost as if Smith had read my thoughts. Looking back, I suppose it was him that put them there. He didn't wait for my answer. He knew he didn't need to.

'Great to have you on board,' he said, slapping me on the back. 'Oh, cheer up! You have a face like thunder. Look on the bright side. This way you get to live. To prosper! And, who knows, you might even prevent a war.'

'Oh my God, just stop. Enough. You had me at "I'll have you killed."'

'But this is important,' Smith replied. 'You need to understand the heroic proportions of your undertaking. I said that we needed something to unite the country, didn't I? And every action has a reaction . . . or is it an equal and opposite? Blunt, what am I after here? Blunt? Where did he go? He's always sneaking off like that, the scamp. Look, either way we don't want a rolling stone gathering moss, and everyone getting all riled up and demanding a war.'

'Why would they do that?'

'Oh, it's only a matter of time when things are tough until someone demands a war with somebody.'

I couldn't fault his reasoning there.

'In our case, Caledon is first in the firing line and you are the catalyst, my dear Mr Macfarlane. You – or, rather, the Wolf of Badenoch – have rather captured the public imagination down here. You are all the evidence they need of a restive nation keen to throw off the shackles of oppression. You are a figurehead behind which people on both sides of the border can rally under the banner of liberation. And it's all so romantic to boot. I understand your Wolf logo has even become a favourite tattoo amongst certain social groups.' He shrugged. 'It's a bit AOR for me.'

'AOR?'

'All Other Ranks.'

'A very military expression.'

'Do you think? Can't think where a pencil pusher like me would have come across it.'

'I have some thoughts.'

'Anyway, here's the thing: His Majesty's Government believes that sooner or later it will be forced to act with – how should I put it? – extreme prejudice against the Marischal's regime. We need something to bring us together. You know, Falklands style. Without it, we may tear ourselves apart. War may be the only way to stop the violence.' Smith returned to staring out the window, and I noticed he was no longer smiling. 'The problem is war is a serious business, what? Yes, I cannot overstate how little we actually want war with Caledon. The consequences would be terrible. Who knows what secret arsenal your dear leader is harbouring? Who knows which of our enemies would use Caledon as a proxy battleground to covertly – or overtly for that matter – engage against us? And above all, we can't afford it.'

'So, to save you a war, I'm going to be the pre-emptive strike? Do your dirty work for you?'

'Dirty work? No! You must think of this as your – the Wolf of Badenoch's – finest hour. England can't just go around knocking off other heads of state, now can we? Must be seen to be keeping the moral high ground. But you can, can't you? That's your birthright. My God, we'll help turn it into a national bloody duty! It's perfect, don't you see? It is everything you have strived for, delivered in one crushing blow!'

He clapped his hands in excitement. I did not share his enthusiasm.

'And it'll be fun to play spy and assassin, won't it? Playing the role of Double O fits perfectly with your sense of the romantic and dramatic, I'd have thought.'

'The role of what?'

'Double O. Ah, I see your history is not quite up to scratch. It's how Elizabethan spies used to sign off their letters.'

'Ah, I thought—'

'Of course you did, but remember, very little of anything is original anymore. It's all been done. And that should be of great cheer to you: none of what we're talking about is new. We're well versed in ARC operations. You're in safe hands.'

'By ARC, I assume you mean Assisted Regime Change.'

'Well, of course.'

There was a pause while I stared at Smith and he beamed back at me.

'So, Mr Macfarlane, what do you say?'

Steam erupted and sparks flew, gears clanked and cogs turned in the Macfarlane brain. All for nought. My earlier plan to talk my way in and then out of this mess now seemed precarious. I would have to return to Caledon soon and had no doubt that if I failed to go along with the plan or tried to pull out of it later, then Mr Smith would tear down the whole house of cards and leave me to the tender mercies of the Mallice. On the other hand, I had been handed another chance to advance the cause of the Wolf. Perhaps even finish it. Maybe this was a blessing in disguise. Jeez, the things we can make ourselves believe when we have to.

'It seems I have no choice.'

'That's the spirit! Capital stuff.' Smith grinned at me. 'We must celebrate our new partnership.'

Right on cue Blunt returned, carrying a bottle of whisky. One of my bottles (fourteen-year-old single cask bourbon barrel, fruity and creamy flavour with a long finish and . . . oh, never bloody mind).

'Hope I'm not interrupting, Chief,' Blunt said brightly.

'You know you're not,' I snapped back.

'Quite so.' He smiled at me, the bastard, before flourishing the bottle. 'Anyway, look who I found out in the corridor: the one and only Jimmy Mac.'

'Let's drink to our new friendship, shall we?' Smith poured Scotch for us all with a merry flourish. 'Now, what is it your lot say? "May the best you've ever seen be the worst you'll ever see"? Yes? Apt, don't you think?'

He raised his glass. There was nothing left to do but stop spinning the bracelet around my wrist and raise my glass too. And with that simple gesture, somewhere a bell rang and the next round began. I couldn't tell for whom that bell tolled, but this time I knew only one fighter could leave the ring.

We drank in silence, savouring the taste. As I took my last sip, Smith erupted back into life, offering me his hand.

'Now then, I've taken up quite enough of your time. Don't want to take liberties, eh?'

'Imagine that,' I replied.

He ignored me. 'One last piece of advice.'

'Yes?'

'Try not to get yourself killed. Or worse.'

'Goodbye, Mr Smith.' I put my glass down on the desk and started walking out of the office.

'Mr Macfarlane!'

'Yes?' I said, turning.

'One more thing.'

Oh God, what now?

'What is it, Mr Smith?' I asked warily, looking back at that simple, happy face.

'Do send my best to Archie, won't you? Lovely girl, that. And do make sure you look after her. Such a tender, fragile little thing.'

I left the room thinking that he was right, as he had been in everything else. Archie was fragile. Not like an antique vase, of course. More like a landmine.

CHAPTER 4

A Dagger I See Before Me

To add insult to injury, Hildy outlined his plans to hurl me into mortal danger at his actual, real-life, working distillery. They even called it 'Smith's', for God's sake. After we had proclaimed *ententes cordiales* and the paparazzi had finished their evil work we sat down in a cluttered office at the back of the plant. Leaning over a large touchscreen table, Hildy proved to be every inch the stalwart, upstanding, poised, and dedicated man I'd been worried he would be. He even tried to console me for being so comprehensively out-manoeuvred, the bastard.

'You are not the first and will not be the last,' he said, with the plain honesty that comes so easily to those who lie for a living. 'Oh, go on, admit it, the idea of bumping off the Marischal is growing on you, isn't it?'

The infuriating thing was that he was right. If we did succeed in killing our dear leader – as unlikely as that seemed – maybe we would light a touchpaper. Maybe we would ignite a downtrodden, tired, and terrified populace, yearning for change.

Sometimes you need to do bad things to make things better, Common Sense reasoned with me. *And ignition is crucial. Killing the Marischal doesn't mean bringing down the regime. The evil runs deep. There are a lot of very bad people deeply invested in the regime's survival. Wildfires must rage. The people must rise. We must burn it all down. And, if nothing else, we've got to admit: the idea of murder appeals to the lazy side of us. It could save days, months – years, even – of trouble and strife. We're all for the easy life.*

Think of the fame, said Pride. *We'll be national heroes. Global icons. Even Lizzy won't be able to resist us then – and imagine how angry that would make Blunt.*

'Are you paying attention?' Hildy's voice cut into my daydreaming. 'Now, have you organised an assassination before?'

I said nothing.

'Well, let's pretend you haven't for now. You'll be pleased to hear it's both easier and more boring than it sounds.'

It's nice to get a pep talk before you start on a new project.

'The first element is the people—'

'You mean "expendable" people, surely?'

'Please, Mr Macfarlane, take this seriously.'

'Oh, I am, I assure you.'

'I'll be coordinating the mission from London alongside a couple of our agents. We want to keep this circle tight.'

'And what do I call them?'

'Smith.'

'Both of them?'

'Yes.'

'Silly question, really.'

'In Caledon we will have a three-man squad. You and two other dissident Caledonians.'

This came as a shock. 'Two others? Who?'

'There's not much I can tell you. One is a former soldier who jumped ship abroad and handed themselves over to us.'

This seemed plausible. I'd heard a rumour not long ago about a soldier who went AWOL in Germany, presenting himself at the English Embassy in Berlin. I had no idea how they were getting him into Caledon and I didn't much care. Then a much bigger shock.

'The second is currently stationed with the Marischal's private guard.'

'He's stationed bloody *where?*'

These guards were drawn only from the most die-hard amongst the Mallice ranks. ('The pigs who wallow in the best shite', as Archie eruditely put it.) Hildy spoke over my stunned silence. I closed my mouth at some point.

'As a private guard, they are privy to a lot of sensitive information, including the Marischal's travel plans—'

'Look, I've got to stop you there. This guy being involved shouldn't set alarm bells ringing; it should set off goddamned air-raid sirens. The idea that one of the Marischal's guard would be a turncoat is, well, nuts.'

'There are many things about the workings of the Marischal's government that you don't know, nor need to know,' Hildy said in an infuriatingly calm voice. 'Rest assured, our vetting is meticulous and our planning airtight. You can be sure that when we set our minds to making something happen, it will happen. Trust me.'

'Oh no, no, no. I won't rest, nor will I be assured. And I won't take any of this on trust either. I don't trust you and you, I presume, don't trust me. This is a marriage of inconvenience, nothing more. Now, I say again: I need to know more about who the shooters are or we are done here.'

'OK.' There was no mistaking the steel in his voice. 'If you're so clear about our relationship, then let me remind you it doesn't matter whether you trust us or not. The big question – in fact, I'd argue the only question – is whether you want to stay alive for any meaningful amount of time.'

It's difficult to negotiate in such circumstances, I'm sure you'll agree. I sat in frustrated silence, while Hildy eyed me as one would a grumpy toddler. Then a smile spread across his face.

'Look on the bright side,' he said, spreading his arms. 'What you don't know can't be tortured out of you, can it? Now come on, let's have some tea.'

Motivation comes in all shapes and sizes.

'Look, if I tell you the names of the others,' Hildy went on, 'then it's only fair they have yours. Wouldn't you prefer anonymity in the circumstances?'

And that was the end of that.

The more time I spent talking to Blunt, the clearer it became that he was indeed what his boss had said: an old-fashioned romantic type, whose courage and resourcefulness made him a willing player in Smith's Great Game. A man who could stare death in the face and know that he's an Englishman and all is well in some corner of a foreign field, etc, etc, etc. With this realisation came the certainty that I was dealing with a true idealist and, like all idealists, Blunt would be willing to kill in pursuit of that ideal. Worse still, idealists share a common delight in others dying on their behalf. No matter how many. They need to survive, of course, or who will be left to drive the ideal on? The fact there's no one left to share their nirvana when the world finishes burning doesn't seem to matter. They could be radical socialists, despotic fascists, or militant stamp collectors, but they're all the same and all terrible for one's health, even in small doses.

For sport, I tried to put Hildy off his stride by mentioning Lizzy as often as possible, hoping to fill his mind with seething, improper notions of nipples and navels. If he was riled, he didn't show it. But I imagine his water bill rose considerably during that period to cover all the cold showers.

Then a terrible question raised its head: was Lizzy in on this whole thing? My God, had she put Blunt and Smith up to this? It seemed too much of a coincidence that all this was happening so soon after she had not only introduced me to Blunt, but also then forced me into that madcap scheme to get Professor Spring out of Caledon, sticking two fingers up to the Marischal in the process. And if she was in on it, how could I find out without alerting her? Again, Hildy interrupted my ruminations before I could try to take control of the situation, even in my own head. It was almost as if he was doing it intentionally.

'One last question,' he said. 'Do you want anyone else on the team?'

Presumably he was angling for Archie and Wally.

'No,' I replied firmly. 'I don't want to complicate this any more. I can't drag anyone else into my mess.'

The first thing I did after leaving Hildy to his tea and murder was to drag the others into my mess as quickly as possible. Doing this without Archie and Wally's support would be insanity, but there was no way I was telling the Smith family that.

Archie was happy to see me back in one piece and positively delighted by the turn of events.

'Well, this ups the fucken ante, eh?' he said, before a note of alarm entered his voice. 'Hang oan a minute: once we've got the job done, will we have tae stop blawin shite up?'

'There will always be something somewhere that needs blowing up, Archie, don't you worry,' I said, patting his shoulder.

Wally wasn't nearly as keen. But out of loyalty and, more importantly, his perennial battle of one-upmanship with Archie, he couldn't leave us in the lurch.

'I think this idea is ridiculous and will almost certainly get us killed. But I can't leave you in the hands of that giant clod,' he said, pointing at Archie. 'The big clod will never let me live it down. But look, there's one piece of the puzzle that's missing.'

'What's that?'

'Where are we going to kill our head of state?'

'Yes, well, Blunt is keen to make something of a statement with that.'

Archie eyed me warily. 'Come oan, oot wi' it.'

'We are to do the deed in our very own capital city.'

'Auld Reekie? Yer bluidy kiddin', aren't yeh?'

'No, I'm not. It's got to be Edinburgh. For maximum impact. Show the regime nowhere is safe from the Wolf of Badenoch.'

'But it's a bluidy fortress! They've got those boxy thingies everywhere. Wally, whit are those boxy thingies called?'

'ISMI*-catchers – they collect identification codes from you.'

'Aye, them things are everywhere, Mr Mac.'

'And don't forget the facial recognition cameras, gait monitors, auto-software downloads, the—'

'You're not helping, Wally.' I needed to quell the dissension in the ranks. 'Look, it's our best option. The turncoat in the Marischal's guard has provided a schedule of our dear leader's movements over the next few months. I've seen the satellite recon and the high-atmosphere drone footage of previous schedules. I've even watched it live. You could set your watch by it.'

'Imagine if we had someone who could get us that kind o' techy intel, eh?' Archie smiled.

Wally ignored him and pressed on. 'But surely the Marischal has multiple route options?'

'You're right. And the exact route won't be decided until they leave. That's why Hildy has picked three assassins. I – sorry, we – only get to know about the route I'll be stationed on. Somehow, we need to discover the other two so you can take one each and monitor what's going on. Wally, I need you to see what you can do.'

'I'm on it.'

'There's one more problem.'

'Och, there's always anither bluidy problem.'

'The Smiths have given each of us a location to make the kill shot from. They say they're picked for easy access and optimal lines of fire. We've got angles, distances, and everything. Take a look.'

For the next hour we pored over films, maps, and 3D schematics sourced from the depths of the dark web. And, try as we might, we

---

* International Mobile Subscriber Identity.

49

kept coming to the same conclusion.

'Yer fucked,' said Archie. 'Aye, it's a prime spot tae get the job done, but nae doot aboot it, yer fucked.'

The site was a first-floor flat halfway along Princes Street, the main thoroughfare that runs through the centre of the city. It offered glorious views of the road, park, and castle beyond. According to the travel plans we'd been supplied with, if the Marischal came my way then his cavalcade would pass right in front of my vantage point. There was even a second possible shot through the rear windscreen if they followed the prescribed route. The view was nothing short of assassin porn. Snipers have naughty dreams involving vantage points such as this.

But, to those who've seen a lot of this kind of thing, it was clear there would be no happy ending. The shot was too close. Far too close. If they spotted me – which they surely would after the crack of the rifle and the muzzle flash – then I would be trapped.

'It'll make a braw* tomb,' was Archie's conclusion, and even Wally couldn't bring himself to disagree with the big man. The only thing for it was to send Wally streaking down the internet super-highway to rent an apartment overlooking the Mound, the road onto which the procession of vehicles would turn after passing the death-trap on Princes Street. I didn't need to tell him to use one of our shell companies.

This new position would put me, at the very least, a couple of hundred metres from the target and give me a panoramic view of Princes Street, opening it up to enfilade fire. If all else failed, I could still go for a shot through the windscreen when the car turned towards me. This plan would give me much more time to choose my target and more time to escape. Which, as we both know, was my highest priority. To the left of my planned vantage point, sitting on its imposing crag, would be Edinburgh Castle. Spread out in

* Fine or pleasant.

front of it, and separating me from Princes Street, was Princes Street Gardens. It is a lovely park to stroll in if you crave an escape from the daily rigmarole of murder and regime change. It is also convenient to fire over, sitting, as it does, in a handy depression between the castle and the street opposite. All in all, a far superior location to that chosen by the English.

But, as with all best-laid plans, it fell flat on its arse. Wally comprehensively failed in his search for such a venue. To be fair, it was getting close to Christmas and New Year, making it an outside shot at such short notice, but that didn't change the fact that I was now left in a very dangerous position. I was stuck with Hildy's location and one hell of a logistical headache. Around this time the golden bracelet covered many miles in its ongoing journey round my wrist. It was a wonder the names of those bastards, exquisitely carved inside it, didn't wear off.

When not property prospecting, I was spending the amount of time on the dark web normally reserved for a committed paedophile, as it was the only way I could securely contact Hildy. Try as I might, I still couldn't get him to divulge the other two routes or sniper locations. Wally wasn't faring any better. Every time I asked for a sitrep the answer was the same: there were hundreds of bits of encryption standing between us and the information we craved. His exasperation at being unable to break in was sad to see. Even Archie left him alone.

Wally was still at it, long into one night, when Archie and I descended into the dark of the secret hidey-hole beneath under the house that my ancient forebear Robbie Macfarlane had built to escape uninvited guests. The air was damp and cold and the air smelled heavily of the braes.

'How's it going?' I asked, breathing in the peaty air.

'Not good; I just can't get in,' Wally said, before listing all the clever and unintelligible techniques he had been using.

'Whit aboot—' Archie began.

'Look, you big lug,' snapped Wally, looking up in frustration. 'Stay out of this. Why don't you go and wrestle a heifer, or whatever it is you usually do at this time of night?'

'Ah, OK, no worries, wee man. Guid luck wi' it.' Archie turned to leave but stopped in his tracks. 'But ah wiz wonderin', cuz, well, we ken where he's startin', aye?'

'Oh, this is going to be good.' Wally rolled up his tablet and sat back, arms crossed, eyes staring out of the shadows. 'Go on, please. Enlighten us.'

'An' we ken where he's finishin', aye?'

'Right . . .'

'Weel, if ah wiz them, I'd just type that intae the route finder oan the internet,' said Archie serenely, a smile dancing round his mouth.

'Maybe,' said Wally, eyes narrowed.

'An' will it no' also tell yeh the quickest ways – yeh ken, the ways that'll ha'e the least traffic, and a' that jazz?' Archie's smile spread. 'Ah'm no' as smart as yeh, but that's whit ah'd dae once ah had ma primary route.'

I was smiling too, because he was right. How else would you choose the routes for a notoriously impatient despot, particularly if you were a busy agent of tyranny keen to sort this most mundane of tasks and get back to meting out state-sponsored terror?

'Well, I suppose it might work,' said Wally huffily.

'Aye, it might,' said Archie. 'But ah suppose it could be a' baws,* eh? Well, guid luck tae yeh wi' a' the clever stuff. Ah'm aff tae wrestle a coo, if yeh'll excuse me.'

I patted him on the arm as he climbed out of the gloom. Wally looked incandescent at being out-thought by Glasgow's intellectual answer to the sledgehammer.

* Dreadful (vulgar).

'Don't worry, Wally, there will come a time when you will out-muscle him somehow, I'm sure,' I said. I couldn't think of any circumstance where this might happen, but it seemed the right thing to say at the time.

After providing this inspirational management and then packing Wally off to have a stiff drink, I turned to singing hallelujahs alongside the fine upstanding online congregation that is God's Motherfuckers. This chat room for militant Christians was my unholy access point for obtaining smuggled goods. Blunt had offered to supply a rifle for The Job, as I was now calling it in an attempt to lend some gangster glamour to the undertaking. However, I had put my foot down at this. I didn't trust the bastard to give me the right kit and there would be too many people in the supply chain. I prayed the other shooters had not been naive enough to accept that offer themselves. Perhaps they had no choice. They didn't have the Reverend.

'Taste and see that the Lord is good,' I said, donning my aug-specs, the retinal scanners swiftly calibrating to my eyes.

'Blessed is the one who takes refuge in him,' came the response, eventually, out of the darkness.

'What have you got for me, Reverend?' I asked as the craggy features of one of Caledon's most dangerous men swam into view.

'Straight down to business, eh? No chit-chat today?'

'I am under a certain amount of time pressure.' I exhaled a cloud of warm breath into the cold air.

'Men who go shopping for illegal high-calibre rifles often are,' came the laconic response. 'Off to shoot a herd of deer, are you? Or maybe an elephant?'

'Something like that. Have you had any luck in the search?'

'Any luck?' he spat in disgust. 'Of course I've had bloody luck!'

I sat quietly in the dingy little room, a wry smile on my face at his indignance. There was no chance at all that Caledon's legendary smuggler would let me down.

'Right, let's see here,' he said, his eyes looking down and out of the aug-specs' range of vision. 'Hell of a shopping list, this. OK, first option: something called a Barrett M107—'

'No thanks; too heavy to get around. What's next?'

'A CheyTac M200. Comes with something called a Kestrel 4000.'

'That's the environmental sensor package.'

'The what?'

'Measures wind speed, air temperature, air pressure, relative humidity, wind chill, that sort of thing.'

'Jesus,' he said in wonder. 'Who'd have thought deer hunting would be so complicated?'

'You'd be surprised.'

'Right, do you want me to go on?'

'Yes, please.'

'Right, third and final offer: a McMillan TAC-50. Comes with "hydraulic recoil mitigation", apparently.'

'That's to ease the impact on your shoulder.'

'Well, anyway, that's your lot. Anything take your fancy . . . *sir*?'

The Reverend had done sterling work, it had to be said. A quite exemplary set of choices. Old tech, admittedly, but reliable and accurate. The TAC-50 – known affectionately by users everywhere as the Big Mac – felt like the best fit for reasons beyond the natty nickname. I was drawn to its long-range accuracy (it famously held the record for the world's longest confirmed kill shot at 2,657 yards; that's over a mile and a half, for crying out loud). It was .50 calibre, too, meaning the bullets were massive and could take out engine blocks, which seemed like a handy option to have. More importantly, it should go through the bulletproof glass that the Marischal would surely be sitting behind.

I placed my order.

'Oh, and there's something called a hyper-imaging scope; do you want one of them?' he added.

'Definitely,' I replied.

'The coordinates for pickup will come when I go,' the Reverend said.

'Of course. Oh, and I'll need ammunition, obviously. Two boxes of .50 BMG orange-tipped tracers. Not the red tips – orange, OK? Then four boxes of ball cartridges and two boxes of armour-piercing incendiary cartridges – that's the ones with the silver tips.'

'Incendiary? So you're gonna shoot and cook the deer at the same time, eh?'

'What can I say? We live in an age of instant gratification.'

'That your lot?'

'No, I'm going to need three, no, four unlicensed drones – quadcopters, ideally. Oh, and three canoes.'

'Canoes? Kayaks are faster.'

'No, it's got to be canoes. I need the width. And paddles, obviously. Double-bladed.'

'That it?'

'Aye.'

'Nice doing business with you,' he said.

'Cheery-bye, then.' I was about to hang up when he spoke again, taking me by surprise.

'Mr Macfarlane?'

'Yes?'

'You be careful, mind.'

'Er, OK,' I said, caught off-guard by the concern in his voice.

'Mr Macfarlane?'

'Aye?'

'Whatever it is you're up to, may yeh gang faur and no' fare waur.'*

'Thanks.'

'Good luck, Jimmy.'

* May you go far and fare no worse.

The hologram flickered and vanished. I sat alone in the dark, trying to process our exchange. I couldn't credit it, but I had the distinct impression the man was concerned for me. My God, it almost sounded like affection. Maybe he just understood my activities far better than I was willing to admit. Maybe I was more like him than I cared to admit. I was about to shoot someone with a rifle so powerful it could kill a car, after all. Food for thought, that. In all our dealings over the years I had grown attached to the Reverend and in that moment I needed him to feel the same. I wanted to be wrapped in his strength and cunning and I wanted him to watch over me and tell me it would all be all right.

'Reverend?' I said, staring into the darkness behind the augspecs. 'Reverend? Are you there?' But I knew he wasn't. In the cold of my underground lair, I suddenly felt very lonely.

CHAPTER 5

The Flower and the Serpent

Archie picked up all the kit a few days later from a barn on a remote farm somewhere north of Inverness. Then I had my secretary put time in the diary for me and Archie to head out onto the hills bedecked in full stalking gear, under the pretence of filming a propaganda film for my whisky line. It would be the usual twaddle, featuring the famous Jimmy Mac climbing hills, leaping swift-flowing burns, and generally doing all the things that whisky is, ironically, designed to discourage. For his part, Wally spent every minute God gave glued to his screens, trying to find me a better vantage point to do the deed.

Cut off from civilisation, Archie and I spent three days trekking in the wilds, passing by sparse larches and wind-bitten rowans and traversing huge boulders that had been thrown carelessly down from the mountaintops in the time of giants. On and on we walked in the freezing air. The ancient mileposts and stone cairns showed us the way and the distance was no matter. There were times when I never wanted to stop.

Lost in the wilderness, we worked hard until I had zeroed the rifle and could nail rocks the size of a car window at a thousand metres with relative ease. We estimated that wherever I ended up, I wouldn't need any more than three hundred and fifty metres to hit the target accurately, and probably considerably less. Job done, we returned home to the distillery, wet and cold and happy. It couldn't last.

Just two days after we got back, a message came from Blunt's executive assistant, over unencrypted email. Hidden in plain sight. It explained that he had been delighted with our meetings in London and would love to pay me a visit to discuss export deals in more depth. To this end, would I mind meeting him on 19 December in Edinburgh? Did I think I would be prepared to strike a deal? Yours sincerely, etc.

So that was the date. In eight days I would try to kill a head of state.

I replied, saying I would be delighted and would make sure all the relevant preparations were made.

After telling Archie and Wally, there didn't seem to be much else to do except throw myself into work to keep my mind off things as best I could. I ate well and exercised hard in the cold grey mornings, just like the good Presbyterian I was brought up to be. Of course, we still had no solution to the minor issue of certain capture and death if we went through with Blunt's plan. But I had a long history of things turning up when I needed them and, at that moment, it was the only strategy I had. Sometimes one must just accept there is no place for thought before action.

Then something did turn up, although it was unclear what bearing it might have on any of my various predicaments. Another dinner invitation. From the Farquharsons. The last of these prestigious offers had led to me getting a faceful of lead, being thrown into a dungeon, and then nigh-on drowned on the high seas. As such, I wavered. The worry was that, no matter what they were serving, I might be biting off more than I could chew.

I went to Archie and Wally for their advice on the matter because I was sick of relying on my own judgement. Not that their help wasn't without its own travails. For safety's sake, we were back in the lair under the disused toilet, where the cold, damp air lay on us like a shroud. It was becoming a bit wearing.

'Whit's the harm, eh?' was Archie's considered response, his breath rising in a cloud in the cold air.

'I can't help you very much,' said Wally. 'They posted the invite so I can't do anything around tracking the correspondence, and their internet usage is nothing unusual.'

'Who posts an invite these days anyway?' asked Archie.

'Wait, good point,' I said, pulse racing a little faster.

'Wiz it? Aye, o' course it wiz. Why's that then?'

'They didn't post the last one, did they?'

'Ah cannae remember.'

'I'm sure they didn't. It would have sat on the mantelpiece. And remember, Loker knew all about it afterwards – he asked me about it when he barged in here and made threatening overtures.'

'Paper and pen is certainly safer than sending anything digital,' Wally piped up.

'Aye, but wi' respect tae the Quality, they're no' exactly runnin' wi' the times, are they,' Archie pointed out. 'Might get a pigeon from them any day the noo.'

'Wally, it doesn't have some kind of cypher in it or anything, does it?'

'Not that I can see, and I'm pretty sure I'd have spotted it.'

'No mentions of kings over the sea, underground railroads, dungeons, phantoms or anything like that? They all featured last time.'

'No.'

'Well, surely, by making it so unsuspicious, that makes it even more suspicious, doesn't it? What are they hiding?'

'Ah think yer overthinkin' this, Mr Mac.'

'So do we go?'

'Miss Burke might be there, eh?'

And so it was that I arrived at Invereiton Castle, seat of Lord and Lady Farquharson. I sent my chauffeur into the bowels of the castle with strict instructions to keep an ear open and not damage anything or anyone unless absolutely necessary. A butler ushered me into the vast hallway but I barely had time to admire the great panelled walls, which were festooned with broadswords, targes, halberds and all the other things you'd expect. He politely bustled me straight past the drawing room (odd), past the dining room without a pause (odder still) and on, deep into the castle. The further we went, the sharper my coward's senses became. Finally I was shown into a cosy little sitting room, with a roaring fire set in the hearth. A group of people stood by it and my mood sank a little lower with each one I took in.

'Ah, Macfarlane, late as usual, eh?' The biggest of them detached himself from the huddle and strolled over.

'Your Lordship,' I said, addressing the master of the house in all his barrel-chested, bearded glory.

'Come in, come in, no ceremony here,' Lord Farquharson said. 'I think you know everyone.'

Didn't I just? All the co-conspirators who had dragged me into exfiltrating Professor Spring were here. Allen Fletcher, Laird of Belleville, and Lady Farquharson beamed at me, which was hardly surprising. All they knew was that I'd succeeded in saving Spring, not that I'd done it largely by chance, while putting equal amounts of effort into sending him to the bottom of the ocean where he would stop being such a bother. Also present was the corpulent figure of newspaper magnate Iain Barclay, who was looking cross, maybe because his glass was empty, or maybe because no one had given him licence to sit down yet. To my knowledge, he hadn't been in on the Spring scheme, so he was an interesting addition. Wait. Someone was missing from this merry band.

'Hello, James,' said a voice from behind that made me go weak at the knees.

'Hello, Lizzy,' I replied, turning around nonchalantly enough to only knock a couple of medieval heirlooms off the table next to me. 'How are you? I see you have chosen to wear clothes you've stolen from a small child, as usual.'

She wiggled herself at me and I had to use all my strength to stop my jaw falling open. The dress gave the impression that she had been dipped in liquid satin and left to dry. Lizzy lazily brushed the hair away from her eyes.

'I'm pleased to see your trip to London hasn't changed your tastes too much.'

I was struggling for a witty retort when Lady Farquharson came striding over, her imperious figure politely but insistently demanding our attention.

'Lizzy!'

'Anne!'

They embraced, before the Colonel (a nickname that her reputation deserves) looped an arm around each of us and said with a cheeky smile, 'Don't you make a lovely couple', before leading us to the group and handing us drinks, served in beautiful, and no doubt ancient, glasses. I listened to the chitchat and could make nothing of it. Something was going on and my blood pressure was rising by the moment. I almost jumped out of my skin when the Colonel tapped a small spoon against her glass and bade us be quiet. Alasdair, Lord Farquharson, moved his mountainous torso to be next to her and stood stroking his great white beard absent-mindedly.

'Welcome to you all and thank you for coming,' she began. 'I wish we were meeting in happier circumstances but we are all bound together by the ties of war—'

'Hear, hear!'

'Quiet please, dear.'

'Sorry, dear.'

'As Alasdair suggests we have done great things together, particularly of late.' She dipped her head towards me and my cheeks reddened. 'But we have word that something is afoot. Something important.' My cheeks went very white. 'We have been given this information by our dear friend Lizzy Burke, who has once again put herself in great danger to do so. Lizzy?'

Lizzy sashayed over to the Colonel and stood next to her, a smile on her face that betrayed no hint of worry. She looked ready to judge ugly babies at a village fete rather than deliver earth-shattering news. Barclay cut in before she had a chance to speak.

'Wait, are we safe here?'

'Yes, Iain, we are,' said the Colonel. 'We are too deep in the castle for any signal to penetrate and I have our best people outside the door.'

'Best people – how can you trust them?'

'Because they're mine and they're Helots.'

'Bloody Helots? They're all guilty of sedition, for God's sake. They have the brand. You trust them?'

'Implicitly. They are loyal unto death—'

'Hear, hear!'

'Please, dear!'

'Sorry, dear.'

'We have taken them in, we have kept them safe after the regime so cruelly marked them and threw them on the midden.* They are ours, as I say, unto death.'

'Jolly good. Hear, hear, I say!'

'Lizzy, you have the floor.'

'I come with a warning,' she said, and the smile never left her face. 'Something is about to happen. I don't know what and I don't know when, but I'm sure it is and I'm sure it's going to be big. I wanted to tell you so it wouldn't catch you unawares.'

'I'm sorry, what?' spluttered Barclay, his face red. 'You've dragged me here for that?'

* Dunghill or refuse heap.

'What else could I do?' asked Lizzy. 'You surely didn't want me to call you?'

'Come now, girl, there must be more.'

For a second a shadow passed over Lizzy's face at the tone of Barclay's enquiry, but I doubted anyone else noticed it. She took a deep breath.

'Hildebrand Blunt is coming back.'

The next thing I knew, powerful arms latched round my stomach and gave an almighty heave, launching the ice cube from where it had buried itself in my windpipe.

'Thanks, Your Lordship,' I gasped. 'Sorry, Lizzy, do go on.'

She was explaining how he had got in touch and she would once again be his chaperone, but I wasn't really taking it in. How could he be so monstrously stupid? The idiotic, lovesick fool! Didn't he realise none of his secrets would be safe when he was in Lizzy's clutches? And who else had he been in touch with? There was moisture on my brow that had nothing to do with the fire behind me.

'Why on earth should we care about Hildebrand Blunt's return? He's a bloody distiller, just like Macfarlane,' said Barclay, looking confused.

'I'm with Iain, I'm afraid,' said Belleville genially. 'I don't quite see what the fuss is.'

'I'm telling you, we need to care. No – we need to worry, because I'm certain he's not who he says he is,' said Lizzy. 'I've tried to find out more about him and his background but I can't – and that by itself should tell you something. If he's coming back then I'm sure something's afoot. And there's no way the English are going to meddle up here so visibly unless that something is something big. And – oh yes, I didn't mention, did I? He says he's here to see James.'

All eyes turned to me. As far as they were concerned I was the hero of the Underground Railroad: only Lizzy knew about the Wolf of Badenoch. Maybe that was enough to raise her suspicions. Either way, it was clear Lizzy had gathered us to put me in a tight spot – to catch me out; to dare me to deny it or backtrack. Clever minx.

'He is,' I said slowly, playing for time. 'But if he is here for anything more than business, then it's news to me. I went and saw him last week in London. We signed papers, memoranda of understanding, that sort of thing. He's totally on the level. There's nothing . . .'

I ran out of steam and just shrugged. It wasn't a convincing performance. Lizzy's eyes bored into me and she was about to speak when the door to the room flew open. A large man stood there, panting. Where his hand was holding the door open, his shirt cuff rode up to show the pale pink scar in the shape of an 'S', the sign of sedition that proclaimed he was a Helot; branded and tossed into indentured servitude for some slight against the regime.

'Helicopter coming in from the south, m'lady. Mallice helicopter. Pickets in the woods say there's cars approaching the driveways too.'

'Alright everyone, nothing to worry about,' the Colonel began. 'Let's all make our way quietly to the dining room and—'

'No, no, no!' thundered her husband. 'I've had quite enough of this. Clandestine meetings. Skulking around in dungeons. When will it end? Who do these people think they are? Invereiton has never been successfully invaded in three hundred years and I'm not having it now. Now, where's my sword?'

With that he strode out of the room, his heavy steps echoing down the hallway.

'Oh Lord, he's off to get *Dìleas Làimh*,' she said with a sigh.

'*Dìleas Làimh?* What are you talking about?' snapped Barclay, looking scared now.

'It's the family sword,' the Colonel said patiently. 'Called the Loyal Hand because it had to be cut from the body of an ancestor who fell at Culloden. Hamish?'

'Yes, m'lady?' replied the man at the door.

'You know what to do?'

'Aye, m'lady, but I'll need some help.'

'Of course you will. Now hurry along, please, before His Lordship gets too, well, enthusiastic.'

Hamish the Helot hurried from the room. I found my voice again.

'I can't be found here.'

'Pardon me, James?' said the Colonel.

'Loker came straight to me after I left Invereiton last time. Almost found Spring. Threatened me. If the Mallice find me here it'll end very badly for us all.'

'Well, you must go then. I suggest—'

Hamish was back at the door.

'M'lady, I'm sorry to interrupt but they're here. They came straight in. The Mallice. Wouldn't wait at the door. Broke poor Alice's nose when she asked them to stop. They're on their way now.'

'OK, thank you, Hamish, that will be all.' She was infuriatingly calm.

'How do I get out of here?' I urged.

'You can't,' the Colonel replied.

'What?'

'That corridor is the only way out.'

'Oh my God, we're doomed.'

'Oh, you're so funny, James.'

'Am I?'

'Ah, my hero of the high seas.' And, as God is my witness, she ruffled my hair like a small child. It's appalling what people can make themselves believe when they have to. 'Come with me.' She led me over to the far wall and pressed on a piece of wood panelling, which sprang open.

'One of the many hidey holes another ancestor put in so he could spy on his guests. Get in, quick, and don't make a sound. You're definitely guilty if you're found in there.'

I crammed myself inside and she pushed the door shut. A single ray of light penetrated from a small hole, which I peered out of, feeling every bit the paranoid feudal warlord. Seconds later the Mallice came in – but not just any Mallice, bloody Thomas Loker. His dark grey uniform distinguished him from the black of his officers. His colourless face seemed to absorb the orange of the fire, while his one good eye ranged over the assembled group, instantly transforming them from guests to suspects. The other eye, milky and grey, moved too, although what it saw or did not see, no one knew. In my tiny chamber the sweat poured off me. I stifled a cough. The only sound was the crackle of the fire in the big stone hearth.

'Good evening,' came the light, easy voice. The Colonel gathered herself first.

'Good evening, Mr Loker. Very nice of you to join us.'

'You do not seem surprised by my arrival. Surely you had no reason to be prepared for it?'

'I am very surprised, Mr Loker, but Highland custom dictates that, as a visitor, you must be welcomed into my home.'

'I hardly feel I need to ask, Lady Farquharson. Are you a Good Citizen?'

She stood erect, her face unmoving, eyes like gimlets. 'Yes, Mr Loker, I am a Good Citizen.'

Loker smiled a thin smile and started walking around the room, stopping at each person.

'What an august gathering. Mr Barclay, hello. Are you a Good Citizen?'

'I am a Good Citizen,' he replied automatically. The ritual continued.

'Mr Fletcher . . .'

'I am a Good Citizen,' Allen stammered. Loker stared at him for a moment then moved on, stopping next at Lizzy. 'Miss Burke?'

'Hello, Thomas,' she said, smiling. 'Oh, I am a very Good Citizen.'

From my cramped vantage point across the room I could see his face change before it became waxen again. Not even Loker was immune. There was much rumour about her relationship with him, and I was one of the few who knew it to be true, because she shared intel that she got from him. Her bravery was breathtaking.

Loker started off round the room, examining its contents, searching for clues. The space was full of the ancient knick-knacks that aristocrats are wont to collect when they govern colonies. He picked up an animal skull with long curved horns that had been peacefully gathering dust, probably for centuries. Loker blew on it and brushed the dust carefully off.

'You must be careful or they lose their colour,' he said. 'I am a collector too, as you might have heard.'

'A rather different collection, I understand,' said the Colonel, standing stiff, refusing to be intimidated. 'You don't get horns like that on a human skull.'

'Quite, quite. Is anyone else joining us, Lady Anne?'

'My husband is elsewhere in the castle.'

'No one else?'

'No. Why?'

'I had rather hoped to find James Macfarlane. You know, *Jimmy Mac*?' He sneered the name. More sweat got in my eyes.

'We barely know the man.'

'But he has been for dinner lately, has he not?'

'Yes, but a lot of people come to dinner, Mr Loker.'

'I suppose they do.'

His eyes were once again ranging around the room. He didn't believe her and he needed proof. The Colonel was looking around too, aware of his intentions. I saw the proof before either of them did. The drinks glasses, all together on the tray. Even with Lord Farquharson accounted for, there was one too many. I was starting to suffocate now. Loker's eye swept the room, searching for something to damn us with. It was only matter of time before our error became plain. But Lady Anne saw it first. A look of regret crossed her face and she gave a small shake of her head.

'Now, Mr Loker, you are most welcome to join us—' She strode forward and threw a welcoming arm out towards him. In doing so, her hand caught the edge of the tray, sending it crashing over and the antique crystal glasses onto the stone hearth where they exploded spectacularly.

'Oh dear!' she cried. 'Is everyone OK? Mr Loker, are you hurt? I am so terribly sorry. Oh dear, oh dear, and those tumblers a gift from Bonnie Prince Charlie. Oh dear, oh dear.'

Loker studied her as she fussed about the hearth and called for a dustpan.

'Operative 1306?'

One of the Mallice officers in the doorway took a step forward. 'Yes, sir?'

'Search the castle.'

'Search the castle, sir?'

Loker stared at him with a look of fury, but his voice was quiet. 'Search the castle, now.'

'But, sir.'

'What *is* it?'

'I think we'll need more men, sir.'

I could see Loker's jaw working. But whatever he was going to say was lost as an almighty roar sounded from somewhere far off. It was repeated, louder still, and followed by loud thuds.

'What is that?' Loker said, his head twisting round to face the Colonel.

'Oh dear,' she said, the weight of the world on her shoulders. 'Not again.'

Hamish had appeared, carrying a dustpan. He nodded almost imperceptibly.

'What do you mean, "not again"?' Loker snapped.

'I fancy that is the sound of Lord Farquharson stuck in the pantry. The door is terribly stiff if it is shut too hard.'

The roaring continued, the thudding increased, as if someone was wielding a heavy object against the door. Loker stared at Lady Anne. He was thinking furiously. He knew it would be fruitless to search the castle. It was just too big to trap someone in. He suspected some kind of conspiracy, although how he'd got wind of our meeting, God only knew. But without his star suspect – one James Macfarlane, Esq. – he knew this could just as likely be another social occasion among Caledon's limited elite. Yes, he could put the guests to The Question, but if he were wrong, the Marischal would be furious. The Farquharsons were pillars of the Marischal's faux romanticism, emblems of ancient and noble Caledon. It just wouldn't do to torture them by mistake.

'I wonder, has my bird flown?' Loker said thoughtfully, before turning on his heel. 'Good evening to you all. Come on, we're leaving.' He swept out of the room, flanked by his goons. The assembled party followed him, Lady Anne in the vanguard, no doubt on a mission to disarm her husband with a minimum of fuss. In my cupboard I gasped for breath and waited and marinated.

CHAPTER 6

A Capital Time

It took an eternity for Hamish to appear and spirit me out of the room, avoiding every inch the Mallice had passed through, to steer clear of any microphones or nano-cams they had carelessly left behind. I wanted to ask Hamish what he'd done to get the Helot brand, but we were manoeuvring round the corridors of the castle in a silent, furtive way that didn't lend itself to small talk. The threadbare carpets soon gave way to flagstones that demarked what had been – and probably still was – the servants' quarters.

'Hush now,' said Hamish as we approached a wooden door and came to a stop.

'I am hushing, what do you think—'

'Hush, now.' I was about to remonstrate when we heard voices from beyond the door. Some were clear, others crackled when they came to us via walkie-talkies.

'Mallice,' I whispered.

'Hush,' said Hamish.

We retraced our steps but stopped again when we heard voices coming down the corridor ahead of us. They also crackled.

'We're trapped,' I hissed, but Hamish ducked into a stairway and, light-footed as a gazelle, mounted the stairs two at a time, stopping at each turn to scout ahead in a very soldierly way. Up we went, one storey, then the next. Hamish led me from one darkened room to another, each time sidling up to the window and peering out, before moving on. Finally, he found a view he liked and threw the window open. He scanned the ground and then the sky.

'Time to go, Mr Macfarlane.'

'Go? What do you mean, go?'

'Out the window, Mr Macfarlane. No Mallice there for now, and Archie has your car about half a mile off through the trees. Just over there, you see? Good luck.'

'What do you mean, good luck? We're two storeys up. The wall is sheer. I don't need good luck, I need bloody wings.'

'Take these,' Hamish said, producing a pair of gloves from his pocket and handing them to me.

'Gloves? So I'll have warm hands when I break my neck?'

'They're geckos, nano-ridge gloves. They let you—'

'Yes, yes, I know what they are and how they work. What I want to know is why on earth you have them?'

'Good to have handy if Her Ladyship has tasks such as this.'

'Wait? You've done this before?'

'I've arranged it. I've not *done* it.'

'Oh God, you're part of this Underground Railroad nonsense, aren't you?'

'So are you, are you not, sir?'

'Yes, I suppose I am.'

There was the sound of footsteps on the stairs.

'Time to go, Mr Macfarlane.'

I pulled on the gloves and leaned out the window. It was sickeningly far down and I was out of practice. The footsteps were coming closer. I put one leg out, then another.

'Goodbye, Hamish. And thank you.'

'You're welcome, Mr Macfarlane. Now remember, the trick is to keep your body weight suspended directly below you, or the gloves won't stick. And it's a long way down.'

'Don't I know it, Hamish. Cheery-bye.'

Praying that the gloves were in good working order, I slapped my hands onto the outside wall and swung outside. I hung there, suspended for a moment against the smooth white wall in the freezing air, before shimmying down to the ground and plunging into the undergrowth. There were no yells, nor whistles, nor pointing of fingers, and I never looked back.

* * *

The next few days in the run-up to The Job were hellish. I spent a lot of time worrying, and I worked so hard to take my mind off it that the staff at the distillery started getting suspicious. There was no further correspondence from Lizzy or any of the others, just a silence that I filled with misgivings and uncertainty. I expected the Mallice to come knocking any moment, but the days passed and still no one came by to cordially invite me for brutal interrogation.

Early on the morning before the big day, Archie drove me south to Auld Reekie, with Wally travelling separately. We still didn't have an alternative to Blunt's death-trap and it gnawed at me constantly. Blunt's stupidity in telling Lizzy he was coming ranked a close second. I wondered how long it would take her to get the plan out of him. I'd wager she could do it quicker than Wally could destabilise a banana republic (and that was pretty darn fast).

I had been booked into the Glamis suite at the Balmoral Hotel, which seemed appropriate in light of my Macbeth-esque ambitions. Archie swept the room for cameras and bugs before I took the Reverend's rifle out of its shiny case, dismantled it lovingly, and put the pieces into another bag before depositing that at the bottom of the wardrobe. Then, carrying the empty hard-shell case, I went straight to the first-floor flat that Hildy had so kindly provided for the purposes of homicide. (By 'straight', I mean with all the doubling back, crossing roads, turning down random side streets, and changing of hats that counter-surveillance requires.) I paused only to pickpocket two separate bystanders, with the aim of leaving their devices at the scene of the crime and hopefully confusing Loker's band for a short while. I abandoned counter-measures only when I was as certain as could be that no agents of the state were watching.

I made the final approach to the flat in as nonchalant but visible a way as I could, doing my best to let Hildy think I was playing along (for I was sure he was watching). Having gained entry, I peered assassin-like out of the window for the benefit of any English observers, before leaving the flat as conspicuously as I had come, no longer carrying the empty rifle case. A rudimentary piece of mis-direction, you'll agree, but the first step to blinding someone is to make them open their eyes.

The rest of the day was spent trying to improve my lot. The visit to the flat had done nothing more than confirm the place was a death-trap – entirely unsuited to someone who would rather kill than be killed. I spent a large part of the afternoon walking up and down my portion of the route – my 'kill zone', or 'corridor of death' if you want to be dramatic – hunched in a big coat, hat, and sunglasses to shield me from the cold, the bright sunshine, and the ferocious surveillance state. The small stone in my shoe was uncom-fortable but did the job of disguising my normal gait. I was off the grid, without any digital equipment. I counted four of Wally's ISMI boxes on the route and didn't even bother with the cameras that looked down from every post, wall, and drone. I just kept my head down and went about my business in as unobtrusive a way as possible, just like everyone else.

The longer I stomped up and down, the more I felt the pres-sure of the big occasion. Cold sweat broke out on my neck. My hands shook for reasons that had nothing to do with the biting cold of the air. Round and round I went, examining every shop, every house, and every window. Searching for my spot. For my salvation.

I hunted and I scouted, but to no avail. There simply wasn't a place that would serve my purposes. I was in real trouble.

Meanwhile, on the other side of town, Archie and Wally pounded the pavements of the other routes we'd second-guessed, looking for likely spots where members of my assassins' guild might ply their trade. However, the lads' search had thus far proved fruitless. I suspected the other shooters would already be *in situ*, lying low. Presuming they existed at all. All Archie and Wally could do was make educated guesses about prime spots for an effective kill zone, of which there were several. All this added to the sense of impending doom.

After another hour of fruitless searching for a new vantage point, I decided to clear my tortured mind and take a turn in the Gardens beneath the castle. As I was pondering life's many banana skins, I was shaken from my reverie by a loud bang – the unmistakable sound of a howitzer being fired. My nerves were as taut as bowstrings by then and the sound of a cannon being discharged was the final straw. Without thinking, I threw myself to the ground and waited for clods of well-manicured parkland to start raining down around me as the gunners found their range.

But all was again silent. Silent, that is, except for an American voice that piped up from my right.

'Well! Will you look at that?' it boomed happily. 'Thought he was under attack from the One o'Clock Gun! Hey, Gladys! Look'ee here! Did you see that?'

Turning my face from its bed of grass, I beheld a most wondrous specimen, stood a few feet from my nose. Trainers – *sneakers*, in the parlance – enclosed huge feet, from whence equally large calf muscles emerged, clad in lovat green kilt socks. It was a swift journey from there to an overly long kilt – the red of the MacGregor tartan, unless I was mistaken. On the front of the kilt sat a black sporran, emblazoned with the Saltire. Above that was a long blue waterproof jacket that was zipped tight over an ample frame. All this was topped off by a large open face, beaming at me in genuine wonder.

Gladys, herself built and clad in a similar manner, replied in singsong Midwestern tones, 'Well, Hank! I ain't never seen nothin' like that before.'

Hank's powerful arm pulled me to my feet, his booming voice enquiring if I was 'OK, son?' and wondering how I 'didn't know about the One o'Clock Gun, fired from the castle every day, Monday to Saturday, since 1861, except during Dubya Dubya One and Dubya Dubya Two'. He waved a paper flyer in my face. 'First done, ya know, so the ships out in the river could set their maritime clocks before headin' out round the world. I could recommend an excellent tour guide if you wanna know more?'

Just to be clear, I like Americans, I really do. I find their sincerity and openness a delight. They're one of the few groups of tourists who still come to Caledon – and my distillery – in any numbers, which says a lot for them. Just you try stopping them coming over to visit the pile of stones on that bleak hillside that surely marks where their great-great-great-grandfather bade a tearful final fare-well to his sheep and set out for the New World. You won't stand a chance. But, as much as I like Americans, being humiliated in front of them really is the pits. The world turned upside down, if you will. So I declined Hank's kind offer, brushed myself off and prepared to beat a swift retreat. To regain some dignity, I nearly told him that I'd fired the gun myself on several occasions. Which was true, but he wouldn't have believed me. Instead, I stammered goodbye and stumbled off.

Then I stopped. I turned back to stare at the Yanks in wonder before gazing up at the castle. Hank began to look concerned. I stared at my watch. *My God, the gun!* It was accurate to the second, as it had been for almost two hundred years. I smiled. Then I laughed. Had you heard that hysterical outburst, you might have recognised it for what it was: the desperate cry of someone from whom the prospect of imminent death has just receded, if only slightly. I turned on my heel and marched straight back to where Hank and Gladys were still standing.

'I'm sorry, where are my manners? Thank you very much,' I said to them, shaking their giant hands vigorously. 'You're right: it is loud, isn't it? Loud enough to be heard all the way out on the Forth by ships. Quite right. And *bang* on time, you might say, eh? Ha! Ha! You could set your watch by it!'

They clearly thought I was bonkers, but since Americans presume the eccentricities of everyone on this little island are simply a result of us being complex, quaint, and intelligent (rather than stupid, confused, and arrogant), they weren't worried.

'Now then, Hank, I seem to remember you were talking about an excellent tour guide. Would you mind sharing his or her mobile . . . Excuse me, *cell* number?' I asked. 'In fact, do you mind if I call from yours, I seem to have left mine at the hotel.'

I called the guide immediately and arranged a private tour for the next day. Then, flyer in hand, I waved cheery-bye to my American friends and marched towards the castle humming their state song, 'Home on the Range', which seemed appropriate for someone with guns on the brain. There was a new skip in my step, a new joy in my heart, a new gleam in my eye. I had an idea, you see. It wasn't yet a fully fledged idea, and it brought with it new dangers and unanswered questions that on any other day I'd run a mile from, but these were lean times and I'd take what I could get. The important thing was I had found a way of not dying in Hildebrand Blunt's dead-end hideout like a rat in a trap. If it came to it, I would die on my own terms, and what more can one ask for than that?

* * *

The evening began positively joyously, given the circumstances. Lizzy looked ravishing and ravishable. Hildy betrayed no sign that he was on a lethal mission behind enemy lines. Nor did he have to work hard to play the part of lovesick fool. I was determined to test his nerves of steel, and he eyed me warily as I knocked back fiendish amounts of booze in the restaurant (most of which surreptitiously went in the plant pot beside my chair). I laughed a good bit. I fancy I even brayed a few times. Behind his inscrutable smile, I could tell Hildy was becoming increasingly concerned at my erratic behaviour.

'We have a lot of work to do tomorrow, old chap,' he reminded me more than once. 'Maybe lay off a bit?'

His discomfort was helpful both in keeping him on the back foot, and in cheering me up. After the meal, I took Lizzy and Hildy to a nice loud bar I knew. This served several purposes. Firstly, it gave us privacy and free speech – no microphone from any of the various regimes I was being messed about by was going to pick up what we were saying. Secondly, I guessed it would mean Hildy would have to leave the premises to relay his concerns to his side, which he duly did. Finally, the cacophony of noise meant Lizzy and I had to sit very, very close in the dark. It had been a long time.

She was in a dark-blue satin dress that, inevitably, looked as if it had been designed to fit a child's doll. Her eyes were painted a smoky black. She caught me staring – leering, really – almost straight away and leaned in close.

'Can you guess what's underneath?'

I replied in my customarily suave way. 'Pfft. Ah. Er. What?' rolled off my tongue.

'I see I can still surprise you,' she purred into my ear, before her tongue darted in there, as if to retrieve the words.

There are times when it's important to realise you can add nothing productive to a discussion and you shouldn't even bother trying. This being one of those occasions, I just nodded dumbly.

Lizzy put her hand on the back of my head, running her fingers through my hair. Then she put her arms around me and hugged me close. I knew I should have pumped her for intel; tried to find out if Blunt had told her anything or, God forbid, actually involved her. But I wasn't in any fit state to be good at my job. At that moment, I wanted nothing more than to leave it all behind. To get lost in that beautiful body.

The music was loud and the air was hot. Lizzy disentangled herself from my wandering hands, while flashing lights from the dance floor swept across her face, turning her into a bewitching kaleidoscope. For a moment I forgot my diary was chock-full of murder.

'You know I . . . I care for you, don't you?' she said, placing her hands on my cheeks and locking her eyes onto mine.

For all our entanglements she'd never professed anything of the sort before. I should have instantly been on guard, but I melted just as Blunt had. The difference was she meant it with me. Of course she did. Definitely, probably, maybe. The eyes softened. I was about to tell her she looked sad, when I stopped. It wasn't sad. No, I'd seen that look before, just never on her. She was scared. Oh my God, she did mean it. And she was choosing now to tell me. But why now? This seemed an appalling development.

'Do you trust me?' she asked.

I have a steadfast rule that you should always tell beautiful women that you trust them when they ask, no matter the circumstances, nor how wild a lie it might be.

'Of course I do,' I said languidly, squeezing her thigh for added impact. But the adrenaline had started to flow again. Something was afoot.

'I know about tomorrow,' she said.

'*You what?*' Thank God there was no ice in my drink. I pulled back and stared at her in shock. A couple of people sitting near us looked over and then away when I scowled back at them.

'Please, come close. I don't want to have to shout over the music,' she said, beckoning me to her.

Another iron-clad rule for a successful life – that I pass freely on to you like the philanthropist I am – is however shocking and appalling the situation, one must always take the opportunity to get close to a beautiful woman with a plunging neckline when invited to do so. I leant closer.

'I'm scared,' she said. 'I'm scared what might happen.'

'How the hell do you know about this?' I hissed, ignoring her fears; torn between anger, lust, and confusion.

'Hildy told me,' she replied, almost surprised at the question.

'What do you mean, he told you? Jesus, *why?*'

'People tell me many things. You should know that.'

'Yes, but this is—'

'No different,' she cut in forcefully.

'But how . . .' Despite my fears, I think I'd always believed Blunt wouldn't be so stupid. So *amateur.*

'Oh, come now, James, don't be naive. Hildy is young and emotional – not an embittered husk like you. And he's profoundly dedicated to a cause, also in a way you couldn't understand.'

'I'm taking all this as a compliment.'

'But that dedication – that patriotism – means that, even if he doesn't know it, he is lonely,' she went on. 'It's a terrible combination if you don't want to fall in love. Which, of course, he has. With me.'

Dear God, I thought. *No matter how much money I have; how many Archies I have at my back with their knuckledusters freshly polished; how many rifles I carefully zero in, I will never have Lizzy's power.*

'I don't want you to do it,' she said, gripping my arm, her long nails digging into the skin under my shirt.

'I don't have a choice.'

'Yes, you do!' Lizzy's eyes blazed and her lips were a slash of scarlet fury. 'If anyone has a choice, it's you,' she hissed in my face, as the music blared around us. 'Run, James! Hide! Get out of the country. But please don't do this tomorrow.'

'You don't understand . . .'

'No! It's *you* that doesn't understand.' She glanced at the door, watching for Hildy's return that would surely put an end to her desperate pleas. 'They *will* find you. They *will* catch you. They . . .' She leaned forward and put her arms round me. 'Please,' she whispered in my ear. 'There are things I've got to tell you. You haven't seen what I've seen. The things they do; how far they're willing to go.'

'I think I've seen enough,' I said. 'In fact, I think I've heard enough.'

'Enough of what?' came a jaunty voice from behind me. Hildy sat down on his chair and sipped his drink. I had no idea how long he'd been watching for.

'Oh, nothing. Lizzy was just offering me another drink. Very naughty of her. In fact, as you've said, we do have a lot to do tomorrow, so you'll pardon me if I call it a night? It's past my bedtime. Want to be able to see straight in the morning, eh? Cheery-bye, one and all.'

As I left the bar I turned back. For an instant I saw Lizzy staring at me with a look of desperation that I'd never seen before. But it was fleeting and melted back behind her smile as Hildy leant in to ask her . . . well, God knows what. At that moment I felt nothing but anger towards both of them.

You might think me foolish to have looked this gift horse in its luscious mouth, but to be fair, there was no way I could have foreseen all the pieces on the chessboard moving as one to encircle me. If I could have, I might not have felt so angry at Hildy's lovesick, puppy-dog idiocy, or at Lizzy's relentless drive for the inside scoop. All I knew at that moment was the power of the adrenaline coursing through my body. I clenched and unclenched my fists in impotent fury at the thought that my life was on the line and the information upon which my continued existence depended was being bandied about like playground gossip.

Yet, even as I stood there, the anger began to recede. For a moment, I almost went back. Almost sat down and heard her out. Her desperation seemed to denote a breaking point: a rare moment when she was on the cusp of betraying her own iron-clad rules on discretion and confidentiality. The very rules that had kept her alive for so long.

And all for me.

If I had taken that first step and returned to my seat to hear her out, it might have changed everything. I have tried to rationalise my behaviour in that moment; tried to convince myself that her information could not have altered my path. I tell myself that what she had up her sleeve – now I know it in full – couldn't have changed the inevitable. I was damned either way. To have heard what she had to say and changed course would have seen Hildy throw me to the dogs. Even Lizzy Burke would not stand between him and his duty. That's what I keep telling myself, over and over. Here, in the dark. Yet the inescapable truth is if I had listened to her entreaties then that information might not have saved us, but it would have given us a fighting chance.

Instead, I left Lizzy miserable and hurt. I carry that with me. I shudder as I think about how truly wretched she was the next time I saw her . . . no, wait . . . *heard* her. Oh Jesus, that bar, in the lights and the noise and the sweat: was that the last time I ever saw her? How long ago was that? Weeks? Months? No matter. That memory will be with me forever. It is my penance. It drives me on and reminds me I can't give in to madness or death. I haven't done Lizzy justice with my misery yet.

We miss you, Lizzy Burke. We miss you now like we never expected to miss anyone. Except Archie, obviously, but the affection between a man and his giant Glaswegian, all fists and scars, is a different kind of bond. It's a well-worn cliché that you don't know what you've got until it's gone, but, in your case, we have a sneaking suspicion that we did know what we had. Or, at least, what we wanted. In the back of our mind, we believed that at some unspecified point – once Everything Was Better – we would be together. When we had achieved . . . What? Would anything have satisfied our appalling, reckless ambition? Would you have been able to put your life of intrigue and danger to rest? Could you ever sit with us and be happy? Be normal?

That was very touching, said Common Sense.

Thank you, replied Pride. *Is there anything you want to add?*

Well, yes, said Common Sense, measuring his words carefully. *I think that knowing both of us – two people who found opportunity rather than despair in that desperate time – 'normal' was just a ridiculous daydream.* Normal people. *It seems laughable when we write it down. Perhaps we were simply both too self-destructive to be satisfied with a simple life, surrounded by peace and quiet. Perhaps, if we were honest, Lizzy, we both saw it as good fortune to live in such evil times. Perhaps, perhaps, perhaps. But it is too late now. All we can do is shut our eyes, see your smiling face, and remember the real Lizzy Burke. And then we realise that to wish for peace or normality would be wrong. You wouldn't want that, and would surely tell us off for trying to impose such an odious state upon you. And so we wish you goodnight, sweet princess; may flights of devils speed you to your lascivious rest.*

When I emerged from the close, sweaty embrace of the club, the cold air hit me like a slap in the face. At least it wasn't snowing. I offered a quiet prayer of thanks for the wonders of global warming. I was suddenly very tired. As my senses attuned to the night and the dull noise of revellers in the surrounding lanes I heard the shrill music of a Christmas fair floating up from nearby Princes Street, gladly picking its way through the net of digital steel and skipping past the ever-watchful eyes of the CCTV. Then I heard that rarest of things: laughter. Down in the Gardens the merry-go-round, the big wheel, bright stalls, and glasses of steaming glühwein were creating the illusion of another time; casting a temporary spell of forgetfulness over the oppressed.

I stared over the Gardens and up at Edinburgh Castle. It reared high above me on its rocky outcrop, dominating the skyline and glowing orange in the giant halogen uplighters. I thought again about the One o'Clock Gun, sitting dark and silent in its battery. It had spawned an idea that had seemed like my salvation a few hours before, but which now made me feel a bit sick due to the extraordinary level of risk involved. I shoved my hands deep into my pockets and felt something there. I pulled whatever it was out and stared in disbelief. How did they . . .? Wait! These were the trousers I'd worn to Invereiton. Archie clearly hadn't been through the pockets when he'd washed them. I looked in wonder at my hands and back up at that massive rocky outcrop. Then, oh-so-quietly, I joined in with that soft, floating laugher. You see, Archie's dereliction of domestic duty might just have provided the final piece of the puzzle that might save my life. I marvelled at how he always got things right, even when he didn't mean to.

I pulled on Hamish's gecko gloves. The laughter had released the tension and now I was calm and focused. Years of well-drilled habit were taking over, removing all distractions from my mind.

A good thing too, since I had a mountain to climb. Well, a volcano, to be precise.

CHAPTER 7

Something Wicked This Way Comes

There comes a time in a man's life when he has to ask himself whether climbing a volcano in the dead of night, under threat of being blasted off it at any moment by hidden defence systems, means things have got out of hand. Unfortunately, this was the only solution I could think of that would give me a middling chance of being alive in twenty-four hours' time. And so I dragged myself up, traversing the large, sharp boulders that were slick with freezing water, and negotiating the precarious overhangs and slippery ledges until I reached my goal. I was there for barely a minute before I began the descent again, hoping in my heart of hearts that single minute would save my life.

The next morning, I woke in my soft bed all stiff and covered in scratches. If it hadn't been for the geckos, which ensured my hands stayed clamped to the wet stone, I'd have surely ended up in a bloody heap in the Gardens below, and not even Gladys and Hank's unfettered enthusiasm would have been able to coax me back to my feet.

For a moment, in that strange time between dreams and wakefulness, I watched the sun stream through the window and wondered at Archie's tardiness. Then reality hit: there was no Archie, nor even one of his famous pick-me-ups – maybe even the fabled No. 1, given the circumstances – as the big man was *in situ* on his designated route and quite unavailable to come to my aid. Today was a day for murder and I was going to have to start it by not only dressing myself, but finding my own breakfast. When would this nightmare end?

I eventually stepped out of the hotel after an austere meal of porridge and eggs because I simply couldn't get my head around the buffet. The air was crisp and the sun dazzlingly bright. It was hard to believe, looking up at the wide, clear sky, that I was off to commit murder most foul. People were milling about, looking calm and inconsequential. It seemed absurd they could be so ignorant of the momentous events soon to unfold around them.

I took a deep breath, tipped back my head, and exhaled a thick white cloud from my lungs into the blue sky, watching it disperse. My face was hidden under a turned-up collar, hat, sunglasses, and week-old beard that was tickling my face something rotten. My every step felt leaden. The question of whether this assassination was the right thing to do weighed heavily. Not the 'moral' thing, you understand. The morality of it was all one to me. Pride raged at being press-ganged into a course of action that had formed no part of my vision for the Wolf of Badenoch. If the Wolf was to be anything, it was to be a symbol, an agent of change. It was not the Wolf's job to fundamentally alter our society, it was the Wolf's job to inspire the huddled masses to throw off their shackles and tear down the edifice of oppression. The Wolf was supposed to quietly sit that bit out and emerge triumphant at the aftershow party. That was the plan.

As such, this assassination just didn't feel right – and not just because I was in the kind of personal danger that I'd normally run a mile from, given half a chance. No, something was missing. If I killed the Marischal, all the structures of oppression would still be in place – and who was to say another would not take his place? Perhaps even the despicable head of the Mallice, Thomas Loker. Common Sense peered out from behind the sofa to suggest that working with Smith and Blunt provided the structure and support needed to get the whole job done, and get it done faster than I could ever have dreamed of. But his tone was uncertain and he shrank from Pride's fierce gaze.

And so it was a conflicted assassin who climbed the Royal Mile that morning, making his way up the old, cobbled street towards the castle, hands shoved deep in his pockets to ward off the cold. I mulled over the professor's final morbid rendition of *Macbeth* as I went. It was difficult to escape the thought that I was now about to be that 'poor player that struts and frets his hour upon the stage'. Was this 'the way to dusty death'? Would I be 'heard no more'?

Soon I came to the New Tolbooth. The country's biggest jail towered above me, passing judgement without humanity or forgiveness. Sorrow seeped out of the dull grey stone. Even on the sunniest of days the granite walls radiated gloom, telling of the horrors that lurked, locked fast, behind them. It was a lovingly rendered copy of its medieval predecessor, itself a byword for misery. A reminder in the heart of the city that They were always watching. The thought that even now some poor soul was begging for mercy as the Mallice put them to The Question somewhere behind that wall brought me out in a cold sweat. Above the prison's huge sheet-metal entrance gates stood a wrought-iron inscription: *Preserve and improve the good; reform or exterminate the evil.*

Like everyone else, I veered away from it as I passed, briefly stepping off the narrow pavement onto the uneven stones of the road. I meandered, glancing from side to side, taking in the sad state of the Royal Mile. I remembered it from my youth as a vibrant place of performers, tourist shops, cafés, and pubs. Back then it was overrun with smells and sounds; a place where flapping Saltires and Lions Rampant jostled with each other in the breeze. The skeletal remains of that time could be seen in the few surviving discount stalls, but the crowds were sparse and the energy was missing. The flags hung limp in the windless air, all the fight gone out of them.

I wondered if this day would change all that. Would this be a shot heard around the world? It seemed improbable. Impossible, even. All around me people walked by, lost in their own worlds, their concerns, their hopes and their fears. I wanted to stop them. Grab them by the shoulders; shake them and exclaim to their amazed faces that everything would soon be different. That by mid-afternoon, the world would be a better place. That I was bringing death so that they might be brought back to life.

Reaching the end of the street, I approached the castle across the wide, open esplanade. I looked up at the statues of Robert the Bruce and William Wallace guarding the main gate and smiled at the absurd notion that my life might, one day, be measured against theirs. A stone banner hung between them, proclaiming *Nemo me impune lacessit* – the Latin motto of the Stuart dynasty. 'No one provokes me with impunity.'

'Great pep talk, lads,' I muttered, passing beneath the two freedom fighters.

Soon I was passing under the raised portcullis gate. I offered a brief prayer that it would still be up when I made my way back and marched onto the battlements. Straight ahead stood Andy, the guide who had come so highly recommended by Hank. He stood straight and simple in his guide's tabard, ready to impart centuries of pre-prepared knowledge.

His plump, jolly visage, framed with thick black glasses, never once altered as he took me from pillar to post. I took some joy from my anonymity and soaked up the views, along with Andy's stories of romanticism, heroism, and enough blood to keep even Archie happy. As he prattled on about the castle's history, I observed how much had changed since I had been stationed here as a young lieutenant. The answer, as I had hoped, was 'very little'. And why should it? The cameras were in the same places. The guard changed at the same time and place as I had once done, years before. Staring upwards, I couldn't even see any drones patrolling the sky. This was the centre of Caledon and the idea that it would be used for infamy was unthinkable. God bless hubris.

The guide's tales were now nothing more than a buzz in my ear as I surveilled the area. Only once did he drag my attention back as he told me about the Marquess of Montrose, for whom the crowds had fallen respectfully silent as he walked up the Royal Mile on his way to his execution in 1650, and the anger of the authorities who had counted on their jeers and boos. Then, in dramatic tones, Andy recounted Montrose's last words before he was hanged: 'God have mercy on this afflicted land.' *Plus ça change.*

I looked at my watch: it was 12.30. Cometh the hour. I thanked Andy and tipped him, but not enough that he would remember me. Taking heart from Montrose's bravery – and trying to ignore his ignominious end – I marched towards my own destiny.

12.35

It was a calm, cool, and collected Mac who walked purposefully towards the battlements overlooking the city. I was a professional with a job to do and the skills to do it. I took in every aspect of the scene around me. The crowds were small; mostly knots of people wandering in the footsteps of their state-appointed guides. Examining the cannons. Taking in the view. The few members of the castle garrison I could see looked even more relaxed.

Moving to the battlements, I placed my hands on the cold stone and breathed out in an unhurried fashion, already beginning the process of slowing my heartbeat. Years of training flowed through my veins, all leading up to this moment. Just off to my left was the One o'Clock Gun that had left me cowering in the Gardens far below, at the mercy of American largesse.

12.40

The seconds passed, then the minutes. The people remained, milling about slowly and infuriatingly.

12.45

Waiting, waiting, waiting. Then, all of a sudden, I was momentarily alone. *Now or never.* I took a deep breath and vaulted over the wall, sliding down the steep incline. I landed on the small flat roof of an outbuilding that protruded from the wall ten feet below and made my way across two further lean-tos until I reached their extremity.

I took a deep breath before dropping off the roof and onto the damp rock of the volcano itself. I crouched there for a moment, looking around for any signs of discovery, but there were none. Hugging the castle wall, I skirted over the granite stones, trying to stay out of sight and in shadow, until I was almost directly under the One o'Clock Gun. The granite of Castle Rock pushed out from underneath the fortress, jutting a few metres beyond the wall, before plunging straight down to the Gardens far below.

I looked up to the battlements above me, expecting to hear a hue and cry break out at any moment; to see heads appearing, silhouetted against the bright sky, eyes scouring the rocks below to find me. But there were none. There was no hue, nor was there cry.

Well, all that was about to change.

12.48

Relief flooded through me as I spotted the waterproof sack still sitting where I'd left it during my climb the previous night. Methodically, I started unpacking its contents and assembling the tools of my trade.

12.53

In position. I lay prone and uncomfortable on the cold, wet granite, staring through the hyper-imaging sight of the sniper rifle.

The sight let me see microwave, millimetre wave, and infrared images – 'superhero vision', as the marketers say. If you've never tried hyper-imaging, then just imagine being able to see through thick fog to spot the stag you've been stalking all day – you terrible cheat – and you'll understand what I'm talking about.

I rubbed the gun down as best I could to minimise any prints or other tell-tale signs, although DNA residue was something I'd have to worry about later. If there was a later, of course. Then, using a small remote control, I tuned my in-ear receiver to an encrypted channel and said, 'Well, hello, you English bastard.'

'Where the bloody hell have you been?' Hildy's voice was full of professional indignation. 'He'll be in range any minute now.'

'I was sightseeing,' I said.

'You were *what*? Goddamn it, James . . . Look, are you in position?'

'I am,' I said, although he wasn't to know it was a long way from Jimmy's Grave, as I'd christened his death-trap on Princes Street.

'Satellite recon shows he is almost certainly coming your way.' Hildy's voice now regained a studied and reassuring note of calm. 'The other two shooters are prepped, but it looks like you are in pole.'

Typical. Bloody typical. But then at least all the effort I'd gone to wasn't wasted.

'Right, I'm going dark,' I said. 'I'll see you at the rendezvous.'

'Roger that,' he replied. 'And, James . . .'

'Yes?'

'Best of British.'

'There's no such thing, Hildy.'

12.56

Christ, this is going to be close . . .

I clicked the remote again and jumped to another channel.

'Good afternoon, men,' I said.

'Hullo, sir,' came a gruff voice, shortly followed by another, softer one. 'Hello, Cap'n.'

It's funny. On any other day, I would have berated Archie and Wally for using the military form of address, but it didn't even occur to me at that moment to criticise them. Instead, a glow of pride was filling me. These were my men. We were back together, doing what we did best. They were following me into the valley of Death once more: theirs not to make reply, theirs not to reason why. And whilst I trusted them implicitly to 'do', it was up to me to make sure they didn't die.

'I hope yer comfy, sir, wherever yeh are,' Archie's voice crackled over the radio.

They knew I wasn't in the flat on Princes Street, but for their own safety I'd kept them in the dark about where I really was. The last thing I wanted was them rushing to my rescue, rather than making good their escape.

'Not really, but you can't fault the view,' I said into the headset. 'I was thinking, Archie . . .'

'Whit's that then?'

'If we succeed with this, then surely it's time you told me the recipe for The No.1, don't you think? I mean, after this a stiff drink ain't going to cut it. We'll need something positively rigid.'

'Yeh must be jokin', sir. Yer nowhere near. Really, yeh should be prayin' yeh never need it. If we *don't* succeed, then mebbe. *Mebbe.* But yeh'll have tae make a proper hash o' things.'

I sighed and went back to the day job. 'Any sign of the other snipers?'

'Not a thing, sir,' his steady voice came back. 'No evidence at a', but it's like looken fer a needle in a fucken haystack.'

'Understood. Wally, anything to report?'

'Not a thing, Cap'n. Very quiet here.' Then, unable to restrain himself, 'I told you, sir, the big lug's plan isn't worth a tinker's curse.'*

---

* Is of no value.

'Yer jist sore because yeh couldnae come up wi' somethin' better,' Archie snapped back.

'OK, calm down, calm down,' said Wally.

'Here's a lesson fer yeh, Wally: never in a' the history o' calmin' doon has any Scottish person bein' told tae calm doon, ever calmed doon. Ye'd do well tae remember that, especially right the noo.'

Lying prone on that cold rock, minutes away from murder most foul, I listened to them bicker and felt truly happy for just a moment. Wally was about to launch into another riposte when he was cut off by an urgent whisper from the big man.

'Somethin's happenin'. Just up the road, aboot fifty metres. Five, nae, *six* black vehicles have pulled up. Looks like Mallice. Aye, it's definitely pigs. They're pilin' oot intae the street, aboot a dozen o' the swine . . . Hang oan, ah'm movin' closer . . . Jee-zuz, whit a racket. They're kickin' a door doon, yellin' . . . They're runnin' inside.'

He went quiet and then we all heard the unmistakable sound of a shot, followed by several more.

'Archie, come in!' I hissed urgently. 'Come in!'

Silence.

'Oh, come on, pick up the phone, you silly bastard,' said Wally, a note of genuine alarm in his voice.

Silence.

'Cap'n, they're comin' back oot,' a muffled voice said. 'They're carryin' someone. They've dumped a body oan the pavement. Goad, he's shot tae shite. One o' the Mallice is carryin' a rifle. It's big. Sniper's rifle, nae doot. Sir, ah think we've been compromised.'

A cold fear gripped me. I swung the telescopic sight away from my kill zone to look at the building I should have been in right at that moment. Sure enough, a convoy of black cars was pulling up outside and spewing black-suited thugs out into the road. Some took up positions around their cars, others by the door. More still smashed their way in and disappeared. I watched them. It was a well-planned, smooth operation. Then I noticed a man with a broadcast camera in his hand disappear inside after them. This was more than an operation: it bore all the hallmarks of a performance.

'They're entering my designated location now,' I said. 'Abandon your positions now, both of you. Meet me at the rendezvous point.'

'But, sir—'

'That's an order,' I snapped. 'Oh, and gentlemen?'

'Yes, sir?'

'Go silent.'

'Leave no shadow,' they replied in virtual unison.

'Over and out.'

I turned off the receiver and offered a quiet prayer for the two of them. We had been betrayed. The question of who had given us up raced through my head, but, finding no takers, went rushing off on its merry way. I watched the Mallice on the street manoeuvring around, looking as capable and organised as ever.

Soon a head appeared at the window where they had no doubt expected to find one James Macfarlane, Esq. The big bald noggin looked around in confusion before disappearing again. I gazed through the little circle of my sight with something approaching pleasure as they brought the empty rifle case, which I had deposited there the previous day, out into the street. I'd been meticulous with that, and if there was any DNA to be found there then I deserved everything I got. He opened it and tipped out the clothes I had stashed inside, purchased from a charity shop shortly beforehand, which would cause no end of confusion for the forensics people.

They looked furious. It warmed my heart to see it. Then they began to look concerned, scanning the street, the park, and even the castle, suddenly aware that there were a thousand places for a sniper to hide. A sniper they had, minutes earlier, been certain was in their grasp.

I swung the rifle left, scanning the length of Princes Street.

There, right on cue and surely timed to meet a recently captured assassin while the cameras looked on, was the Marischal's cavalcade.

Four powerful 4x4s with blacked-out windows shielded a huge car with – saints preserve us – large, clear windows, designed to display the Marischal to his adoring public. I stared at his face, blank of emotion even in his moment of triumph.

I looked for imperfections, or any warping of his features that might denote thick bulletproof glass. There were none. Yet it *must* be bulletproof – surely his vanity was not so great? You just never know with these despots. The line of vehicles came to a stop. I began taking deep, slow breaths and felt for the trigger. When he got out, he would die.

But he didn't get out. He sat there.

12.59 and 35 seconds

Time ticked by with agonising sluggishness. My eye flicked rapidly from the Marischal in his car to the digital display in the imaging sight that was counting down the seconds, and back again. And then it happened: a Mallice officer walked to the rear passenger door and bent to grasp the handle. To me it felt like the most momentous opening of a door in all of human history. It swung wide in perfect clarity. The crosshairs in the sight adjusted automatically. Then the Marischal stepped out. I could clearly see his face. No longer calm, he was looking around in fury. He scanned the street, as his men had moments before, taking in the Gardens and Castle Rock, until I could swear he was gazing straight at me.

Come on. Come on. Come on. Stay there, you bastard . . . Just a few seconds longer.

12.59 and 50 seconds

But he wouldn't stay, damn him. He turned and signalled to his Mallice lackey to open the door once more. He ducked back into the car, pausing to take one last look around, the disappointment and anger etched onto his face. Just five more seconds . . . He was back in his seat, still perfectly clear in my crosshairs through the open door.

'Three, two, one,' I whispered.

The One o'Clock Gun boomed out above me at the exact moment I pulled the trigger. The rifle smashed back into my shoulder and the scene in my telescopic sight dissolved into a charnel house of blood, bone, glass, and metal, as the bullet struck home. The Marischal sat still in his seat, eyes wide in shock, his mouth opening and closing in disbelief, covered in blood and gore.

But it wasn't his own.

On the ground lay the shattered wreck of a body. There was a gaping, gushing hole where the left side of its torso had once been. It sent a torrent of blood over the pavement and into the road. That missing portion of the body was now liberally decorating the car and our country's leader. The doorframe was badly bent and the glass of the window was covered in a heavy lattice of cracks.

Looking back, I can only presume that at the precise moment I fired, the bodyguard had leaned over to close the door and taken the full force of the bullet. Then it must have ricocheted into the door or the window – I just don't know.

All I knew was that I had failed. By inches. But how close I had come to success didn't matter. The Marischal was alive and I was no hero, no liberator. I was a fugitive. The most wanted man in the country.

CHAPTER 8

A Cup to the Dead Already

There was no time to think. I disassembled the rifle with practised ease, slipped the bag over my back, pulled on my geckos, and started scrambling, sliding, and dropping down the giant rock as fast as I could. It would be just minutes before lockdown began in earnest and the Wolf hunt started.

My thoughts on that desperate descent were odd, inasmuch as I wasn't scared. Rather, I was appalled that I had killed the man. I didn't regret killing one of the Mallice – he was fair game – I was enraged that I'd killed the wrong person, and frustrated beyond measure at how close I'd come. A mere second or two's difference and I would have changed the fate of the nation. It's on such trifles that history turns, I suppose.

The revelation that we had surely been betrayed filled my thoughts as I descended. The geckos saved my life several times as I darted, scrabbled, and leapt from outcrop to overhang.

Reaching the bottom, I turned left and started walking through the Gardens as nonchalantly as I could manage. Everyone and everything felt like an enemy. The trees lining the path, stripped of their leaves for winter, looked ominous and gaunt, their branches emaciated arms that might reach out and grab me at any moment. The air was full of sirens, as the apparatus of the state mobilised.

Forcing myself to take slow deep breaths – in through the nose, out through the mouth; you know the drill – I processed my current circumstances. First, I had to get rid of the rifle. I turned out of the Gardens and onto the main road that ran on the far side of the park from where the twisted wreck of the Marischal's car stood. I walked swiftly up the hill, putting Castle Rock between me and the forces of evil, before turning into the network of streets beyond. In a rare piece of good fortune – long overdue, you'll agree – there was some kind of road improvement project going on. Normally, I would curse the absent construction workers as overpaid layabouts, but in this case, they had helpfully left a large hole in the road, surrounded by barriers.

I marched up to it and peered in. A dank smell rose up to greet me. The fissure was deep and dark and disappeared into a tunnel running under the road. A sewage system? No matter, it would have to do. I tipped the pieces of the rifle out of the bag and into the darkness, hearing a series of satisfying splashes as they landed. That would keep the rifle hidden for a while at least. The water would also hopefully wash away any DNA I'd left on it. All I was left with now were the comms gear and a pistol, now tucked into the back of my trousers.

The ease of my escape from Edinburgh seemed too good to be true. I couldn't risk using my getaway car in case it was compromised, so I stole a car from near the construction site and was away. But, by God I was foolish. It's difficult to rationalise how stupid I was. How few counter-surveillance measures I took. All I can say is a failed assassination plays on one's mind in strange ways. I was shaken by events; by the accidental murder I had just committed; by our betrayal. I was sloppy, maybe even arrogant, as I flew up the motorway to the North and towards safety. And because I didn't think, I killed us all.

The drive north took more than two hours. I wanted nothing more than to hurtle up the motorway, eating up the miles until I was back in the Highlands and home. Then we could plan to get the hell out of the country. But I did do some things right: I drove slowly and unremarkably. I scanned the channels and waited for news of the attempt on the Marischal's life. There was none. Instead, I listened to some propaganda about Caledonian manufacturing prowess, supported by the usual lies, damned lies, and, of course, statistics. On I drove, uncontested and unconcerned. I even sang along to some music.

Our rendezvous point was a pretty cottage on the south side of the Cairngorm mountains. The two-storey whitewashed building sat just off the highway, on the edge of a wide floodplain that extended either side of the River Spey, off to the left. Tough brown grass stretched out across the flat land. The house itself was hidden behind a small, independently minded wood that stood alone on the plain, screening the cottage from the road. Behind the cottage, the plain met the steep scree and heather-covered hills, which rose majestically up into the deep blue sky. It was a beautiful winter's day.

I turned off the road and rolled to a stop by the trees. Killing the engine, I took my pistol from the glove compartment and opened the car door. Then I slunk into the shade of the tree trunks, crouching low in the bracken and heather, before putting the earpiece back in. I saw no signs of life, but someone had been here recently, judging by the fresh tyre tracks.

'This is Ptarmigan,* come in,' I whispered into the encrypted airwaves, using the call sign we had agreed.

There was no reply. *Please God, let them have made it out.*

'This is Ptarmigan,' I repeated. 'I have reached the rendezvous, please confirm your position.'

Silence.

Then, 'Ptarmigan: Grouse and Snipe at the rendezvous. Perimeter secure,' came the welcome growl. 'Confirm yer position.'

'Look out the window.' Relief flooded through me: Archie and Wally were safe.

---

* A game bird, famed for its camouflage and ability to survive cold environments.

I stepped out of the trees as the cottage door opened. They appeared on the threshold, looking for all the world as if they were heading off on a rambling trip, dressed in waterproof trousers, jackets and heavy walking boots. I strode over, reaching out and shaking their hands warmly in greeting. We went into the cottage and I took in the large open-plan ground floor, the white walls and dark wooden beams in the ceiling. A small seating area to our left held battered chairs, while a dilapidated kitchen, shamelessly flaunting its melamine surfaces and cupboards, was to the right. An old oak table filled the space in between the two rooms and, behind that, a thin staircase, covered with frayed blue carpet, wound up and out of sight.

It was a credit to Wally and Archie's professionalism that they made me a cup of tea before asking any questions. I raised my mug, Jimmy Mac's sardonic smile on my face.

'A cup to the dead already, eh?'

'Aye, and hooray for the last bastard who died,' Archie said, a big grin now on his face.

The smile dropped from mine. Of course. They didn't know.

'There hasn't been a word about it on any of the channels,' Wally chimed in excitedly. 'I can't find a bloody cheep. Everything should be going batshit crazy now the Marischal's dead.'

'He's not dead,' I replied slowly, casting my eyes to the floor. They both stood mute and shocked. 'I had the perfect shot, but a bodyguard walked in front of him as I pulled the trigger.'

'Aw shite,' said Archie, summing things up in his usual concise fashion. Wally was swaying slightly, his eyes wide. He looked like he might be sick. Not for the first time, I keenly felt how much like a child he seemed in this most adult of worlds. Archie saw it too. He put a reassuring hand on Wally's shoulder and squeezed.

'We have to assume we were compromised,' I said. 'Now, as far as I know we are the only ones, aside from Hildy, who know about this place. But we have to work on the basis that he betrayed us and we have to get organized and get out of here.'

'But that disnae make sense,' Archie protested, and I could almost hear the gears turning inside that massive head. 'He wanted the bastard deid, right? Gie'in us awa' widnae help wi' that, would it?' He mulled over the conundrum, before concluding philosophically: 'On the ither hand, the bastard is English, so yeh never can tell.'

'It has to be him, doesn't it?' Wally asked. 'It was Blunt's plan. And the Mallice knew exactly where the second gunman was and they blew him to pieces . . . Jesus, they knew exactly where *you* were supposed to be.'

'It still doesn't feel right,' I said. 'The English want the Marischal gone; there was no benefit to them in giving us up . . .'

Then it struck me.

'Oh shit, of course! The third gunman – the guardsman! He must have been a plant. I told them! I bloody told those goddamned spooks not to trust a Mallice guardsman; it was insanity.'

'Aye,' said Archie, levers once again clanking into action. 'But how wid he ha'e known aboot where the ither two wid be? He knew the routes, fer sure, but no' the exact properties. Blunt wisnae sharin' that intel wi' the team, wiz he? We only found the ither guy by sheer blind luck—'

'I thought you said it was common sense?' Wally cut in, unable to help himself.

'Och, awa' an' bile yer heid*. . .' Archie replied and, even now, they fell to bickering in the usual fashion.

I ignored them, lost in thought. The truth was, none of it made any sense. There were clearly pieces to this jigsaw that were still missing. I wracked my brains, but only became more frustrated at being unable to solve the puzzle.

It was well over an hour later – when I was changed into my

---

* Go away and boil your head, i.e. get lost.

hiking gear, all ready to take flight into the hills if the circumstances demanded it – that Hildebrand Blunt arrived. He walked straight in and almost got himself shot. By the time the old wooden door had creaked open and he had stepped inside, two pistols were levelled at him. A third appeared from behind the door and was pressed into the nape of his neck. He hardly flinched.

'Easy, chaps,' he said, with infuriating calm.

God, but he was a cool customer, this one. He didn't even seem surprised to see Wally and Archie there.

'Is everyone OK?' he asked.

'Aye, nae thanks tae you,' snarled Archie, grinding the pistol barrel into his skull. 'Yeh gave us up, didn't yeh?'

'What do you mean, "gave you up"?' he asked, looking surprised.

'It doesn't look good,' I said, with the measured assurance of someone who has a gun and is speaking to someone who doesn't. 'They knew where we were. They killed at least one of the other snipers.'

'They killed both of them, actually,' Hildy said quietly.

'What?' I said in astonishment. 'The guardsman too?'

'I told you,' he continued, 'that was a good man. A brave man. Now, may I have a seat? We have to talk and we have to do it fast.'

'Archie, please remove your pistol from Mr Blunt's neck,' I said.

Then déjà vu overcame me. We'd been here before. My mind flew back to that cold afternoon at Invereiton, as I lay stricken on the ground with Archie about to do bloody murder to Blunt for trying to kill me with a shotgun. It seemed there had been a lot of people trying to kill me since Blunt came into my life. It felt wise to keep my pistol on him.

'Archie, Wally, would you give us some privacy please?' I asked, quietly assured by my continuing status as Man With Gun. 'Wally, I need you to keep listening to the chatter. Archie, keep an eye on the drone feeds: make sure we've got good coverage of the hills and we've got the approach covered. I don't want any more surprises. While you do that, I'm going to have a word with Mr Blunt. Oh, and before you leave, pass me the teapot and a spare cup.'

They shambled off, unhappy at leaving me with the man they suspected had betrayed us, but still professionals with a job to do. And then we were two. A spy and an assassin, sitting at a kitchen table in a beautiful rural cottage drinking tea.

'Talk,' I said, the pistol levelled across the table.

Blunt sat looking pensively at the stairs until the creaking floorboards in the ceiling above us fell silent, revealing the others were in position and out of earshot.

Then he moved and it was so fast I hardly even saw it. There was a sharp pain in my right hand and all of a sudden, I was staring down the barrel of my own gun.

'That's better,' he said, smiling.

'What are you doing?' Really, this was all getting a bit much.

'I'm going to kill you, obviously,' he replied, still as cool as ever.

'Whatever for?' I asked, more interested than concerned. The pistol wasn't silenced. If he shot me, Archie and Wally would hear it and that would be the end of Hildebrand Blunt, a fact he was surely aware of.

'Because you cocked up Plan A and now we're on to Plan B, although if we're counting, it's really more like Plan F. You, dear fellow, have consistently managed to mess things up for us and we are, frankly, out of patience and out of options,' he replied. 'You've been on borrowed time longer than you know. A lot of people are terribly cross with you right now.'

He studied me for a moment, his head to one side. I would have butted in, but when an enemy is spilling his guts, you keep schtum, no matter what. When he didn't continue, I decided to give him a prod.

'Why did you betray us?'

'Lower your voice, if you please,' he murmured. 'If I hear those floorboards creak just once upstairs, then our conversation is over.'

'You'd never make it to the woods without a bullet in your back,' I said. 'My men will see to that, you English bastard.'

'Oh, come, come. You're better than that sort of low-grade racism.'

'Don't you believe it,' I said through gritted teeth.

I was angry. I hadn't known either of the men who had so recently paid the price of Hildy's conspiring, but I suspected they were both just like me: good men at heart, trying to do the right thing. Comrades-in-arms.

'Why did you do it?' I asked, almost in a whisper. 'After everything. Why betray us?'

'I didn't,' he replied in that easy tone. 'I solemnly promise I didn't – and the man with the gun never needs to lie. Although when I come to think of it, their deaths are – partly at least – on you. If I'd got you the first time, the others would probably never have been involved.'

'Just more pieces in the Great Game, eh?' I accused him, before clocking what he'd said. 'Hang on, what do you mean, *the first time?*'

Then it came to me like a bullet from the blue, which, I suppose, it was – both literally and figuratively.

'Oh God, Farquharson's shoot,' I stammered. 'You actually meant to kill me?'

'Well, yes, of course – and if it hadn't been for Lizzy appearing out of nowhere and giving me such an awful fright, I'd have done it, too.' He smiled. 'That dear, silly little thing.'

How little you know, I thought. But I'd keep that revelation for emergencies. In the meantime, I had to keep him talking. There was no way, after everything we'd been through, that I was going to die so prosaically, over a cup of tea in a chocolate-box cottage.

'No, you have to do better than that,' I said, crossing my arms in a way that said *there's no way you can shoot me now, I've got my arms crossed.* 'I don't get it – what on earth had I ever done to you? Why did you try to kill me?'

'For the good of England, why else?' he replied, a puzzled look on his face, as if he couldn't possibly comprehend why I needed to ask. (I've said it before: you have to watch out for these zealots and their penchant for putting others in the line of fire for the sake of their own fanatical ends. God, patriotism really is the last refuge of a scoundrel, ain't it?)

'That's crazy,' I shot back at him. 'Killing me doesn't make any sense! You, Smith, everyone – you all wanted the Marischal gone – and I was the only one to do it. "Stop a war", you said.'

'Well, yes and no.' He leaned back in his chair, as cool as the proverbial cucumber. 'We certainly did – *do* – want him gone, for both moral and practical reasons. But, at the time of the Farquharsons' shoot we weren't ready. Far from it. In fact I'd argue we aren't ready now. You see?'

Well, of course I didn't see, and so shook my head blankly.

'I can't see anything of the damn sort. First you wanted me dead. Then you wanted me alive to make someone else dead. And now it's me you seem to want dead because someone is alive whom you wish dead. How on God's green earth am I supposed to make sense of any of this?'

'Do I really have to explain it all? Come now, aren't you keen to put the final pieces in the jigsaw yourself? To square the circle . . . to solve the riddle?'

'No, I am not,' I replied with finality. 'I don't even have the pieces to solve any bloody jigsaw. For God's sake, please just explain so I can die, if not happy, then at least with a sense of context.'

'I admire your balls, James.'

'Leave my balls out of it.'

'OK, have it your way,' Blunt said, glancing up at the ceiling where a floorboard had creaked. No more sound came. 'The thing is, we are having a harder time of it down south than you realise. The economy is shot to pieces, the Europeans are making our lives a misery – they blame us for the bloc's collapse, you know? Which is nonsense; it's their fault for ignoring their own people for so long—'

'Please, enough of the geopolitics,' I said.

'But this is *all* about geopolitics, James,' he replied, arching his eyebrows. 'Look, as we told you, we are dedicated to the reunification of the United Kingdom; that much *is* true. But – and it's a big but – we're not really prepared to take that step yet. We need to do it, as best we can, on our terms and in our own time, and, I'm going to be candid with you here, that time has not yet come. Unfortunately, our hand has been forced. Forced by you.

'You see, Mr Macfarlane, you are ahead of your time and ours. If you'd asked me a few weeks ago I'd have told you we simply aren't ready for the Marischal's regime to collapse. I'd have said we don't have the finances or the structures in place to sort out the mess; that we couldn't sustain the vast numbers that would stream over the border through that hideous Wall of yours. The north of England has enough troubles of its own without thousands of Caledonians infesting it, including those ghastly Reivers from the Newmarch, no doubt. There'd be riots and God knows what else. So, the fall of the Marischal was the last thing we wanted. Meanwhile, you – the Wolf of Badenoch – were causing us real worries. Your – what shall I call them? – *antics* were making some quite serious waves.'

'That's nonsense,' I replied, and I meant it. 'Jesus, I was only just warming up before you lot came along and ruined everything.'

'Ah, now that's where you're wrong. I totally understand why you'd think that, but we do extensive – and I mean *extensive* – surveillance of communications north of the border. We have a whole team of clever people monitoring and interpreting a vast range of data. Your man Wally is good. My God, he's good. But he doesn't have the resources to read the patterns and join the dots in the way we do. The long and the short of it is, you've got people talking and not in the way you might think. More often than not the really interesting stuff goes on in the same dark corners of the web where you talk to the Reverend' – that he knew about my dealings with the Rev was a hammer blow, I'll admit – 'but you've started *something*.

'It may just be a murmur for now, but the signs are that at any moment it might turn into a roar. There are tremors. And tremors presage earthquakes. And if that were to happen, well, that's when all bets are off. Again, if you'd asked me a few months ago, I – in fact, everyone back at the office – would have said that if it did all kick off, we were not ready. That the consequences for England would be devastating. That's why I was sent up to Invereiton Castle to kill you. We needed to delay this breakdown in society in Caledon and the only way to do that was to take active steps to shore it up in the interim.'

He looked at his watch and back to me.

'I'm terribly sorry, but we are running very short on time. As much as it pains me to say it – and do it – I must now kill you,' he concluded, with an apologetic shrug. 'And it does pain me: I have huge admiration for you. We are very alike, you see.'

'We are *nothing* alike,' I spat back at him. Keeping him talking was proving easier than I thought. If there's one good thing about zealots, it's that they feel obligated to explain why they're killing you.

'Aren't we, though?' he continued, with appalling self-certainty. 'We both believe passionately in our countries and in what we perceive to be right. And we are both thoroughly intolerant of anyone abusing those things. Our methods aren't even that different.'

My mind was reeling. Weirdly, I wasn't thinking about dying. Rather, I wanted to know what Hildy really meant when he'd said I had 'started something'. Was the touchpaper truly lit? The thought of it filled me with elation after the recent spate of disappointments. It offered a glimmer of hope that the whole shambles might have been worth it.

But in those moments of optimism I had forgotten one thing: the conversation had ended. Blunt raised the gun.

'One last thing!' I yelped. 'Just one last thing. You haven't answered my question. Why go to all this trouble? If you wanted me dead, why not do it yourself when we were in England? Why run this whole Marischal assassination charade?'

'*Seriously?* Have the famous *Jimmy Mac* die on English soil?' he said in disbelief. 'It would be a huge propaganda victory for the Marischal and an excuse for our enemies – the ones who are already in unholy alliances with your government – to exert more pressure on us. The truth is, once I'd missed you at the shoot, I did suggest giving it another whirl. But, aside from the fact it would be incredibly difficult to organise, by then politics had moved on, as they are wont to do. The British public—'

'Hildy, for the last time, there's no such thing.'

'I do wish you'd stop interrupting. Look, in the corridors of power the feeling was the public in both Caledon and England was lapping up the adventures of the Wolf of Badenoch. It seemed that if you died – by our hand or, as seemed more likely, the Marischal's – there would be unrest and we'd have to step in anyway. The public would demand it. So the Chief wasn't lying to you about averting a war, you see. Nor was he lying about having to leave it to you if we wanted the cleanest option possible. But we still needed to do it on our terms so we'd have a half-decent chance of managing the fallout. Hence you taking the matter into your own hands, with, well, a little bit of direction from us.'

'So you wanted to have your cake and eat it.'

'There, I knew you'd get it in the end.'

'But what about that death-trap flat you tried to set me up with?'

'Yes, I feel a little bad about that,' he said, a look of contrition on his face. 'Christmas time was a terrible time of year for it and it was the best we could do. Again, though, a calculated risk. If you'd died a martyr that had its upsides too.'

'Which leads us to the final question: if you didn't give me up how did they know where I'd be? How did they know about the others?'

'Now, that, I admit, is vexing. I don't know how the Mallice found them. I don't know how they found you or, rather, where you were supposed to be. Perhaps we underestimated them. Don't you worry though; we will get to the bottom of it.'

'Of course, you underestimated them. With your arrogance and your goddamned national superiority. You'd think you'd have learned from hundreds of years of this kind of behaviour and everything it's brought, but apparently not. Anyway, what if we'd been captured? What if they'd tortured your involvement out of us? What if we'd given you up freely? I certainly bloody would have done. I would have sung like an overly oxygenated canary.'

'Oh, if necessary, you would have been killed,' Blunt said. 'We had booby-trapped the flats in case the Mallice were less, er, *thorough* than we expected them to be. Of course, with a bunch of thugs like that, you can usually rely on their predictability. A very capable lot. And even if they had gone in with orders to capture rather than kill, we presumed there was no way you guys were going to be taken alive.'

'You'd be surprised what a premium I put on staying alive,' I told him.

'Well, indeed, but don't you worry yourself,' he said patronisingly. 'As I said, we honestly didn't want you dead; we really wanted you to succeed. But if it came to it and you were caught, there were secondary – Lord, even tertiary – plans in place to deal with such circumstances. We do not do things by halves, Mr Macfarlane.'

'Evidently,' I said, before lapsing into silence.

Hildy sipped his tea and then lifted the pistol slightly towards me once more. 'No more questions?' he asked politely. 'I am answering truthfully out of respect for you and because this is a very good cup of tea and it seems a shame to waste it.'

'It is one of Archie's many skills,' I said, shifting in my seat. The barrel followed me.

'Oh, please don't try anything,' Blunt said, taking another sip. 'Let's end this with dignity, shall we? Please, rest easy in the knowledge that there is nothing you can do that will stop the bullet from this pistol passing through your brain. Nothing whatsoever.'

'That's all very well, but you still haven't explained why you want to kill me now.'

'Oh, this is just one of those tertiary plans I mentioned. I don't want to be prosaic about it, but you are far too much of a nuisance to leave alive. It's all got quite out of hand. I mean, crikey, I'm the one telling this story and I'm struggling to keep up.'

Now, your genuine assassin would have a clever way out of this, I have no doubt. Pre-determined distractions would be engaged, gadgets activated, enemies rent asunder. But, as I've said before, I've got no head for the assassination game – nor, clearly, for this level of political intrigue. So instead I just sat and looked at him. Blunt, for his part, raised the pistol a fraction higher.

He put down the teacup with care and clicked off the safety. 'Goodbye, James. It really has been a pleasure working with you.'

I stared at him in what I'd love to say was one last act of defiance, but it was actually all I could think to do at the time. I waited for the end. I knew there'd be no warning. The bullet would travel considerably faster than the sound of the shot. There would be no final fanfare: just silence. Forever and ever. Nothing could save me now.

Then the phone rang.

CHAPTER 9

Toil and Trouble

I kid you not: I was saved by the bell. For a moment at least. First my pocket vibrated and then the old-fashioned ring called out.

'What the hell,' Hildy spluttered in disbelief. 'You're not serious? You've still got a *mobile phone*? In this day and age?'

He was so surprised by this anachronism that he forgot to kill me. Instead he actually laughed. Then the phone stopped.

'What? You think I'd get one of your bloody implants?' I snapped back. 'Would you choose to live under a totalitarian dictatorship with a GPS tracker under your skin?'

'Yes, of course, I suppose you're right,' he began, as my phone rang again, before cutting off after just a few rings.

Then it happened a third time. Perhaps it was just the tension in the room, but these short blasts felt as if they had an urgency to them. An air of desperation. Then things got properly out of hand. The heavy-duty device on Hildy's wrist lit up as someone tried calling *him*. He glanced at it and back at me. A look of deep concern had come over his face. I imagine my face was the same. Only one person I could think of had both our numbers.

'Who is it?' I asked, praying I was wrong.

The wrist strap stopped flashing. After a beat, it started again.

'Answer it, for God's sake,' I urged. 'I'm not going anywhere.'

He switched the gun into his left hand and kept it levelled at me. 'I'm just as good with this hand,' he said, unnecessarily. Folk like that usually are. He pressed a finger against the cochlear implant beneath his ear. 'Look, this isn't a good time,' he said. I looked unsuccessfully for the tell-tale scar that would reveal the sub-dermal chip at his voice box. 'I'm . . .'

He stopped. And he listened. The pistol did a rare thing: it wobbled in his hand. His slow, steady breathing turned ragged.

'What's going on?' I pressed, an empty feeling filling my stomach.

He pressed a button on his wrist and the room filled with a voice. A woman's voice. A woman in agony.

'Oh God, they made me tell . . .' It subsided into coughing and moaning. 'Oh God . . . They know where you are . . . They know all about the plan . . . About Mac; about everything. I didn't want to tell them but, oh God, I couldn't let them hurt—'

Her words were lost as another coughing fit racked her. Then it hit me like a bucket of iced water: I knew that broken voice. But I had never heard it in such despair. Blunt was way ahead of me.

'Lizzy, where are you?' he said urgently. 'What have those bastards done to you?'

'Hang up,' I said, equally urgently. 'Hildy, for God's sake, hang up *now*! They'll be tracking us.'

'It doesn't matter . . . They know . . . You've got to run . . .' Lizzy's voice faltered, before another voice replaced hers. It was a cold drawl I knew too well.

'Oh, you can run,' the voice said. 'In fact, I'd rather like it if you did. Yes, please do run. But, rest assured, you can't hide. I don't think there are enough trees for that around your little white house, are there? I suppose you could head for the mountains, but it'll take you an age to get yourself properly lost in there. And you don't have an age. So, start running, my little rabbits. I shall be seeing you shortly. Goodbye.'

The line went silent.

'Lizzy!' Hildy yelled in impotent misery, before rounding on me, stabbing the pistol in my direction. 'Who was that?' he shouted and pleaded all at once.

I marvelled at him: this man with ice in his head, who, like so many before him, had been undone by the fire in his heart.

'That was Thomas Loker, Director of the Marischal Police Division – the Mallice,' I said, anger growing inside me. 'What exactly did you tell Lizzy?'

'What? I . . .' he stuttered.

Suddenly, I had him by the lapels of his jacket and was shaking him, the gun flopping and flailing in his limp hand.

'What did you tell her?' I shouted in his face, as the floorboards above came alive with the sound of running feet. The empty horror in the pit of my stomach at hearing her tortured voice had been replaced with a white-hot fury.

'Oh God, *everything*,' said the lovesick fool. 'I knew I shouldn't have, but it just seemed like the right—'

'Save it.' I pushed him back in disgust. 'If we don't get out of here, then she never gets out of there. Wherever there is.'

'She can't have told him everything.' Blunt's face drained of all colour.

'Oh, trust me, she can and she will have,' I said, turning to shout up the stairs. 'Archie, Wally, we—'

Before I could finish, big boots trampled down the stairs.

'They're here, sir!' cried Archie. 'Ah've counted at least a dozen o' the bastards comin' doon fae the hills at the back.'

'The drones are tracking a convoy of black vehicles coming up the road from the south, Cap'n,' Wally called out. 'No more than a few minutes until they're here. I didn't get any signals. They must have been blocking me. They must know we're here.'

'They know we're here alright. We need to get out of here now,' I ordered. 'We're executing Operation Styx. Straight to the boats.'

'The boats?' said Hildy in bewilderment.

'Like you, I have secondary and even tertiary plans,' I said, stuffing a couple of final bits into a rucksack.

He was standing, completely lost, the pistol now hanging limp at his side.

'May I have that?' I asked, putting out a hand to take the gun. 'I imagine you have another.'

He handed it over in a daze. 'But what about Lizzy?' he said plaintively.

'Don't you worry. I'm going to find Loker and beat him until he tells me where she is, then I'm going to hand him to Archie so the fun can really begin. But if we're going to save her, we must get out of here; we must live to fight another day.'

The front door banged open as Archie and Wally clattered out. Through the warped glass of the cottage windows I could see them heading for the trees at speed. Wally even contrived to stay on his feet.

'What about me?' Hildy said.

'Divide and conquer,' I replied. 'I have no doubt you have plans to get away from here – you're a resourceful chap. Once we're safe, I'll consider whether I need your help again. Goodbye, Blunt. I can say with utter certainty that it has not been a pleasure.'

As I dashed across the gravel in front of the cottage to the trees, I looked back for a split second and saw Blunt standing motionless in the doorway. Perhaps it was my furious glance, but he seemed to snap out of his trance and disappeared into the house. His day was shaping up as badly as mine, which offered some comfort.

I was into the trees in seconds, through the pines and out across the road almost as quickly. After that we were into the wide-open space of the floodplain, with about a hundred and fifty metres to cross before we reached the river. The ground was covered in short, stubby grass and pocked with rabbit holes, while the earth was soft underfoot. I can't think of worse terrain to have to run over.

I was rapidly closing on Archie, who was himself a few metres behind Wally, when there was a horrible crack and the big man crashed to the ground, just twenty metres short of the canoes tied up on the riverbank ahead.

Wally stopped in his tracks and doubled back to him.

'Get tae yer boat, yeh silly bastard,' Archie yelled at him, struggling to his feet and growling as he put weight on a broken . . . ankle? Tibia?

'Oh, shut up! Just, for once, shut up,' came the response as Wally yanked off Archie's rucksack and dropped it with his on the ground. Squatting down, he lifted a big arm around his little shoulders and heaved until both he and Archie were upright, the wee man now acting as a crutch for the hobbled giant.

'Yer a bluidy idiot,' Archie was saying to him. 'Ah wouldnae come back fer you, yeh know.'

'Aye, I'll bet you wouldn't – typical Weegee,* came the response. 'Come on, you lazy, fat git. Jesus, can't you give me a hand here? You've still got one working leg, don't you?'

The bickering continued as I passed them, scooping up one of the fallen backpacks and heading to my canoe, where I intended to drop the kit and return to take Wally's place.

Something whistled past me, making a dull thud as it hit the turf ahead. I stopped dead. Another projectile sped past my face. I felt the air shift as it shot by, hitting the river at subsonic speed. I looked back to the road, where four, maybe five, black 4x4s had pulled up and were disgorging Mallice. Two or three were leaning on the bonnets of their cars to steady themselves for the shot. To the left and right more were fanning out, looking to outflank us. Capable, you see?

'That one!' a piercing cry rang out. 'The one by the canoes. We only need that one. Anyone who hurts him will answer to me!'

* Derogatory term for someone from Glasgow.

As these instructions were delivered, I was covering the ground to where Wally's small frame was struggling to heft Archie's mighty bulk across the grass. Flattering myself that I was the one they wanted alive, I put myself between my boys and the shooters as Archie tried to hop along. But the soft ground gave way beneath his feet and he kept stumbling, almost dragging Wally onto the pocked turf each time. We were covering the distance at a hellishly slow pace, the bullets thumping in the earth all around us. Again Archie went down and again Wally put an almighty effort into heaving him to his feet. But the strained grunt that came from Wally's mouth was cut unnaturally short.

'Whit is it, pal?' Archie's eyes widened in shock.

Blood coursed out of Wally's neck and down over his chest. He gagged and spat bloody saliva over his chin. A look of complete surprise came over his face and he turned to stare up at Archie. Then, without a word, he collapsed on the ground and was still. I froze, appalled, before throwing myself down next to Archie, who was already on the ground cradling Wally's body, blood slick on his waterproof jacket. I felt for Wally's pulse as it slowed and then died.

'Come oan, pal,' Archie groaned. 'Jist a few more steps, eh, wee man? Ah'll pick up the pace, ah promise . . .'

The Mallice advanced on us from behind and on both sides: a net closing in. I stared at Wally. His eyes were wide open, crystal clear and blue. But the questing light that had always danced within them was gone. I threw my arms around the two of them, acting as a human shield.

'Archie!' I said firmly into his ear.

Archie just knelt there, swaying slightly, staring at the body of his nemesis and best friend.

'Archie, we have to go!' I commanded, trying to shake him out of the trance. I dashed the tears from my eyes and tried to lift him. It was like hefting a fallen tree trunk. 'We can't help Wally now,

Archie,' I implored him. 'We have to go. We will repay this, but we can't do it now. And we can't do it if we're dead.'

I looked from side to side at the closing perimeter. Then something strange happened. The agents directly behind us started falling: some silently, others screaming as they crashed to the ground. Yells of confusion were mingled with hurried orders and I wheeled round to look behind me.

There, in the trees before the cottage, and standing square like a target shooter, was Hildy, calmly picking them off with a pistol. I caught his eye and he nodded before downing another of the Mallice. I returned the gesture automatically, before turning back to Archie and wondering how on earth I was to get him – and myself – to safety.

That, incidentally, was the last time I saw Hildebrand Blunt. I couldn't tell you why he did it or how long he kept up the cover fire. At some point I glanced back and he was gone, as if he'd never been there at all. I can only presume he tried to save me as a way of increasing our chances of saving Lizzy. Or perhaps the scenario offended some inbred sense of fair play. Maybe it was all just part of the plan. Whatever the case, I like to think he's rotting in a ditch somewhere, riddled with Mallice bullets. But then people of his ilk tend to survive and prosper. The bastards.

'Archie, you are to leave with me now,' I said, quietly but insistently.

'You go on, sir,' he said in an absent-minded way, as if he had bigger thoughts to mull over. 'Ah cannae leave Wally . . . Ah jist cannae. And yeh'll no' git awa' fae this lot if yer carryin' me. As yeh said, there's nae point in us all dyin'. Best if I hang aroond tae hold 'em aff, eh?'

'Archie, that is a direct order.'

'We're a bit late fer that, Mr Mac,' he said, looking up from Wally for the first time as another bullet zinged past us and hammered into the soft earth. Then, as God's my witness, he stood up straight and came to attention. Throwing up his hand, he saluted as the bullets rhythmically beat out a retreat on the ground around us.

I stared into the eyes of that meeting of unstoppable force and immovable object. They were clear and focused. There was not one ounce of fear. There was only determination to complete one last job.

I realised he was right. I wouldn't get him to the boat in time. And if I went down in a blaze of glory, who would save Lizzy?

'Go silent, sir.'

'Leave no shadow,' I whispered, swallowing hard and returning his stiff salute.

He thrust out his huge hand and grabbed my forearm. 'It's been an honour, Mr Mac.'

'The honour has been all mine, Archie.' I went to withdraw my arm, but he held it fast.

'One last thing,' he said, looking briefly from side to side at the net, which was closing again now Blunt was gone. 'The No. 1.'

I looked at him, baffled. Then I realised what he was talking about: the legendary hangover cure that was so potent he hardly dared speak its name. He wouldn't let the secret die with him. This was his last gift to me.

I had waited so long for it. But I didn't want it. Not now. There must be another time. A better time. A happier time. I told Archie all this in a garbled stream. Archie listened to my pleas for a few seconds, like an indulgent parent, then began to talk over the top of me.

As he spoke, it was as if the whole world around us had stopped. No, that's not quite right, the world didn't stop, but it just seemed a great distance away. All the yelling and screaming, muzzle flashes and whining bullets were no more than a pack of dogs barking in some place far off, their howls carried to us on the lightest of breezes. All that was clear in my mind – then and now – was Archie's voice as the world took a step back out of respect for this moment.

'One third cognac. One third dry vermouth. One third absinthe. Stir and strain. Noo repeat it back tae me.'

'One third cognac. One third dry vermouth. One third absinthe.'

'Stir an' strain. Dinnae shake it, fer Goad's sake.'

'Stir and strain.'

'Dinnae shake.'

'Don't shake.'

Archie looked down one last time at Wally then back to me. 'Time tae go, Mr Mac. Remember tae raise a wee toast, eh? A cup tae the dead already.'

Tears clouded my vision again. When I blinked, one rolled down my cheek.

'Hooray for the next to die,' I said, at last finding the strong voice that Archie deserved. 'Cheery-bye, Archie.'

'Aye, cheery-bye, Mr Mac.'

'Archie?'

'Aye?'

'Sorry it has to end like this.'

'Och, we've done OK, haven't we? In the end we knew it wiz a' baws, eh?'

We both smiled.

'You're right, Archie. As ever your gift of clarity is unmatched. A' baws. Yes, it was. Goodbye, Archie.'

We held each other's gaze for one more moment before both turning away. The spell was broken and the world came rushing back at me, filled with shouted orders and pungent nitroglycerine from the pistols wafting in the breeze. I ran the short distance to the canoe and started undoing the mooring rope. But my hands were shaking and I was making a mess of it. Looking around, I saw the agents closing in from both sides.

Archie was back cradling Wally's body, brushing the hair from his lifeless eyes, and whispering something into the ear of his fallen friend. Bullets continued to hammer the ground around him but Archie paid them no heed. Finally, he laid Wally down on the grass, passed his hand over the eyelids, closing them for the last time. Then Archie drew himself up to his full height and looked first to the left, then to the right, and finally back to Wally. At that moment he seemed to inflate: to take on even greater proportions as he inhaled a massive breath. The enormous roar that burst from his chest instinctively checked the advance of both flanking parties. Seemingly impervious to the pain of his shattered bone, he took off, half hobbling, half running, towards the team approaching from the left.

Smart guy, I thought as I leapt into the canoe. Archie had approached the group that was downstream from me and therefore stood the greatest chance of cutting off my escape. They seemed baffled, quite incapable of response, as the oncoming behemoth called down ancient, guttural oaths upon them.

One of the Mallice finally found his wits, unholstered his pistol and shot at Archie at almost point-blank range. If the bullet hit him – and I can't see how the pig could have missed – Archie didn't seem to notice. Without even checking his stride the big man tore into them, downing bodies with enormous swings of his arms, smashing faces into a pulp with that solid head of his. For a brief moment I wondered if Archie could have found a better way to go out than this.

The Battle of the Spey didn't last long; there were just too many of them. As the unsightly pile of men grew around his feet, those left standing gathered themselves and gave Archie a mighty heave, pushing him away from them towards the river. This gave one of the agents enough time to pull out his pistol, which barked three shots in rapid succession. Archie staggered back, a look of shock on his face. The breeze carried his last words to me.

'That's nae way tae fight, yeh cowards. That's bluidy cheatin' . . .'

Then, like a mighty oak, he toppled slowly backwards, into the river, and was gone.

Barely had the water covered his body when I struck out into the strong current in my canoe, searching, tears blinding my eyes. I cast desperately about, but the river was high and rough and I didn't see it – I mean, *him* – surface.

I yelled at the despicable men on the shore as I sped past on the swell. I cursed them and wept at the loss of my friends. No. Of my *family*. Without warning, an enormous force slammed into my side. Time slowed down once more. The noise of the river faded and I could hear a high voice screaming from somewhere far, far away. 'You'd better not have killed him, you idiot! You'd better bloody not have . . .'

All around me the grass, the mountains, the men, and even the sky started to sway and eddy, matching the flow of the river. It was as if the whole world was being borne away on the swirling current. Yet, unlike during Archie's momentous sermon on the hallowed No. 1, the silence brought nothing of import at all. In fact, nothing seemed to matter in the least. I felt so very tired. *Yes, sleep*, I thought, *that cures all, doesn't it? Or is that apples? No matter . . .*

I looked idly at my right arm, which seemed to be covered in warm liquid. Someone had splashed my face with the same. It was running into my eyes, stinging and blinding them. I lay forward on my rucksack. The canoe rocked from side to side and I smiled at the thought of the Reverend suggesting I do this job in a kayak. A ridiculous thought. Darkness came and I closed my eyes, wondering if Archie and Wally – or, yes, my grandparents! – would be there when I woke up. Maybe all of them together. We would share a drink and laugh about all this. I was at peace. Ready to meet my Maker.

Unfortunately, my Maker seemed quite unwilling to meet me.

CHAPTER 10

Sound and Fury

The serenity didn't last. It never does. When I woke, I opened my eyes – only to be plunged into a new terror. It was black as pitch, and at first I thought I had been blinded, so complete was the darkness. I reached out my hands and felt a sharp pain in my right arm. Exploring it tentatively, I found it to be bandaged. Then I touched my face, which was dry. The tenderness of my right cheek revealed some heavy bruising around what felt like butterfly stitches.

I stretched out again and felt smooth walls on either side of me, just beyond my shoulders, and then another, a couple of feet from my face. Oh Jesus, they hadn't buried me alive, had they? My breath came fast as I hammered on those smooth walls, sweating from fear and exertion, shouting out to invisible saviours, preferably those in possession of spades. The noise echoed around me, but no answer came. I forced myself to be calm. Forced my pounding heart to slow as I let the environment wrap itself around me.

Just then, after an extended absence, Common Sense popped up to point out it was very unlikely that I was buried since I was sitting on some kind of bench. I did the old avalanche trick and let some spit drip out of my mouth. It slid reassuringly down my chin, meaning I was upright. I sensed a rocking motion. A distant hum crept grudgingly into my ears.

We are in some kind of vehicle, Common Sense kindly pointed out.

I stood up and banged my head hard on the roof, cursed loudly, and sat down. Again, I focused and let my senses take over. I was being transported somewhere. But why, and where we were going, remained a mystery. I banged over and over on the wall in front of me. Nothing happened. I sat down, panting hard, my bandaged arm throbbing.

The impenetrable darkness and the silence – only broken by that dull engine hum – brought the memory of Wally and Archie's murders charging out of the darkness. A gut-wrenching grief made me double over and hit my head on the wall in front. There was nowhere left to go. The game was up. I had hit rock bottom.

Enveloped by darkness, my ears picked up a new noise. It sounded like a dog whimpering. Slowly, it crystallised into a sobbing sound.

'Hello?' I shouted, banging on the walls again with renewed vigour. 'Is someone there? Can you hear me?'

I listened again. The crying had stopped. Was this some psychological torture technique of the Mallice?

'Hello!' I bellowed, as loud as I could. 'Is there anybody there?'

A small, halting voice drifted into my blackened cell. 'James? Is that you?'

I pinned myself back against the wall, breathing fast. I wanted to curl into a ball; be lost to all of this. I didn't know whether to laugh or to weep myself. Because there was no doubt: it was Lizzy's voice.

'James?' she repeated, her voice unsure.

'Lizzy, is that you?' I shouted back, shocked into action.

'Yes,' she replied, before coughing violently and moaning.

'Are you OK?' I asked carefully. None of this felt right. Nothing was coincidence. Everything was planned, devised, coordinated, and controlled. But to what end?

'What happened to you?' I asked. 'Do you know where we are?'

'I'm so sorry, James . . .' she said, before lapsing into silence again.

'There's no need to be sorry for anything,' I said, my concern for her replacing worries for my own well-being, if only for a moment. 'We need to work out how to get out of here.'

'We can't get out of here; there's nowhere left to go,' the voice said quietly. Sadly.

My brain hurt. I felt as if I was back trying to build Blunt's jigsaw, but now with no idea of the picture and half the pieces missing.

'Lizzy, please, try to take some deep breaths. I need you to tell me what happened.'

'I tried to warn you, James. I tried to stop you, but you wouldn't listen.'

'Look, you've got nothing to apologise for. It was Blunt. It was me. But it's not your fault.'

'I tried to warn you,' she said again. 'You wouldn't listen. You don't understand. I couldn't let you go through with it. I need him alive. But I never wanted this.'

'What? Why? Who?' I spluttered.

'Without him, I lose everything.'

'For God's sake, Lizzy, without *who*?'

'The Marischal. Duncan Finlay. Who else?'

'I don't understand. You hate the regime more than anyone else I know.'

'No, I don't. I'm not you, James. Not everyone sees the world like you do. Without the regime, I'd be nothing. Everything I have I've taken from the opportunities afforded by this regime. The regime suits me fine. I need the regime.'

'I don't understand.'

'Yes, you do. You understand better than anyone. You've done better than all of us. You seem to have forgotten that it was only recently – only after you'd become the most famous person in the country – that you developed a conscience.'

I let that go, mainly because the truth hurts. 'But you helped me. Without you, the Wolf was nothing. Everything the Wolf – everything *we* did was to bring the regime down.'

'No! Everything *you* did was to bring the regime down. You just presumed I was in it for the same reasons. You and your goddamned ego can't see past the end of your nose.'

'My God, why then?'

Lizzy paused for a long time. 'Everything changed when I had my daughter,' she murmured at last from her place in the dark.

'You have a what now?'

'It's all for her.'

I was stumped. I sat in the rumbling, swaying gloom and waited.

She paused again. I thought I heard her take a deep breath, but in that silent black tomb it could have been my imagination.

'Three years ago, do you remember a crazy rumour that I'd spent a year with a German prince?' she began.

'Yes, of course.'

'It was a lie, but one I made up to cover the fact I was . . . pregnant. A crazy lie, but who can tell the difference anymore? I just needed to be away, so no one could know. For my sake, and for the safety of the baby.' She paused. 'A little baby girl, James!' she came back, her voice all love, longing, and fear. 'I did everything I could to hide her, but Loker found her and threatened to kill her. Saw it as a betrayal, you see. Somehow, in his warped mind, it was OK for me to sleep with other people; he could endure that. Out of sight, out of mind, you know? But a baby? That was something different.

'He came and he raged at me and then he went off. Two days later he came back and took her away. I kicked and screamed and fought but his thugs held me while he rocked her in his arms, the bastard, and told me if he couldn't have my body to himself, he would at least have my mind. He actually said that! "I will have your mind." What kind of person demands another person's mind?'

I sat in mute fear as she raged.

'He took her. Told me she would be safe as long as I became his informant. It started harmlessly enough – tittle-tattle, gossip, that kind of thing – and she was returned to me. Everything went on as before, except that now, chunks of information were being funnelled to Loker. He even made me swear not to tell the Marischal about our arrangement, as he called it.

'To start with, gossip was all he wanted, but it was like a drug for him. I had to feed his habit with more and more information. He's obsessed by knowing *everything*, you know? He's terrified of not knowing, being cut out, being isolated. Knowledge is his power and what I know is more than most, as you're well aware. What I gave him meant he could manipulate, compel, and coerce some of the most powerful people in the country.

'I wanted to end it, but as long as Loker could threaten my little one, there was no way out. In the end I realised I would never really get her back – get myself back – unless I could get rid of him. The only way to do that was to prove to the Marischal that Loker was untrustworthy. Unreliable. Incompetent. A liability. That's why I helped you. Why I did everything else. I don't care about the Marischal – but I do care that he survives, at least for now. Don't you see? Getting rid of Loker is the only way I can get my little one back and the only person powerful enough to do that is the Marischal. I couldn't let you kill him. My God, I tried to warn you. I tried to stop you, but you wouldn't bloody listen.'

Images of her desperation at the club came flooding back. 'Lizzy, what did you do?'

When Lizzy spoke, her voice was strong and even. Unapologetic. 'As soon as Hildy told me about the plan I knew I had to stop you. If you killed the Marischal, who would step into his shoes? Loker. Who else? Where would that leave me?'

'What did you do?' I demanded through gritted teeth.

'I tried to keep you safe; to give them just enough to stop you, but not enough to catch you.' Again she paused. 'But then Loker—'

'Lizzy, what did you do?' I begged, my voice loud and echoing, in stark contrast to her controlled tone.

'Yesterday I contacted the Marischal's office. I did it anonymously; told them there was a plot against the Marischal. Told them when it was planned for. That was it.'

At the word 'anonymously' I put my head in my hands.

'They came for me early this morning. Hildy had gone from the hotel when I woke up. I was still in bed when they came through the door. They didn't break it down, so they must have had a key.

'They were on me before I could move. They dragged me off the bed, put a bag over my head, tied my hands, and carried me out of the room. I tried to kick them, bite them, anything I could. They stood me up in the corridor and one of them punched me in the stomach. I couldn't breathe. Couldn't see. I was so scared, James.'

I sat listening in silent horror to her account of the mechanical, well-practised violence.

'Then they took me by the arms and dragged me along a corridor, down the stairs, and threw me into a car. Then they drove me to . . . God, I don't know where. They pulled me along corridors, through doors, up and down stairs. I begged them to stop. To take the bag off. I could hardly breathe. They threw me in a chair and handcuffed me to a metal ring on a table. Then they pulled off the bag.'

She stopped, unable to go on.

'OK, Lizzy,' I said in as measured a tone as I could manage. 'Tell me everything you can, any detail, no matter how small.'

The voice came back softly: 'It was so bright in there. I was cold. Shivering. It wasn't a very big room. The paint was light green and peeling from the walls. It smelled musty. And it was bright. So bright I had to squint to see. Loker came in. I remember the look on his face so clearly. He looked calm, but – it was weird – he looked *sad*. He told me he was "so disappointed in me". I told him I didn't know what he was talking about. Then he got angry. So angry. Told me he knew what I'd done. Yelled at me: asking why I didn't come to him about the plot. Asked me if I knew how much damage I'd caused.'

There in the darkness, I heard her laugh at this small victory.

'I told him I was trying to help. Begged forgiveness for my *mistake*. Then Loker asked me for more detail. When I said I didn't know, he didn't say anything. A calm seemed to settle on him. Then he hit me. Again and again. I couldn't even defend myself – that bloody coward – because my hands were cuffed to the table. The worst thing was it was so mechanical. He kept saying how disappointed he was, then hitting me again. Then he stopped and asked what the plans were. And do you know what? I realised I wasn't scared any more. I was angry. Certain I wouldn't let him win this time. I spat blood at him and cursed him.

'Then he stopped hitting me and left the room. I don't know for how long, but it seemed like hours. By the time he came back I was so cold, shaking uncontrollably in that horrid, bright room. I wanted to stop. Didn't want him to think I was scared. But I couldn't. Instead, I called him a coward. Told him to let me go. Repeated everything I had told them already. But he said it wasn't enough. He said the assassination had failed; that you were on the run and he needed my help to track you down.

'My God, it made me so happy! I realised the Marischal must be alive and you must be alive – and you had a chance of escaping. So I said I didn't know anything else. And he just stood and looked at me for a long time. I thought he would start hitting me again but he didn't. Instead he said, "You have done this", and he turned and banged on the big metal door of the room.

'It opened and . . .' She tailed off and the fury was gone. I could hear her taking big gulps of air, trying to steady herself. 'It opened and they brought in Fiona . . .'

'Fiona?' I asked, confused.

'My girl, James, my wee girl!' Lizzy groaned. 'She was so scared. When she saw me all bloody and bruised, she started crying and struggling, fighting to get to me. But that bastard Loker just held her there.

'I begged him to leave her alone – to take her out of there. But all he did was take his hand from behind his back and show me a hammer. Oh Jesus . . .'

She faltered, trying to find words to describe the horror. When she spoke again it was rapid and unbroken as if rushing to finish the story as fast as she could.

'He forced her hand flat onto the table, James. He said if I didn't tell him what he wanted then he'd smash her fingers, one by one. She was so scared. I kept telling her it was going to be OK. She kept pleading with me – with *me*, not *him*, James! – to make her safe. And I couldn't, James. Oh, James . . .'

Faster and faster, higher and higher her voice went as the terrible events unfolded in our inky void.

'He lifted the hammer up and, I swear, I couldn't believe someone was capable of doing that. I just couldn't. So when he asked me again, I said I knew nothing. He held the hammer up high in the air, unmoving, just hanging there. And there was no humanity in his eyes: they were just cold. Completely cold. It was then I knew he *would* do it. I snapped. I was hysterical. Screaming at him to leave us alone – to do it to *me* and not Fiona. And then . . . Oh God, he did it. He raised the hammer and brought it down . . .'

She released a long, deep moan. A sound of utter despair.

'Wee Fiona . . . Oh, she screamed and screamed. She cried and kicked at him, but he held her tightly, with that precious little hand still on the table. One finger still beneath the hammer.'

Suddenly, Lizzy was screaming, banging against the walls of her cell; channelling the fear, pain, and hatred she was describing. God, but she was brave, that one.

'I was pulling at the handcuffs, yelling at him, calling him a coward. Pleading with him to stop, but he just raised the hammer again . . .'

And suddenly she was quiet. When she spoke again, she was calm. Resigned.

'I'm so sorry, James, but I just couldn't watch him smash her little hands . . . I couldn't. So I told him about the rendezvous point. And do you know what he said? He turned to one of the guards and said, "Location confirmed. It is the stolen car." They'd followed you, you fool! Who steals a car in bloody Caledon? They already knew. He smashed Fiona's finger not to find out something new, but to corroborate the evidence. He did that just to double-check! What kind of monster . . . Then he made me call you, and you wouldn't pick up! Why didn't you pick up?'

I said nothing, appalled by what she had told me. In the silence, the story tumbled out of her again.

'He forced me to call Hildy instead and almost as soon as it had connected, the horrid shaved head of one of those awful Mallice men appeared at the door – they must have been working just outside – and he nodded at Loker, so they knew Hildy was there and must be in on it too. And then he had you all in his net. Now you're here. We're here. In the dark.'

'Lizzy,' I said, as calmly as I could. 'Listen to me carefully. What you did was understandable. Forgivable. God, it was bloody noble. If I'd only listened to you . . . There is no blame on you for where we are right now.'

'I know there's no blame, James. Do you think I'm asking for your forgiveness? My God! You did what you needed to do. I did what I needed to do. Neither of us wanted this. Neither of us planned it. We fought and we lost. We bloody lost.'

It was tough to argue with that assessment. We lapsed into silence, each crammed into our own little hell. Not long after, the swaying of the vehicle stopped. I sat up, muscles taut and mind alert. There was the sound of a lock opening, a bolt sliding back, a heavy door being wrenched open, creaking on its hinges, footsteps. Within four or five paces they were at my door and an electronic lock hummed. As it opened, my pit was flooded with light and I screwed my eyes shut as strong hands dragged me up and out of my cell.

'James!' Lizzy shouted, banging on the walls of her cell like she was possessed. I began shouting to her. I told her . . . Well, who knows? In truth it's a bit of a blur; it happened so fast. I probably told her that everything was going to be all right. That I would come back for her and . . . Well, you know.

Who knows what I might have said if an enormous fist hadn't slammed into my stomach, driving the breath out of me? All I know is I wish I'd said goodbye.

CHAPTER 11

Fire Burn and Cauldron Bubble

They dragged me into the sunlight, gasping for breath, slamming the heavy door behind me, once again burying Lizzy in the darkness. It still galls me that they wouldn't even let me see her, say goodbye to her. That seems a particularly cruel icing on an already despicable cake.

Looking around, still doubled up and fighting for breath, I saw I was in a small, nondescript courtyard, surrounded by high granite walls topped with razor wire. We could have been anywhere, but I knew with utter certainty where I was. I was down the road from Edinburgh Castle – a few hundred metres from where, just a few hours before, I had tried to kill the Marischal. I was in that dread place whose notoriety had made me shy away from its walls as I'd walked past that very morning. I was a resident of the Tolbooth.

Turning to look at the vehicle from which I had just emerged, the latest in an ever-growing line of shocks hit my well-shaken system. It's a wonder I've not gone mad, really it is. Unless I have. But that's far too big a topic to address right now.

The thing is, I had seen that mobile prison before. In fact, I'd seen it, or one like it, dozens of times. It was a medium-sized lorry, decked out in the livery of a laundry company and looking, for all the world, like a normal delivery vehicle. But looking now, with the scales falling from my eyes, I could see that the rear was made of solid steel. Large rivets ran up and down the side of the lorry, marking what I now knew to be the lines of cells inside.

How many prisoners and dissidents were being moved secretly around the country in this way? Sliding past us as we walked along the street. Stopping next to us at traffic lights; their terrified, isolated, and anonymous passengers just centimetres away, yet unable to see us out in daylight. Out of sight and out of mind. Out of their minds. These observations lasted just a few seconds. The two Mallice officers on either side of me pulled me swiftly through a pair of thick metal doors into the Tolbooth proper and along a thin white corridor blazing with stark strip lights.

The next moments passed in a blur. From what I remember, those enormous specimens took me to a large tiled room and stripped me of my clothes, which they laid in a meticulous pile to be catalogued later. They even took off my delicate little golden bangle without so much as scratching it and placed it on top. Only I was to be damaged, it seemed. They dragged me to a large tiled pool of water, just like the communal bathtubs you used to see footballers cavorting in. They threw me in and waded straight in after me themselves, without even stopping to roll up their trousers or grab water wings.

Then they did their best to kill me. Over and over again they held me under the water for a minute at a time, pulling me up just in time for me to take a desperate breath before I was plunged under once again. This kept them entertained for a good while before they half-carried, half-dragged me out of that room, still naked, and then down a set of stairs into another one.

As we entered, I recognised it immediately from my mind's eye. The musty smell, the dirt, the peeling green paint, the table with the heavy metal ring screwed into it. This was where Loker had interrogated Lizzy. I was forced into the same chair and my hands dragged out in front of me and secured to the table by a man of quite extraordinary size. Then, I was left alone. The room was exactly as Lizzy had described it. My bare feet slipped on the floor and I recoiled as I looked down to see that they were sliding on a patch of blood. Was it Lizzy's? Or that of some other poor unfortunate who had been here in between our visits?

The memory of Loker sitting on my exquisite sofa in Glenlairig rushed back. He had come there to scare me into some kind of admission that I was the Wolf of Badenoch. He had asked all sorts of questions but he seemed most interested in my thoughts on coercion and, in particular, torture. I remember his voice had not been aggressive or snide, only full of psychiatric enquiry: *The very idea of being put to The Question fills most people with terror. You, on the other hand, don't even register it. The notion is alien to you . . . You do not for one moment truly believe you could ever be put to The Question!'* Well, I did now and the idea made bile rise up my throat. Oh God, what had he said about unleashing a *symphony of despair*?

Then two things struck me that gave me a little boost. Firstly, I could *smell* her. Snatches of her perfume had infused the room. Lizzy had left a bit of her old self behind and it was as good as a hug at that moment, I can tell you. Secondly, it was immediately apparent that something about the place was wrong. In fact, the *whole room* was wrong. The peeling paint, the exposed old piping on the walls: it just didn't add up. This wasn't a medieval prison; it was positively postmodern. The New Tolbooth had been built fairly recently, which meant the decor had been *prepared* to look like this. It was a sham intended to intimidate and disorientate.

I thought of my time in Lord Farquharson's designer dungeon and a small smile crept across my face. One of the keys to a successful interrogation is making the victim feel hopeless. This room had been purpose-built for that. They'd even removed all the light switches so the resident would know there was no escape from the burning halogen strip light above. Admirable craftsmanship. In situations like this, the intended victim must find whatever slivers of hope he or she can to keep their spirit from breaking. And I'd already found two. A strong start from the underdog.

The Man of Quite Extraordinary Size came back a few minutes later. I looked up at the towering figure and thought him lucky: he'd surely only just made the cut when God decided to move on from gorillas to humans. A metal chair grated on the stone floor as the giant dragged it, protesting, to the other side of the table.

'Hello, Mr Macfarlane,' the man said in a voice that was surprisingly light. 'Or should I call you James?'

He placed his huge hands on the table, spreading his fingers on the metal, then opened his mouth to speak again. I screwed my eyes shut and, trying not to be sick with fear, did the only thing I knew how to do when cornered: I came out fighting. Or, rather, Jimmy Mac did.

'Oh, just stop right there,' I said, a pained note in my voice, eyes cast to the ceiling. 'I mean, *really*.'

He sat back, looking confused.

I ploughed on. 'Let me save us both the excruciating awkwardness of this charade. I am well versed in how this goes. Firstly, you're going to try to create a rapport with me. Establish trust, yes? Then you're going to create a "baseline" against which to judge my future behaviour, now that I am relaxed. Am I right so far?'

He stared at me impassively, saying nothing. Studying me for the baseline, I suppose, just as he'd been trained to do. It was surely a technique he'd used to great effect on previous occasions. Well, he hadn't tried interrogating me before.

'Once you've got – or you *think* you've got – a handle on the *real* me, you're going to start asking lots of questions, right? Ones that you think will reveal whether I'm using the power of recall or just creativity to make it all up. Yes? Am I still warm?' I raised my eyebrows. 'You might even study my eyes to see if I look right when I answer – a sign that I'm remembering something – or left, suggesting I'm making it up.' I leaned in conspiratorially. 'Now – just between us friends – that's nonsense. An old wives' tale. But keep it under your hat.'

I tapped my handcuffed finger on my nose, which must have looked odd as my cheek was almost on the table to complete the manoeuvre. Then I sat back up as brightly as my naked state permitted, warming to the task.

'After that, you'll probably get a bit nasty, eh? You'll be moving on to the confrontation stage. Then you might have a go at "theme development".' I made inverted comma signs with my cuffed fingers.

He sat, impassive, no doubt wondering what the bloody hell to do next.

'You'll throw some theories out there about what I did and why I did it, to see if I latch on to any of them. They'll get starker and the consequences more terrifying, because you'll be hoping they'll make me feel hopeless. You'll give me no opportunity to reason with you. Oh, the misery! Oh, the humanity!

'If you haven't broken me by then, I can look forward to touching levels of compassion and understanding: you would have done the same thing in my circumstances, et cetera, et cetera.'

I paused to smile at him.

'Now, isn't that better? Hasn't that saved us both a lot of time that could have been wasted on such a lovely day?'

He betrayed nothing on his capable face. Instead, he got up and left. As he closed the door, the lights went out, plunging me into darkness. Touché.

And so the curtain came down on my little piece of theatre and I took small consolation that my gambit to keep control seemed to have worked. That was important because, my insurgent apprentice, when they have you in custody and want something from you, they will do their best to make you feel hopeless. You must fight this with everything you've got. But that's just the starting point. If you are to win the day and fight another, you have to do more than that. Because, when they come to interrogate you, they are going to impose their reality on you. You must push back and thumb your nose at their *tedious* grasp on the truth. Instead, you must impose *your* reality on *them*. In my reality – as ludicrous as we know it to be – I was brave and wronged, faultless and maligned. In my reality, I would maintain an unwavering claim to innocence – the only defence against my ubiquitous guilt.

Not long after, the door was thrown open and in the rectangle of light that split the darkness stood the man of the hour: one Thomas Loker, Director of the Marischal Police Division, and the nation's greatest sadist. Considering the company he kept, this was an impressive accomplishment. He stood there, smoothing down his uniform as if he had rushed to make our appointment. The dead fish eye stared in mute accusation.

'Now, look here,' I began with as much affront as I could muster, squinting as the stark strip light above me flickered back on, filling the room with harsh light. 'This is an outrage! I demand—'

Loker silenced me with a disinterested wave of his hand. 'Be quiet, Macfarlane,' he said, in the sniping voice I had last heard shouting orders by the river where Archie and Wally had died. 'You are guilty. The case against you is open and shut. No amount of your famous charm or bluster will change that.'

'Guilty of what, damn you?' I said with force and confidence as fear washed over me.

'I have no idea,' Loker said, surprised. 'I haven't decided yet.'
Oh bugger.

He stood there appraising me, his thin ferret-like face frozen in concentration. I studied him silently in return. Perhaps 'ferret' was unfair, I mused. His face could equally be described as like that of a fox.

'I have just returned from Holyrood Palace,' he said. 'There I reported the successful capture of the terrorist known as the Wolf of Badenoch.'

I was about to start denying everything when he raised a hand again, gloved in grey suede, and said, 'Oh, don't bother denying it; it won't make any difference. It will just be boring and cause you a lot of unnecessary pain. You can avoid that. For now, anyway.'

You won't be surprised to hear that I am against unnecessary pain, particularly when it is being inflicted on me. Indeed, the notion of unnecessary pain seems a total oxymoron. I said as much to Loker as I changed tack and confirmed I was guilty as charged. I moved on to battles I might actually win.

'I'll admit: your admission disappoints me,' he responded. 'I had hoped you'd try to deny it, at least for a while. But never mind. I'm sure there will be other reasons we can devise to hurt you.'

He walked round the room and there was a definite spring in his step. I wondered if he was about to burst into song.

'Oh,' he said, throwing his arms out, 'but who needs a reason, when you've captured the nation's Public Enemy Number One?'

I stared at him, trying to push my fear down deep so I could think. As ever, I'm at pains to say this was not an act of bravery, but one of survival.

'I know what you're thinking,' he said. 'Will the mixture of truth and lies my men will beat out of you be of any more use to me than the half-truths you will volunteer immediately?'

It was a good question.

He continued his foray around the room with the lightness of foot usually reserved for people winning the lottery or being given the all-clear from cancer. God, I wished he had cancer. A really nasty strain, too. He stopped by the wall, peering at it as if conducting an examination.

'What do you think of my pride and joy?' he said, turning his head to face me. 'Did you know that the original Tolbooth was built in the fourteenth century? This very spot has been the site of countless episodes of pain and suffering. Isn't it joyous?'

He placed a hand on the wall again and closed his eyes. It was as if he was trying to commune with the stone. It turned out he was.

'Shh . . .' Loker whispered. 'You can almost feel the tormented souls crying out over the centuries for mercy, longing for release.' He exhaled, as if in the throes of passion, as he channelled the spectral anguish.

I began to suspect he might just be mad. The Mallice guards stared straight at me, either pretending not to notice – or worse, buying into it all.

'I have done what I can to recreate the old building,' the maniac went on. 'But I wanted more than a crude medieval place of terror. I wanted to bring the very best lessons from the masters to it as well.'

'Masters of what?' I asked, keen to keep him talking. While he was talking, he wasn't hurting me.

'Oh, you know, control, coercion. But I'm not talking about wanton, simple, unconstructed brutality, of course.'

'Of course.'

'There must *be* brutality, naturally—'

'Naturally.'

'—but it must be crafted, shaped, and moulded into an art form. So, I turned to the greatest ever defenders of state against infiltrators, deviants, and traitors.'

There wasn't a note of anger in his voice. Rather, it felt like a sermon. He was educating me.

'It might surprise you, but I consider specimens like you as my inspiration. You offer so much that I yearn to know so I can build on what the masters have taught me.'

'You've lost me, I'm afraid.'

'But surely you must know? They are the Stasi – the shield and sword. It is their spirit that lives on. In here. In *me*.'

I knew virtually nothing about the Stasi, other than that it had kept East Germany under its iron fist for a decent part of the twentieth century. It was said they created the most perfect surveillance state of all time. I told Loker of my ignorance, hoping to engage him, to create a human bond between us – to keep control and keep the pain at bay.

'Oh, but how I would love to tell you it all! Did you know that in the Third Reich they estimate there was one Gestapo agent or informer for every two thousand citizens? They say the Stasi had one informer for every seven! But *I* have gone even further. The dissidents in East Germany used to say, *Die Gedanken sind frei* – whatever the government did to them, they still had their private thoughts and desires. Nothing could reach in and take that. But I see *everything*. I have a hundred different ways of seeing what you like, what you want, what you feel. Day after day, people pour out their hopes and dreams, their feelings and their fears, through nothing more than their habits, their digital footprint. And I am there, recording each and every step until I have their essence, everything they do and everything they desire – their very soul – in my grasp. How can you tell me then that *thoughts are free?*'

Loker threw his arms up in mock apology.

'Ah, but look at me, I am lecturing after all!' he said, smiling. 'Fear not, though, for there is no rush. I hope to spend so much time with you. Teaching you. Breaking you. Rebuilding you. Yes, so much time. But I think it best, so you truly appreciate your lodgings – really *feel* them – to explain that I have based my New Tolbooth on one of the most infamous of Stasi prisons: a place they called Hohenschönhausen. And not just the rooms; their processes. Everything! From the truck that brought you here—'

'The laundry truck,' I interrupted, keener than ever to keep him talking.

'Yes, yes,' he said in delight. 'That was the Stasi, hidden in plain view. Genius! Then on through Processing, to the point you arrived here in this room. And this is only the beginning.

Downstairs – where you shall visit soon – there is even a replica of the Hohenschönhausen U-boat, the custom-built torture chambers, which we have, of course, updated. You, as a businessman, know that we can be nostalgic for the past but must move with the times.'

'Of course,' I replied, unable to fault his perverse logic and unable to stop the cold sweat breaking out on my body.

'Oh look, you are keeping me talking. How clever of you.' The smile vanished from his face as if it had never been there. 'But enough, now. It is time to get down to business.'

So the introductions and small talk were over, which was a shame. A terrible, terrible shame.

'I'm going to be clear with you and I am not going to ask for much,' Loker went on, still standing on the far side of the room. 'For although you have caused me many sleepless nights, I also recognise that I must respect your background and training if I'm to get what I want, in the time I need it. And I don't believe I have much time. We are shutting down online rumours about your attempt on the Marischal's life. But we won't get all of them, and I need all the chickens before they fly the coop.'

I wondered what he would ask. Given everything Hildy and Lizzy had already told him, combined with the huge edifice of state surveillance he presided over, there surely couldn't be many things he didn't already know. This was helpful in its own way – it meant I could make an intelligent guess about what he might want from me and how best to go about giving it to him. Loker glided over to sit at the table, hands resting lightly on the top.

'First, an easy one: who were your accomplices for the destruction of the dam?'

'Only two,' I replied quietly, my heart beating faster at the thought of my dead friends. 'Archie Fraser and Wally, sorry, Graeme Finney.'

'No others?'

I gambled. 'No others,' I confirmed.

'Lizzy Burke?'

'What? No. It was only today I learned she was – what's the word? – working with Hildebrand Blunt,' I blustered. 'I mean, I knew that she had been *working* with him before, but that's a different story.'

His one bright eye flashed with anger, but the face remained stony and impassive.

'Look, it was only today I learned the English prick had been spilling his guts to her. That doesn't mean I was working *with* her. Not now. Not ever.'

Lies, of course, but I was gambling the story would be close enough to reality. He looked at me for a long time with a level gaze. I held his gaze as if my life depended on it.

'Very well,' he said. 'Tell me about the Underground Railroad.'

I can't say how much of a relief it was that this was to be the first real test of my knowledge and mettle. Firstly, in a life that has been marked with notable acts of cowardice, arrogance, and selfishness, here I was being given a chance to go some way to redeeming myself. Secondly, I might be able to limit the vicious abuse that was surely about to start.

'I don't know anything about the Underground Railroad, except for the rumours and hearsay that everyone's heard,' I said. 'It's a movement that tries to get dissidents out of Caledon. But that's all I know.'

Loker leaned forward and stared at me before starting to rattle off names, presumably of people who had also been hidden or spirited away by brave folk like the Farquharsons. Perhaps even unwilling volunteers, like me.

Black clouds were mustering on my horizon. A thunderstorm of pain was about to break and, just like someone putting a pin in a balloon, I knew what I had to do: I had to precipitate the down-pour. Every fibre of my inconsiderate, thoughtless being begged me to stop. Common Sense called me names that would have made Archie blush. But I stood strong. Pride gave me a manful pat on the back and then slunk off to hide.

Amid this inner turmoil, I still had enough presence of mind to notice that Professor Spring's name only came up mid-list, while the Farquharsons didn't feature at all. People like Loker have a habit of leaving names you know until last, lulling you into a false sense of security before hitting you with the damning information and watching your response. If this theory stood up, the lack of sucker punch made it unlikely that he knew about my – or their – involvement.

'I don't know any of those people,' I said. 'And I've never had anything to do with the Underground. Not my style.'

'Oh, good.' His one clear eye lit up and his cheeks flushed as the prospect of inflicting pain made the juices flow. 'We can have some fun. I knew you wouldn't disappoint me.'

'Look,' I entreated, 'you know you can torture me – put me to The Question as you so quaintly call it – and eventually get me to say anything, but it won't be true, don't you see? I want to give you the truth, I want to avoid unnecessary pain, but *I can't give you what I don't know*. All that will happen is I'll start telling you more and more absurd things, and after a while you will start *wanting* to believe them and it will all get thoroughly confusing for everyone and be utterly pointless.'

'So you want me to just move on to my next question?' A cold smile flickered on his face.

Now, this caused me a dilemma as what little plan I had to get through this relied on Loker asking a very particular question next and then believing the answer. For that to work, I had to convince him of my utter desperation to speak the truth. So, with my heart hammering in my chest, I knew it was time to do the one thing I wanted least: to make him hurt me. Badly.

'I don't know anything, so let's get this over with, you rat-faced prick,' I said, with considerably greater defiance than I was actually feeling. In fact, I was feeling quite sick.

The smile faded from his face.

'I shall take great enjoyment from this,' he said, before banging hard on the table. At the signal, the door opened and another man entered. He was not quite as big as the Man of Quite Extraordinary Size, but still huge, with closely cropped blond hair. He was dressed in the regulation Mallice dark suit and tie. *He's very well dressed for a torturer*, I couldn't help but think. *A credit to his profession.*

Loker stood and walked to the door. Then, in a loud, almost manic voice, he shouted out into the corridor: 'You vermin! You traitors in your cells! Do you want to hear a wolf howl? Well, we have the greatest wolf of all: the one who you whispered through the cracks in the walls would come to save you. He is here now! Yes, listen well.'

I watched in fascination at Loker's frenzied outburst, before being distracted by the large man, who had moved to stand directly behind me. My heart slammed against my chest as he reached round me and placed a pair of pliers on the table, followed by a black baton. The latter was indistinguishable from an old-fashioned police baton, except for a couple of discreet buttons that glowed menacingly on its handle.

To be honest, I don't want to go into too much detail about what happened next. It's not one of my happier memories. So, I shall be brief. Not-Quite-As-Big-But-Still-Huge Man came forward and grabbed one of my hands. There was little I could do as they were firmly attached to the table. However, I accepted the opportunity for a moral victory, leaned forward and headbutted him hard on the nose, just as Archie had taught me in front of that roaring fire, a long time ago.

'A gift from Archie, you bastard,' I spat as his bones cracked satisfyingly. I felt a genuine rage that, for a brief moment, replaced my fear.

He groaned and gripped his face in a futile attempt to stem the bloody flow. It streamed over his well-ironed white shirt.

'That'll be hell to shift,' I growled at him.

Seconds later, another man dashed in and hit me hard on the side of the head, making sparks explode in front of my eyes. My head – and the world in general – was spinning. Both were brought violently to a standstill by an incredible pain from my hand that shot up my arm. The bloody-nosed Mallice officer had taken my hand in his enormous paw, forced my fingers straight and started pulling out my fingernail with the pliers.

I screamed. A lot. As I did when he took the next two nails off. I strained and bucked and pulled at the cuffs, but there was nowhere to go and no chance of escape. Loker asked me again about the Underground and, bathed in sweat, I prayed that my plan would work. I couldn't keep this up for long.

'Please . . . I don't know anything,' I pleaded.

'I don't believe you.' That cold smile again. 'No, wait, I *might* believe you, but I don't *want* to believe you.'

'Ask me something else! If I can tell you, I will,' I begged, breathing fast.

'No. Tell me what you know about the Underground Railroad.'

'I can't,' I said, hoping I wouldn't break.

'As you were,' he instructed the man opposite me.

Without a word, the officer took up the baton from where he had left it on the table and pressed a button on its handle. He towered over me, a slight smile playing on his flat, merciless, blood-spattered face.

He didn't hit me, as I'd expected, but instead pressed the baton against me. A huge electric shock passed through me, causing my body to spasm and shake. I started screaming again.

I don't know how long it went on. I don't suppose it was all that long, since Loker was a busy man on a tight schedule. But it felt like eternity. When the blood-spattered officer stopped applying shocks to me – *everywhere*, the vicious bastard – I slumped on the table in a pool of my own blood and sweat. My arms were bleeding badly from where the handcuffs had carved the skin from my forearms as I did my merry dance.

'Please,' I gasped, lying exhausted on the table. 'I don't know about the Underground. Please, *please*, ask me something else. I'll tell you anything I know.'

'Lift his head up,' Loker ordered.

The man behind me grabbed my hair and pulled me upright. Loker walked over and stood close. Then he bent forward and looked into my eyes. God knows what he saw there. I can report that there was nothing but cold, merciless enquiry in his.

He nodded, my hair was released and I slumped back down on the table. I didn't think I could hold out much longer. Pride had long since packed his bags and fled. Common Sense was yelling that I'd bought the Farquharsons enough time to flee and it was time to fess up. When you indulge in that kind of rationalisation, you can be sure you are nearing the end of resistance.

'Let's try something else,' Loker said. 'Tell me about the one they call the Reverend.'

Rarely in my life have I felt that level of joy. This was the question I had gambled everything on. Relief flooded my body. Pride and Common Sense reappeared, joined arms and started singing 'Kumbaya'. I stared at Loker for a long time, praying he would take this pause as indecision – an internal struggle against an act of betrayal – rather than the theatrics it actually was.

'I don't know . . .' I began.

'OK,' he said, frustration creeping into his voice. 'Start again.'

I steeled myself for another shock. This was duly administered, after which I started to babble like a baby. I not only promised I'd give up the Reverend, I swore eternal brotherhood; I cried; I begged. It was quite a show, if I say so myself.

With a small movement of his head, Loker sent both the Mallice men loping, knuckles dragging on the ground, to the other side of the room. He sat down once again.

'How do you contact him?'

'Aug-specs . . . Dark web . . .' I mumbled from my vantage point on the blood-slicked tabletop.

I must have bitten my tongue during the shocks as it felt swollen and sore. I coughed violently, projecting specks of blood across the room. Loker recoiled and looked at me with disgust before examining his uniform for stains. Then he beckoned one of the officers over and murmured orders I couldn't hear, prompting the latter to trot dutifully from the room.

'Tell me how and where you talk to him,' Loker ordered.

'Chat room,' I said. '*God's Motherfuckers . . .*'

'God's what?' he asked in disbelief.

'There are some pretty angry people in there,' I said, attempting a smile before coughing once more and moaning at the burns and aches that seemed to cover every inch of my body. The Mallice guy came back in with a set of aug-specs. Slowly and tenderly, I peeled myself off the congealing pool of blood. The ogre placed the aug-specs on my face.

'Call him,' Loker said.

'What if he doesn't answer?' I asked in ragged tones.

'You'd better pray he does,' Loker replied. 'Now call him and arrange a meeting with him for tomorrow.'

'Look, I can't promise that,' I murmured, before a strong muscle spasm took hold, leaving me groaning on the table again. 'If you know anything about him, which you clearly do, you'll know he does all the arranging. I have never dealt with him on *my* terms; if I tried, he would be suspicious.'

'Call him.'

We sat in silence while the retinal display calibrated. It took longer than usual due to the swelling and constant blinking brought on by my muscle spasms. Nonetheless, I was soon diving headfirst, and for the last time, into the recesses of the dark web. It was time to give up the closest thing I had to a father: the Reverend.

Passing by the Christian fundamentalists with ne'er a wave, I entered the private room and sent out an invitation. Then I sat and prayed as I have never prayed before that he would answer. I almost forgot to give the password.

'The name of the Lord is a fortified tower,' I said.

Loker snatched the glasses off my head. 'What are you doing?' he demanded.

'It's a password,' I said quietly, careful not to put a foot wrong. 'He won't talk to me without it.'

Loker looked at me hard; something he was beginning to make a habit of. Then he returned the glasses. 'Do it.'

I decided a show of good faith would be helpful. 'Do you want me to turn off the video feed? He'll see where I am otherwise. I'm not at my prettiest either.'

Loker's eyes widened, betraying the fact he hadn't thought of this. He really was in a rush to get this done, it seemed. I turned off the visuals. It must have been thirty seconds before the Reverend answered. It felt like an eternity.

'The righteous run to it and are safe. Hello, Macfarlane,' came the gruff greeting. 'What do you want?'

It occurred to me I had no idea what to say to him.

'We need to meet,' I said as steadily as I could. 'I want to discuss more . . . cargo.' I looked at Loker and shrugged stiff shoulders. My mind was in no place to be coming up with creative solutions (which was hardly my fault, I hope you'll agree).

'You know we don't meet, except under very limited circumstances, Macfarlane,' the Reverend said. 'This had better be good.'

'It is,' I replied, 'but, look, I can't talk more about it now, you'll just have to trust me. Is there any chance at all of a meet tomorrow?'

'Ha!' he laughed disdainfully. 'You must be kidding!' He paused and I pictured him flicking through an old-fashioned diary, glasses perched atop the end of his long nose, teeth chewing on a pencil. 'Two days, that's my best offer.'

I looked at Loker. He gave a curt nod.

'OK, I'll take it.'

'Right,' he replied. 'Coordinates should be coming up on your aug-specs now. Remember them. Don't save them.'

'OK,' I said, capturing them immediately using the photo function on the specs to show to Loker. 'I'll see you then, Reverend. What is it you say? God speed, no? Can't say I care for it. I'll just say cheery-bye.'

There was a pause.

'Aye,' he responded, 'and to you. I'll be seeing you, Jimmy.'

Then he was gone.

Loker was so delighted with this that he clapped his hands in delight. 'How quickly you are willing to betray the last of your friends, Macfarlane. Perhaps rebuilding you will be easier than I thought.'

The chair scraped back across the floor and he snatched the glasses off my face, before holding them aloft like a laurel wreath. Then he turned on his heel and strode towards the door, handing the aug-specs to one of the guards.

'Make it happen,' he said to the man, who nodded and left. At the same time another monstrous Mallice agent came round the doorframe carrying a small wooden box.

'Sir,' he said, addressing Loker, 'your trophy has arrived. We brought it as soon as it was ready, just as you ordered.'

Loker clapped his hands again. What a day he was having. Taking the box, he returned to the table and sat opposite me. The container looked like polished rosewood.

'Now, I don't really have time for this, but I simply cannot miss this opportunity,' he said. 'Have you heard of my little hobby?'

I had no idea what he was talking about. Slumped in the chair, I shook my head.

'Oh, come now! Surely you have heard what they call me: the Headhunter?'

'Yes, of course. Everyone has.'

'Well, I have rather taken this to heart. I realised keeping the skulls of the vanquished was one thing, but we must always strive to better ourselves, mustn't we?'

'Must we?'

'Of course, we must.' His hands moved to the lid of the box. 'Behold my latest achievement!'

He lifted the lid and, as he did so, the front of the box fell down to reveal a round object. It was the size of a small melon, with leathery skin and some kind of roots spilling down from the top. Like hair.

Oh God. It *was* hair.

I stared at the appalling orb, taking in the eyes, the nose, and the mouth, which was sewn together with dangling strings. Bile rose in my throat. Oh God, it was a shrunken head. But there was something else about it. Something terrible. Something I couldn't place.

'Ha! I see you have recognised my *tsantsa* for what it is! Behold the legacy of the Jívaro headhunters of Ecuador and Peru.' He cupped the horrible sphere, lifting the shrunken head gently from the box and turning it in his hands, staring into its taut face.

'I have worked hard to adapt their art for the twenty-first century,' he said reverently.

On even my most loquacious of days I doubt I'd have found anything to say.

'You see, traditionally you have to remove the dead man's skull and all the muscle and flesh from the skin – no mean feat. Then you boil the carcass. *Then* you have to fill it over and over with hot pebbles and sand until the skin shrinks. It's an art, but it's time-consuming. If you need a head prepared quickly then it is of little use. So I have developed a technique using rapid microwave vacuum drying, very similar to the method used to make your old army ration bars. All the hard work is beginning to pay off, don't you think?' He lifted it close to his face, looking long and hard at the remains of the eye sockets. 'The Jívaro did it to harvest the souls of their enemies, and, while I do not believe in anything so crude and superstitious, I do believe that a person's very nature is rooted in their head. It is the head – the brain – that makes us human, is it not? It is the home of the *self*.'

Loker lowered the shrunken head, cupped it under its chin and peered over it at me.

'So, even if I don't believe in harvesting souls as the Jívaro did, I think the message that will be sent when my new hobby is revealed – which it will be soon – helps me construct a very practical equivalent. Control through obedience. Obedience through fear. I can go one step further than the Jívaro: why wait for death when I can harvest the souls of the living? Progress, you see?

'I can only apologise that I did not complete this one myself and I hope you will not see it as a mark of disrespect. But my apprentices have worked miracles to get this ready for you, take my word for it.'

He kept talking, though I wasn't listening anymore. My hands were shaking.

'Oh, no,' I whispered.

Loker stared at me, a look of triumph on his face. 'Ha! You have seen it!'

And it was. It was the lank hair that had revealed the identity of the head. The rectangular face was more rounded now and the bright eyes gone. But there was no doubt: it was Wally.

A moan escaped my lips.

'I shall leave you alone to say goodbye to each other.'

He softly – lovingly – placed the head in the box and slid it towards me, just out of reach of my fingers. There it sat. Staring. Accusing. At the doorway, Loker turned. He considered me in silence, pursing his lips and tapping a finger thoughtfully against them.

'U-boat. Room 4220,' he said to the guard before sweeping from the room.

CHAPTER 12

Supped Full with Horrors

I was too weak to stop them when they dragged me out of the room and down into the U-boat – the subterranean torture chambers. For a few seconds, it had felt as if the plan had worked. I'd kept the Farquharsons safe, at least for now, and denied Loker any more evidence against Lizzy. They'd laid off me once I had given them the Reverend, just as I hoped. This offered the prospect of respite while they planned his capture, and the chance they'd take me with them on the operation – out of this terrible place and into the realms of daring escape bids. Then they'd gone and put Wally's shrunken head on the table.

No doubt you are thinking I deserved this, having just betrayed the Reverend, the last friend (of sorts) that I had, and a massive thorn in the side of the regime to boot. He had been a light in the darkness for me; the closest thing I had to a father figure and, in these times of oppression, almost unique in his relentless pursuit of free will. Well, free markets at least.

The thing is, I hadn't actually betrayed him, so you can rest easy. Using a password we had long ago reserved for sticky situations such as this, I had told him to play up. To play the game. If Loker came even close to finding the Reverend now, it was through no fault of mine. The ball was in the Reverend's court, and that was tremendously bad news for Loker. If he thought the Mallice was the real power in the north of Caledon, he was about to get a rude awakening. And while I doubted the Reverend had the resources or inclination to launch a rescue bid, it meant someone outside Loker's merry band knew where I was. Knew how my story ended. Knew I'd tried to do the decent thing. That was no small comfort. Then, *goddamn it*, they put Wally's head on the table.

We turned right, my poor feet dragging along laminated tiles, before banging painfully down a flight of stairs. We emerged into a new corridor, identical to the last, with the same tiles and blinding strip lights. This one, however, was lined with heavy metal doors, painted a creamy white. I struggled weakly, but I'm not sure the men either side of me even noticed.

We continued to one of the doors, marked 4220 in big black numbers. They dropped me on the floor between them as one pulled back the heavy bolts and heaved the door open. It must have been six inches thick and had a high step (against which my shins crashed as they dragged me in) that meant it could be completely sealed when closed. I hadn't time to wonder at this because they deposited me on the floor and, with nothing more than a friendly kick of farewell, slammed the door behind them. I thought it strange the bolts made no noise when they were locked.

I curled into the foetal position and lay there, hugging my knees to my chest, my eyes screwed shut, urging the world to *just bloody leave me alone for a moment*. After a short time, I opened one eye, expecting to see some desperately unpleasant instrument of torture in front of me. But there was nothing. Nothing at all, except that the walls and the ceiling were covered in spikes. No, wait, *not* spikes, more like sharp wedges, all pointing inwards. I wondered, bleakly, if the walls were about to start closing in to impale me. I waited. And waited. Still, nothing happened.

The longer I lay there the more I became aware of a peculiar feeling; of the air being dense, as if someone were ever-so-gently squeezing my head. The room was completely white and the light, which was coming from a source I could not identify, was unbearably bright. Try as I might, I couldn't get a proper sense of how big the room was, which was disconcerting. The only other thing was the silence. A silence so complete that it was unlike anything I had ever experienced.

I started hearing noises. Strange noises. Scurrying, gurgling, rustling noises. I scanned the room for the sources of these peculiar phenomena, but could see none. Then I realised they were coming from *inside me*. It was as if my hearing had been turned inwards. I swore I could hear my muscles contracting and expanding every time I moved so much as an inch. Then I heard a scraping noise. What was it? It happened when I lifted my eyebrows. My God: it was my scalp moving across my skull.

These and a myriad of other noises – my digestive system working, the coursing of blood around my head – began to take over my existence. It should have been horrific, terrifying. But it wasn't. Rather, I felt a sense of disassociation from the world, as if I had split from my environment and was orbiting reality in my own self-contained ecosystem. After the day I'd had, it was just what the doctor ordered.

Minutes, hours, or days might have passed before anything more happened. When the door opened again with a noise that had been inconsequential before, it was now thunderous to my ears. I clamped my hands against my head, thinking my brain might burst. Then the door slammed shut and the silence returned.

When I could bear to open my eyes after this explosion of sound, I saw in front of me a metal bowl with some kind of food in it. I stared at it for a while before crawling over and putting a handful of what looked like meat into my mouth. The deafening grinding of my chewing was almost unbearable, while the act of swallowing sounded like a large rock being forced down a shaft that was impossibly small for it to pass. I might have been sick, but the thought of the roar as the tsunami crashed out of me made me break into a cold sweat. That, in turn, slipped and slopped across my skin, like an all-encompassing slug. I resolved not to move and demanded that my body cease all non-essential functions. The sense of calm returned and, after a while, I even made peace with my heart, which was beating at a rate that made me fit for hibernation. That's when the music started.

The cacophony smashed into me like a hammer, shocking my brain into wakefulness. Again, I put my hands to my ears, begging for it to stop. A hoarse whisper was as loud as I dared speak. Eventually, my wishes were granted and the sound ceased to be.

Yet again the silence reasserted itself. I felt exhausted and disorientated. Were the walls moving? Yes, the spikes were surely closing in! But, if they were, it was so slow – slower than the tardiest snail that e'er mounted its thorn. I rose and went over to touch them – the grinding, crashing noise of my tiptoeing almost unbearable. Holding out a hand to measure their progress, I found beyond doubt they were solid and immovable. Still, I eyed them with distrust.

I lay flat on my back in the vacuum of this inner space, while my bodily orchestra began warming up once more. My eyes closed. I was falling asleep, embracing the void . . . Then the music started again and I curled into a ball, rocking backwards and forwards, begging for it to stop. And so this ritual went on. And on. And on. To what felt a lot like the 'last syllable of recorded time' that Professor Spring had kept banging on about before I broke him into pieces on the high seas.

Sleep deprivation is a terrible thing, but it is also a highly effective technique, should you need to impose control on somebody. It can cause appalling physical and psychological damage. But if you're considering inflicting it on someone, then you probably don't care too much about that.

Conversely, whatever you might hear, it's rubbish as a form of torture to extract information, because the effects it has are counterproductive. One of the first things that happens is you become emotional and can't concentrate. Your thoughts and memories become irrational and disordered. You find yourself disorientated, your ability to speak becomes impaired, and your body temperature drops. Then come the hallucinations, followed by severe lethargy. You can't move and don't want to anyway. You begin slowly but surely to make your final break from reality. Beyond that, it's a short hop to total organ failure.

I tell you all this because, so far in my tale, I've tried to be completely honest with you. But when I recount the next episode in this comedy of horrors, it comes with the warning that I am not sure how much of what I say is true. All of it may have happened exactly as I will say it. But there's a chance none of it happened at all, for all the reasons I've just set out. So, here is what I remember and I shall dispense with any attempts to quantify the time periods involved in between incidents. It's pointless even to guess.

Time passed in some fashion or other and I found myself conversing at great length with all sorts of people. Archie and Wally came and stayed for a long chat, which was nice of them, even if it was difficult to understand Wally, what with his lips sewn shut and his head the size of a large coconut. I had to admonish both of them at one point for leaking so much dark blood on the pristine white floor.

After that, I had an emotional reunion with my grandparents. I begged them to tell me they were proud of what I had achieved, before asking a tearful forgiveness for my cowardice and failure to protect Granny from the vultures. Then Abraham Lincoln, of all people, dropped by to discuss politics, although it seemed strange that he had the legs of a flamingo. Each to their own, though, I've always said that.

At some point everything changed when the door opened again. The noise of it crashed over me like a wave, the ferocious impact sending me scurrying to the far wall, where I sought sanctuary by trying to burrow in amongst the wedges. A Mallice officer, with whom I was so far unacquainted, entered carrying a chair. I remember being pleased to see there wasn't an ounce of flamingo about him; it would have ruined the cut of his suit.

Still curled in a ball in the corner, I peered through half-closed eyes to see what he was up to, my hands clamped over my ears. He placed the chair on the floor by the door and stood aside. After a moment, another man entered the room. And not just any man: it was the man himself. Duncan Finlay, Marischal of Caledon. Alive and kicking.

He ushered the guard outside and we were alone. Then he sat and stared at me. Again, I was struck, as I had been when I saw him on the TV after the Pitlochry job, by the sense that he had lost weight and was looking unwell. Finlay's eyes had dark rings around them and his clothes were hanging off him. Such are the stresses of oppressing a nation, no doubt. There can't be enough hours in the day.

Without a word, he stood up and walked over to where I was, his footsteps clattering about my ears. I made hushing sounds as loud as I dared, warning him in desperate whispers and with waving hands that his raucous pacing would surely bring the roof down on us.

The Marischal bent over, studying his specimen. His proximity was terrifying. Finlay towered over me, scowling like a monster ready to tear me limb from limb. I curled more tightly into a ball and screwed my eyes shut. I whimpered.

He seemed content with this little exchange and returned to his seat. Then he started to talk. The first words were lost to me as the storm of soundwaves crashed relentlessly into me, utterly indecipherable after all that time I'd spent in the silence and the searing light. But the longer he spoke, the further the sound of my banging heart regressed. The roar subsided and his voice became that of a man, as if some kind of sonic equilibrium had been restored.

'. . . they call it an anechoic chamber,' he was saying, looking around with interest. 'I'm told it's so quiet that the background noise is actually measured in negative decibels. That, as a concept, is beyond me, I'm afraid. But one of the scientists who designed it did put it rather poetically when he said that, "when you are in here, you *become* the sound".'

For the first time in what felt like an age I could understand what was being said. I was returning towards a reality of sorts; something I could cling to, if not fully understand.

'It is said that forty-five minutes can be enough to make a man hysterical. I am intrigued to get your insight, as you've set a record. Two days. Most impressive.'

Two days! The thought of it was baffling, appalling, beyond comprehension. It felt like mere minutes had passed and it felt like years; like a lifetime or no life at all. My subconscious tried hero-ically to rally. Two days *meant* something . . . But what? I tried to think. To drag a memory back. Soon I gave up, instead willing a philanthropic synapse to fire and relay the information to me. At some point it did, and I began to gabble out loud.

'The Reverend! They go after him today. Maybe they have already. I do hope not, as I must be there in an advisory capacity or at least as collateral? Please take a message to Mr Thomas Loker, good sir. Come on now, aren't you going to write this down?'

The Marischal stared at me. It was difficult to decode the look. At first, I thought he was appalled, but it may equally have been disgust.

'Loker and his men are already on their way to find the man they call the Reverend,' he said slowly, as if not wanting to excite me. 'Although I doubt he'll be there. Loker can be foolish. Too con-fident in his powers of coercion, his powers of persuasion. I don't believe you would give someone up that easily.' He waved a dismiss-ive hand. 'No matter; he will be caught soon enough. Anyone who challenges the will of the people shall face their punishment.'

Perhaps it was the sleep deprivation stripping me of self-control, or maybe a rudimentary survival mechanism of the mind, but it was around this time I found myself robbed of any sense of nuance or perspective. Instead, my brain adopted a sort of binary thought process where everything was made simple. Where everything was either black or white. Where everything was linear and made *total sense*, shorn of doubt or complications. I'm not sure I've ever thought with such clarity. There was no doubt at all. Only certainty.

'Duncan, you mustn't be so sure. He is a clever and elusive man,' I said, like a small child reciting facts to his teacher, keen to impress.

'James, you know I don't like you calling me that,' he said sternly in return. 'I know I said you could when you were twenty-one, but I've never been comfortable with it.'

His neuroses were intruding on the simplicity of my narrative. 'OK, Uncle Duncan,' I replied.

The Marischal exhaled and momentarily closed his eyes. 'I am . . . so very disappointed in you, James,' he said at last.

'How so? Pray tell, Uncle,' I responded brightly, feeling an ardent need to engage, to learn, and be edified.

'Loker suspected you for a long time, did you know that?' he said, as if I hadn't spoken (which I may not have, of course). 'But I told him I couldn't risk moving on you – what with your personal status – until there was proof. Even then, he was under the strictest of orders not to kill you.'

'That's nice.'

'Please do not be mistaken: this has nothing to do with our blood. No, killing you was just the wrong solution. I couldn't create a martyr and, as I told Loker, we could make the Wolf of Badenoch work for the country. We could make him great for the country. And I still believe that. Even if that Wolf tried to kill me.'

'Why is that?'

He studied me for a while. 'Have you ever heard the old adage about a family business?' he began, choosing his words carefully. 'How it takes one generation to found it, one to build it, and one to destroy it? I think the Americans say "From shirtsleeves to shirtsleeves in three generations".'

'I have, indeed,' I chipped in, keen to be of service. 'Although I'm afraid I couldn't tell you where I heard it first.'

'I think that is an appropriate analogy for Caledon. The nationalists founded it and it was then up to me to build it. But I have been receiving increasing reports of disturbances across the country – an undercurrent of dissension.'

Out of nowhere, one of his famous rages broke.

'I will not let my work unravel!' he cried, his face red and body shaking. 'I will not let the foundations be undermined. I will not let everything we have strived for collapse – not now, not ever!'

Finlay stopped and sat back in the chair, rubbing his temples with his fingers.

'I saw the Wolf of Badenoch as a godsend. This terrorist—'

'Freedom fighter.'

'Be quiet.'

'Sorry.'

'This terrorist gave me a figure the people could hate. Someone the country could rally against to rid them of their doubts about our future. That is why we flooded the internet with your exploits after you blew up the dam at Pitlochry . . .'

I interrupted him by giggling, and it must have been out loud because he asked me what was so funny.

'Because the English thought exactly the opposite,' I said with delight. 'They wanted to kill me to cement that very same stability! They said I would rally the people and they couldn't afford the national collapse that such a movement was likely to precipitate. We really are the playthings of the gods, are we not?'

'Did they, indeed? What game are they playing, I wonder? And why didn't they just kill you in that case?'

'I am surprisingly hard to kill,' I chirped.

'We shall see about that. But I want you to understand, James: I didn't want all this for you. I was happy just to make you disappear. Make the problem go away. But then Loker said something to me and it was impossible to dismiss – impossible even to deny.'

'And what was that?'

'He said that to focus on just getting rid of you was wrong. It wasn't *you* that needed killing: it was the Wolf of Badenoch. In his eyes, we needed to destroy the *meaning* of the Wolf. What it stood for. I found his argument compelling, his logic hard to fault.'

'He makes a good argument.'

'Loker convinced me we must use the Wolf, first by building it up into a monster to be feared, then by tearing it down. It was not enough, he said, for you to disappear or die. It was the *ideal* that must die, and with it the hope of those who would use the Wolf as a rallying cry. The mere mention of the Wolf must become anathema, a trigger for despair and not hope. That is why you are here. That is why they have done what they have done.

'But do you know what? I clung to the idea of sparing you all this. I strove to maintain some sort of humanity in the face of Loker's barbarity, which just felt too simple. Too easy. Ill-conceived. I wavered, I delayed, I really did. But then you tried to kill me, James. To *kill* me. You showed you would deny me the clemency I might have shown you, and from then on, my mind was made up. We tried to stop the story of your assassination attempt getting out, but people proved surprisingly adept at circumventing the algorithms. Another of Loker's failings. There needed to be no further nail in the coffin, but now I must do it publicly.'

'Quite so.'

'You must understand the news of your treachery cannot stand.

If I cannot demonstrate that retribution for such a crime is swift and final, then there will surely be another attempt within days. The simple truth is: I can't afford *not* to kill you, I'm afraid.'

'You could always do the whole "magnanimous" thing. You know, be the bigger man? Just a thought.'

'No. It would only be seen as weakness.'

'A good point, well made. Death does seem the best course of action.'

'The people are sick of weakness. It was weakness from our leaders – their corruption, their indecision, their prevarication – that dragged this country into the mire in the first place. I must show strength for the good of the nation.'

'Strength. Yes.'

'I must appear resolute: to know my mind, and to do definite things.'

'You mean lose your mind and do monstrous things?'

His eyes bulged, and I thought he would hit me. He didn't. He wouldn't. He had other people for that.

'I have just one question,' he said at length. '*Why?*'

'Why?' I replied, confused. My dilapidated mind couldn't process such an ill-defined enquiry.

'Why did you do it? Why would you try to destroy what we have worked so hard to build? We have created an ordered society, where everyone is used to the best of their abilities. Other countries collapse and burn under the weight of globalisation, population movements, social inequality, and, yes, the intransigence of their own political elites. Meanwhile, we stand tall! We have stability.'

'You keep saying *we*, but—'

'We have done away with the tyranny of the committees that were corrupt, incompetent, and at the mercy of whoever shouted the loudest. The country was choking on too much liberty, like a child overfed with sweets. It had to be stopped. And then you . . .

You decided you would undo all that. Why, in God's name?'

He was rising, the fury returning, somehow filling the clothes that had previously been hanging off him. The passion and self-belief that had swept him to power flowed from him. It was intoxicating. I felt awe. I would vote for him next time, for sure. Maybe even do some canvassing.

'Are the roads not better? Are the streets not safer? Have we not done away with the oxymoron of democratic elections, which were merely a merciless cycle of campaigning, propaganda, and manipulation – all at vast cost – and so transitory that we did it all again just a few years later? All so we could give our leaders the excuse – no, the imperative – to serve short-term populist interests, rather than push through changes that, even if unpopular, were ultimately for the greater good of the country?'

'You speak many truths.'

'And most importantly of all: have you not been one of the greatest beneficiaries?' he yelled in exasperation. 'You: who was successful, rich, and famous. You, who wanted for nothing!' His stare bored into me. 'Your hypocrisy sickens me, James.'

'How so?'

'In the early days, all that kept the movement together was the money you were so ably making from the family business. The vast dividend you created with your apparent marketing genius kept us going. And where was your revolutionary zeal then? Your social conscience? Your desire to stop me? Hidden deep in mounds of money and adulation, that's where! Without you there would be no Marischal. Without you, no Caledon.'

It was difficult then, as it still is now, to argue with this terrible truth. But I had no time to consider it as a dam broke inside Finlay and he leapt forward in a rage, grabbing me by either side of the head.

'Why, for God's sake, James, why?' he roared. 'I did it for the people. I did it for you!'

Again, my thinking was crystal clear, perfectly delineated; perhaps in a way it had never been before. It's a strange thing, sleep deprivation.

'Dunc . . . sorry, *Uncle* Duncan, come now, you didn't do it all for the people – and least of all for me. You did it for an *ideal*. And, as we both know, idealists are people who kill people. The end will always justify their means. That is why the country was forced to suffer the sanctions, embargoes, and withdrawal of investment. To suffer the Devil's Wind – the Mallice's reign of terror. In a world that was falling to pieces, we needed *less* isolation, *more* dialogue and *more* interaction. And definitely fewer big fuck-off walls.'

'Don't be so naive. My God, look at your beloved English paymasters.'

'It wasn't voluntary employment—'

'Be quiet.'

'Sure thing.'

'That grandeur you so enjoyed in London – yes, I saw the news reports and press releases – that grandeur only came when the Victorians cast the poor and undesirable aside. Crushed their filthy houses and cleared their stinking streets so they could build towers to their own vanity. And do people now remember those people who were swept away in the name of progress? Of course not. It was a necessary evil so a new order could rise.'

'Oh, come now, Uncle Duncan. That is surely a false equivalence. Surely we have moved on in the last century? Surely we can improve the lot of the people without having to kill them?'

'The people? Are you saying you – the Wolf of Badenoch – did this for the people? For the country? Well, did you?'

'Oh no, nothing of the sort. That's not at all why I created the Wolf – which wasn't my choice of name, although I do rather like it—'

'Enough!' he cried. 'Why *did* you do it?'

'That's simple – you were on my list.'

'The list? What list?'

I glanced at the golden bangle that was no longer on my wrist.

'The list of the cheats and the thieves. You know, the family.'

'Wait a minute. What you're saying is—'

'Yes! It was all about you!' I chirped happily. 'Helping the people of Caledon was a nice bonus, but that's nothing to do with why I did it. It was you: it's always been about you.'

And whether I said that or, indeed, whether this meeting even took place, doesn't matter, for it is the pure truth. Why we're all here.

'It was all about *purpose*, you see?' I continued in business-like fashion. 'When you and my other relations were asset stripping my dying grandmother, I didn't know what to do and I fled—'

'How dare you judge me or my motives! You have grown fat off what my mother left you. I took nothing more than I deserved, and while you were getting rich on the spoils, I was rebuilding a nation! Was I to leave all that to chance as she began to lose her mind and the vultures were circling, robbing her? And all the time looking to rob *me* of my destiny?'

'But that wasn't your choice to make, as much as it wasn't theirs. You *all* manipulated and took advantage of her. You all had the same aim: to steal from her to feather your own nests.'

He looked as if he was about to interrupt again, so I continued apace.

'As I was saying, I didn't know what to do and I ran away. I have hated myself for it from that day forth. Then, one day, I came across the solution to all that self-loathing. A solution that would give me the one thing I had been looking for but could never seem to find: *purpose*.

'And that purpose was simple: revenge. Of course,' I said, wagging a finger at him in admonishment, 'you made it all very complicated by using the money that you stole to establish a dictatorship. That meant my aspirations had to change, as did the level of the stakes we were playing for. Quite considerably.

'Nevertheless, the goal remained the same: I wanted to destroy you and do it in as public a way as possible. Admittedly, it would have been much easier if you had just been a businessman, MP, doctor – you know, some upstanding member of the community – and I could merely have outed you for having an affair with the au pair or the pool boy or the dog or something, but there you go.'

Uncle Duncan looked at me through narrowed eyes. He was shaking with suppressed rage. 'Let me get this absolutely clear: you took it upon yourself to alter the fate of a nation because of a *personal grudge*?'

'Yes, you've got it!' I said, delighted that we were of one mind. 'It was a pretty big grudge, if that helps.'

He shook his head in disbelief and, again, I felt the need to help the poor man.

'Is it so unusual or implausible? No one really does this kind of thing for the greater good, do they? You've got to do it for yourself, surely? Do it for love, for hate, for whatever – but always for self. If you do it for a church or a state or a system you're just part of the machine. Part of the problem. It's got to be self, I've always said that. Self, self, self.'

This seemed oh so clear to me, but Uncle Duncan's mouth was opening and closing in silent bewilderment. I pressed on.

'Powerful families have fought in this way and decided the fate of nations for centuries. I didn't pick the board on which the game was played: you did. You made us the Medicis. The Tudors. The Kennedys. I just played the hand I was dealt.'

I stopped. The Marischal was staring wide-eyed at me, shaking. I wondered if I should give him a hug. Then he spoke in a strained hush that seemed to be holding back a tidal wave of energy.

'Why me? Did I do you some particular wrong? Am I so different to the rest? Where is your revenge on them?'

'Ah, well, you've got me there. Just poor planning, I'm afraid. Went too big too early. I was never that good at thinking things through. More of an ideas man, really.'

The Marischal's jaw tightened and a muscle in his cheek twitched.

I ploughed on. 'I started with you and, as you might have guessed, it all got out of hand. Some of which was not my fault, by the way. Anyway, rest assured I still have every intention of chopping down the family tree.'

'Enough!' Finlay's fists were clenched tight, the knuckles white. 'Enough.'

He stared long and hard at me but didn't say another word. He just stood up and left, the chair grating as it slid across the floor. It was over. The door swung shut and I began, once again, to become acquainted with the internal to-ings and fro-ings of my body. The one difference now was that I felt a sense of elation, as if an enormous burden had been lifted from my shoulders. The fact I had failed so comprehensively didn't seem to matter. Perhaps I'd become reconciled to that already and the joy came from finally coming clean; finally revealing my guilty secret. The selfish, awful reason that had got all my nearest and dearest killed – or worse. I had stood in front of the Marischal and declared that I was James Macfarlane. I was the Wolf of Badenoch. I had made my confession. And, although I didn't know it, it was just in time too. The problem with soundproof rooms is you can't hear Death knocking at your door.

CHAPTER 13

Tomorrow and Tomorrow and Tomorrow

I don't know how, when, or where it happened, but in the brief period that I had been removed from the world, Great Decisions were being made on my behalf.

I have no idea how much longer I was in that chamber. It can't have been that long or I'd have died. When they hauled me out, I vaguely remember giggling and repeating 'never get out, never get out, never get out' over and over. Which tells you everything, really.

I can't tell you what happened to Loker's bid to capture the Reverend, because no one thought to let me know. They didn't take me along as I'd hoped, thus ruining my dramatic bid for freedom long before it started. Nor do I have any other news of Lizzy. Dear Lizzy.

What I can do is put the events that followed into a rough order, even if, in my mind's eye, they are just a series of divorced episodes. Firstly, they took me back to that footballers' bath and half-drowned me again. The noise of it all, after all that time in the chamber, smashed into me. I thought my eardrums would burst. Then they shaved my horrid beard off and dressed me in a white shirt and some loose-fitting blue trousers. I'm still wearing what's left of them now.

At some point, I was taken back out into the courtyard, where the demonic delivery vehicles had been replaced by two lines of dark-suited Mallice pigs making a tunnel – a guard of dishonour, if you will – leading to a large metal gate. No one spoke. It was a cold, crisp day and I shivered in the thin shirt. The sun was dazzling in the clear sky.

They pushed me forwards, blinking in the sunshine. They seemed to want to make me walk down this hellish, if sartorially elegant, channel. Of course, this was plain silly. I meandered a few steps, much like Archie after a successful Saturday night, and collapsed on the floor. I wish I had sung 'I Belong to Glasgow'[*] in his honour, but sadly didn't think of it. After that, two large men, indistinguishable from the rest, took an elbow each and led me forward. I didn't thank them for their kindness.

As I stumbled and zigzagged forward, the huge metal gates ahead swung open. The sight that greeted me was confusing and terrifying. On the road outside leading up to the castle, hundreds of people stared at me in silence. As we came out of the gate and turned left, I saw there were hundreds more – maybe even thousands – lining the road.

Faced with this silent, motionless mob, my bewildered mind was overcome with fear and I tried to back up, tried to pull myself from my captors' grip. I just wanted to return to the peace and quiet of Room 4220. But my guards bore me easily forwards, up the hill towards Castle Rock.

It was the blankness of the faces that scared me the most. Their features were implacable, as if they were automatons in need of new batteries. The children, who were there in sizeable numbers, stood stock-still beside their parents. And even with those thousands of souls on parade, there was no noise except the whisper of the wind as we made our way up the cobbled road. I shrank from every sound – the wind, a cough in the crowd, the click of every phone – even though my ears were now reaccustomed to the noises around me.

As we passed, a new emotion hit me: anger. All these people here, together – why didn't they rise as I had? Why didn't they fight

[*] An early twentieth-century song by performer Will Fyffe.

as I had? Why wouldn't they risk everything in this moment to throw off the yoke of oppression as I had done for them? OK, I hadn't really done it for them, but they weren't to know that. At that moment, we had the numbers, there was no doubt. Yet there they stood, impassive, just as they had done over four hundred years before when the Marquess of Montrose had been brought silently to the scaffold on this very same road. But the comparisons ended there: I wished not one ounce of mercy, from God, or anyone else on this afflicted land.

Soon we were approaching the Esplanade, the big open parade ground that stands before the entrance to the castle. A new wave of confusion washed over me as I saw it was all set up for the August festival, when the Esplanade becomes a place for crowds to watch musical concerts, military displays, and the massed ranks of pipes and drums. There were stands of seating on three sides, with a giant screen in one corner that obscured the figures of William Wallace and Robert the Bruce guarding the gate to the castle behind.

August? Surely I haven't been in that prison for eight months?

My heart began palpitating at the thought that it had been so easy to make me disappear; to eradicate my existence for such a length of time. Then I registered how cold it was. Colder than the average Caledon summer, certainly. I was shivering. Hugging myself as best I could, I noticed thick clouds appearing every time I exhaled. There was a light covering of snow on the ground and the crowds were dressed in thick winter coats. Hats. Gloves. No, this was a one-off. Some kind of fundraiser, no doubt, with the Wolf of Badenoch as star prize.

As we approached, all became plain. In the middle of the Esplanade sat a large clear box, rectangular in shape. A wide tube came out of one corner and disappeared under the seating.

So this was how it ended: my very own O-Tank.

I almost felt admiration for Uncle Duncan. He had contrived

to anchor this travesty in law and order to undermine the Wolf: to present me as nothing more than a common criminal. Yet, at the same time, he was injecting a sense of occasion, affirming the importance of the event, and reminding everyone of the consequences of disobedience. On we marched, closer and closer to the yawning gap in the stands that waited to welcome me to a modern-day coliseum.

Stillness. That's what I recall. The air. The people. The sound. All still. I didn't struggle as I was put inside the box and the door was sealed behind me. I was done fighting. Quite literally on my knees. Instead, I stared in silence around this bizarre cell. It seemed odd that a couple of inches of plastic were all that separated me from the thousands of people staring from their appointed places at the star of the show. I wondered if they had to pay more for a front-row seat. Were there touts outside offering to buy and sell tickets? *At the very least*, Pride said, *it seems to be a sell-out.*

Staggering to my feet, I leaned my hands against the clear walls, hoping they were another hallucination and that I would be able to walk through them and away, perhaps to find a place to have a lie-down and a snooze. They were disappointingly rigid, and even more disappointing in that they didn't seem clean. There were other handprints in there. For a moment I was appalled at the lack of standards. I flattered myself that this kind of occasion called for five-star levels of execution. I resolved to have a stern word with the staff after everything was over.

Then a noise intruded on my thoughts. It was little more than a deep vibration behind the hermetically sealed plastic, and recognisable as a voice only by its cadence. Outside the box, the volume must have been spectacular. It must have carried across the city and out over the sea. Just like the One o'Clock Gun. The voice came from speakers placed around the Esplanade. There, on the giant screen, was a judge in full raiment. He was reading out indictments, charges, pleas, verdicts, and sentences. Justice was now being seen to be done. Then the camera left the judge and the screen changed to show a close-up of some poor unfortunate, features drawn and a manic look in his eyes. The figure on the screen stared back at me, looking like a trapped and bewildered animal. But a familiar animal . . . Ah yes, it was me.

Again, I couldn't help but admire the artistry of it. How the Marischal had stripped this creature of any personality or any other ambiguities that might prove a distraction to the audience. Before them all stood A Traitor. Nothing more. Nothing less. Certainly not the kind of man a nation could feel pride in, or support for. All around, rows and rows of people stared blankly at me. Many were filming the event on their phones.

A peculiar rushing noise infiltrated my observations. It went on for mere seconds before my confusion turned abruptly to panic because *I couldn't breathe.* It wasn't as if I was breathing and taking no benefit. No, there was just no air to draw in, as if invisible hands were clamped over my mouth and nose. I staggered around, my arms flailing, clawing at the walls, hitting myself on the chest as if to kickstart my lungs. Then I was at the door clawing weakly at the seals. An acute sense of anxiety gripped me. My lungs were screaming for help and a curious ringing began in my ears. I felt an extraordinary – and quite undeserved – moment of calm, before I passed out.

Suddenly, I was awake, lying on my back, taking in enormous lungfuls of air. It was better than any food I'd ever tasted. Better than any whisky I'd ever drunk – and that's saying something. With one hand on the tank wall, I pushed myself to my feet, staring wildly around at the assembled masses. Almost immediately, the rushing noise began again and I realised in horror they were creating the vacuum once more. My desperate polka around the cell recommenced.

They did it again and again until it became a regular routine. Panic. Serenity. Darkness. Awake. Repeat. I thought I would go mad. I was desperate for them to let me die. After three or four episodes, all I could think of was how I could push them to kill me.

Then: an epiphany. All I needed to do to end this carefully stage-managed occasion was not stick to the script. More than that: I must shred it. After a lifetime of giving everyone what they wanted, their poster child would become everything they didn't want to see. I would not be their poor player, that struts and frets his hour upon the stage. I would refuse to signify nothing. I would give them sound and I would give them fury.

With a fresh injection of oxygen, I struggled to my feet again. But this time I abandoned the thoughts of escape that had seen me scrabbling desperately at the walls, just like the trapped animal the regime wanted everyone to see. Instead, I stood as straight as I was able, shoulders back, head raised. I raised my hand to my temple to salute the crowd. But not any salute: Jimmy Mac's salute.

Standing at attention, managing a parody of Jimmy Mac's sardonic smile, I set myself a challenge: could I stand there until the darkness claimed me again? The rushing sound duly began and the whole terrible saga repeated itself. I thought keeping upright would be impossible. Every fibre of me screamed out for action; for some kind of self-preservation effort. But I stood and I stared at the crowd, my face twitching terribly as I suffocated. Soon my legs gave way as I passed out once more. But, before I did, I fancied I saw some of the crowd starting to shift uneasily in their seats. I imagined that I could even hear a murmur of discontent from the assembled masses. When I came to, I dragged myself to my feet once more, taking time to find the lines of government officials and turn to face them. Yes: both the Marischal and Loker were there. Sitting in state. *Morituri te salutamus,* *you bastards*, I thought, pleased I had remembered another bit of Latin. That classics-spouting prig Professor Spring would be proud.

* Those who are about to die salute you.

Then I saw them: sitting directly in front of Uncle Duncan. The Farquharsons.

So they got you too?

I prayed it hadn't been me who had given them away during one of my chamber rants. His Lordship was grim-faced and stared unblinking at me. He looked every inch the nobleman of old: straight-backed, unbowed, defiant. The Colonel was staring at me too, poorly disguised affection on her face. Yet there was no fear in either of their expressions. If anything, they looked proud.

As I swayed on my spot, I gave a small nod. I fancied I saw them both offer the barest of nods back. A secret bond of solidarity; of fellowship. Then I fixed my eyes firmly on the Marischal and threw my fingertips to my temples in salute again.

At that moment, something changed. There was movement in the crowd now. A growing clamour was perceptible through the walls of my plastic tomb. But what for? Were they baying for the blood of a traitor, who was so shamelessly mocking them? Or were they appealing for clemency? I looked around and saw large numbers of the audience standing up, pointing and shouting. Jesus, a few idiots were saluting me back.

I raised my eyes to meet the Marischal's, but he wasn't looking at me anymore. He was looking around the stands on the Esplanade. He looked confused. Then Lord Farquharson was on his feet, also standing to attention. Staring grim-faced at me, unblinking. His left hand was raised in a clenched fist: *Dìleas Làimh, the Loyal Hand;* that symbol of centuries of Farquharson heritage, dominance, and defiance. I found myself smiling – the old bastard had his Culloden, at last. *Dìleas Làimh* to you too, I thought, and raised a half-clenched, shaking fist in exhausted respect.

Then the Colonel rose to her feet, putting her arm through her husband's. She smiled. It was a small, sad smile, but it spread so that steely face radiated unrepentant pride. If I didn't know better, I would have sworn there were tears in her eyes.

There was movement everywhere now. Loker was barging his way from the Marischal's side, climbing over the assembled dignitaries to get to the aisle, waving his arms like an orchestral conductor while curses and orders poured from his mouth. Mallice pigs streamed out between the stands in well-ordered lines, pointing and yelling at the crowd. Some snatched phones from those who were still filming; others swung and stabbed with their electric batons, scattering crowds of panicked onlookers.

There was a rushing of feet, a banging on the walls of the tank, a dull thud reverberating around my hermetically sealed world, as bodies pressed against it. More and more faces were pressed against the tank, eclipsing the bright sunshine, shouting quietly, as the muffled thumping on the walls grew louder. I looked around, from pigs to men and from men to pigs, and in the melee, it was impossible to say which was which.

I looked above the mob to where the Farquharsons stood. A Mallice officer was tugging at His Lordship's raised fist. Farquharson gave me the smallest nod, politely disengaged his arm from the Colonel's and punched the man square in face, sending him toppling over the spectators in front. I pushed my fingers firmly into my temple and turned my mouth up into that rictus smile. Then the rushing noise started, but this time it didn't seem to matter. Nothing mattered. I was floating, rising easily above the O-Tank. Below me Jimmy Mac was laughing wildly, his head thrown back. Higher and higher I went above the manic sea of humanity. And then I was gone.

* * *

I cannot tell you any more of the immediate aftermath of my execution. I can't say who took me from the O-Tank – or why, since they effectively saved my life in doing so. Nor do I know who was responsible for the plane, car, or even this stinking hot concrete hellhole I now call home. There's no more to tell. No more friends. No more foes. No more about me, no more Farquharsons, no more Reverend, no more Lizzy, no more Marischal or Loker. The rest is silence.

We have reached the finale. The show can't go on. Of course, dear reader, we both knew – or at least suspected – there would be no happy ending. Wait, that's not quite true. I started recounting this story because I thought it might save my skin. And who knows? Perhaps it might still. The number of beatings has dropped off to a trickle. It feels as if my African guards, the stick-thin one, Spurtle, and the behemoth Big Yin, are doing nothing more than assuaging their own boredom. Their hearts just don't seem to be in it. It's sad to see such high levels of professional dedication and passion wane. They come only to deliver food and collect my freshly typed manuscript, which I dutifully leave in the middle of the floor. Also, the rations have improved since I started writing. Fattening the lamb for the slaughter, perhaps? Funny that, when you think about it: from Wolf to lamb.

The thing is, I realise now that this has been about more than one last attempt to save my own skin. There is a greater good to telling this tale – and that is what really matters. Maybe that's why the ghosts no longer come to visit. They seem content to live in my memory now. I've even let Archie go, so he might raise holy hell in peace – wherever *that* may be.

I've recounted faithfully what I did, how I felt and why. In doing so I have come to realise that, yes, my motives were mostly awful, but they were also immaterial in the scheme of things. Either I did the right thing for the wrong reason or the wrong thing for the right reason. I'm not quite sure which, and I'm not sure it matters. Only one thing truly does matter and that is, if you are reading this, you know what we did. Or at least what we *tried* to do. This story is not for me, it's for those courageous few that I left behind. Theirs was to question why. Theirs was to do and to die. It's also for all the other unsung heroes I never met. They are still out there I'm sure, battling the Marischal however they can, taking each day as it comes. Fighting and dying. Where is the person to write their stories?

I have grown used to my new surroundings; to this new existence. Even the blistering heat doesn't matter much anymore since I am, to all intents and purposes, nocturnal. The cold, dark night, once full of terrifying sounds and crushing doubts, has become my friend. I have become moulded to the surroundings. I am part of this place. My own message is now carved into the walls forever, detailing my identity and my crime, alongside those who came before me. Mufunga, who stole the bobojani. Crispen, showing defiance with his crudely carved AK-47. Stephan Chororume, who . . . what? His crime, such as it was, is lost. And, of course, their shining message of hope: *Mwari inzwai tsitsi nhamo ini muno . . .* May God have mercy on me here.

When I added my names to their silent cries I realised I had finally found freedom. Here, unlike in Caledon, my *Gedanken sind* very much *frei*. Sharing my story with you has given me a feeling approaching redemption, however unmerited that may be. I feel at peace. Well, almost. I can't forgive the typewriter. If I don't have arthritis in my fingers after this, it will be a bloody miracle.

But we must address the elephant in the cell: when shall we two meet again? 'In thunder, lightning, or in rain?' No, that will never do. 'When the battle's lost and won.' Yes, I like that. Having already lost – fairly comprehensively, you'll agree – it means we're already halfway there. I have enjoyed our time together and flatter myself that you might worry about yours truly. You really mustn't. I certainly don't. In fact, I find myself borne along on an unexpected gust of satisfaction. That bastard Pride is firing on all cylinders once more. He has found consolation in the knowledge that we are the architect of our own misfortune. Lord knows what he'll get up to next. Common Sense, too, has found a measure of peace in our failures and humiliations. I think he sees it as a form of penitence. Add the two together and we all might be on to something.

And so, I pass my story on to you for safekeeping; not to save myself, but to immortalise those whose lives were played out fleetingly within it.

Out, out brief candles.

For life may be a walking shadow and perhaps I will be heard no more. And there is surely no doubt that this has been a tale told by an idiot, full of sound and fury.

But, I hope, signifying *something*.

Cheery-bye.

Mwari inzwai tsitsi nhamo ini muno

James Macfarlane

Wolf of Badenoch

CHAPTER 14

Epilogue

Was the old James Macfarlane left behind in that infernal bunker when that louse-ridden carcass was dragged out, tumbling into the sunshine? Was the staggering, bewildered creature that emerged a butterfly materialising from a chrysalis? It's hard to know – but if it was, it was a damned ugly butterfly.

Perhaps the opposite was true and this dirty, grasping savage was a more accurate representation of the man than ever there was. Only time will tell. One thing's for sure, all the famous bounce was gone, glorious autumn day though it was.

But we must endeavour to see the bright side, like the mortician who looks upon a decomposing body, takes a deep breath and smells the sweet aroma of job security. And it has to be said, bright sides are easier to come by now than they have been in quite some time. To start with, I'm alive. The witch doctor says I might even get my sight back.

The eye went early: just a few hours after the final instalment of my memoirs had been written and delivered to my agents, Big Yin and Spurtle, who I hoped were negotiating hard on my behalf with the publishers. Job done, I eyed the typewriter venomously, kicked it, hurt my foot badly, then limped off to a corner to settle into an exhausted slumber.

I was woken sometime in the mid-morning by the bolt on the door, which protested loudly as it was dragged back. Groggily I stirred, before snapping awake. Something was wrong. I had heard the heavy grinding sound of the bolt many times, but this was different. There was an urgency to the scraping and grinding that had long been lacking. It spoke of the same anger and violence that had spilled through the heavy iron door in those early days, leaving me beaten and bloody on the floor.

Common Sense and Pride shook hands, apologised for any misunderstandings and gave each other a hug. So, this was it. The end. I had told my story and my usefulness – whatever that might be – had expired. Pride, his moment of weakness forgotten, was demanding I sell my life dearly on behalf of the memories I was leaving behind. On behalf of the Wolf. I had one purpose left: to go down fighting.

As the door opened, I came roaring out, determined to repay Spurtle and Big Yin for their tender ministrations. But after weeks – months? – in that hellish cell, the mind was willing but the flesh was as weak as a politician's promise. In moments I was battered down onto the floor and Common Sense and Pride were back to arguing over what to do next.

After the batons ceased their tireless rise and fall, I was dragged out onto the sharp earth where I had first taken in the magnificent view of the lake that spread out to the horizon, far below this little plateau. The ground was warm against my cheek and the balmy air embraced my battered flesh. Pieces of dry mud and dust mingled with blood to create an unholy paste that I coughed and spat onto the hard ground.

'Get up,' said a high, clear voice.

The words came like an electric shock, making every muscle in my body tighten. This couldn't be right. Oh God, had I actually gone mad in the cell? Oh please, I begged, don't let this all have been a dream. I couldn't bear such a lazy plot twist. But *surely* this just couldn't be real. I mean, he wouldn't . . . couldn't . . .

'I said, get up.'

I pushed myself up onto my hands and stared, willing my eyes to prove my ears wrong. Sweet Jesus, it was him all right, dressed in spotless khaki fatigues and desert boots. There he was: just a few feet in front of me. In the flesh. Making mine crawl. The thin face was burned by the African sun and the hair longer and less austere, but the dead-fish eye stared with a grey malevolence that defied time and geography.

'You have disappointed me, Mr Macfarlane,' said Thomas Loker, standing straight-backed, hands clasped behind him. 'You really have.'

Ever so slowly I got to my feet, breathing hard and swaying on the spot. 'What the hell are you doing here?' I managed.

'I had hoped to learn so much from you. I hoped you would prove to be the specimen that completed my thesis on the human condition – on fear and acceptance and control. But, no, you only brought me more questions.'

He marched forward, pulling dozens of sheets of paper from behind his back and shoving them into my face. I staggered and almost fell. He grabbed me by the tattered remains of my shirt and hissed into my face.

'But this . . . this . . . *monstrosity* has left me further away than ever before.'

Dear God, it was my memoir. My confession. All of it, bound with thick string.

'I don't understand . . .' I began. I really didn't.

'What is so difficult? I am a man of science, of psychology. Of understanding! You were supposed to be the final piece of the puzzle, but no! You were to be the final part of my collection. You were going to finally give me that insight that would complete my treatise on control. Ha! I almost said coercion. No, my control would require no coercion. It would be complete. It would be universal. But you couldn't play that part, could you, *Jimmy Mac*? You had to be a renegade to the last.

'What have you left me with? Nothing. Why did you do it? All of it? Surely it was more than an elaborate temper tantrum by a spoiled, arrogant man-child? Tell me it was not just some arbitrary, clichéd quest of purpose? My God, even you must understand that purpose is nothing more than a different set of shackles to the ones you so ostentatiously tried to break? Surely, Macfarlane, you have not been so stupid as to mistake purpose for free will?'

He stopped and took a deep breath, composing himself.

'I am abandoning this project into which I have invested so very much time and personal sacrifice. So very, very disappointing,' Loker said. His voice trailed off, ending in a sad shake of his head.

I almost felt bad for him. I didn't know the answers – although I imagine they were probably something to do with the indomitable human spirit, or some such. What was clear to me was *why* he wouldn't get them. Loker's desire for order and obedience was forcing him to make connections where there were none. His warped mind needed a balanced mathematical formula that neatly joined bravery and purpose and nobility and desire. Instead, there was something in the equation – the missing integer – he could not find because he could not countenance it: chaos. The final flap of a butterfly's wings as it died, pinned to his board, leaving behind a hurricane. Or to put it another way, he was dealing with a human being – and an idiot at that. Even an idiot like me cannot be defined in black and white. You can try to define a population, of course, but individuals are not so binary; there is no inevitability to their behaviour, no rigorous structure of choice. We are stupidity and greed and fear and longing. We are confusion and uncertainty and arrogance and love. We are chaos.

Of course, it's easy to engage in such pseudo-philosophical ramblings so long after the event. At the time, I did little more than stare – and open-mouthed at that. Yes, any musings on the human condition came a distant second to me gaping alternately at Loker and the manuscript. It was prefaced and dotted with strange scribblings, as if Loker had been studying it, making annotations as he went. Like a teacher marking a student's work.

'I have one question,' I croaked, taking Loker by surprise.

His eyes narrowed but there was a gleam in them; that same eagerness to extract the last piece of the jigsaw, little knowing it was long since lost down the back of the sofa of eternity.

'Why the typewriter? Why the bloody typewriter, for God's sake?'

The disappointment on his face was palpable and lovely to see.

'Frivolous to the end, Macfarlane,' he said, unsmiling but looking at my bent and blistered hands. 'But I will grant your last request, and I hope you find the prosaic nature of what sits behind your pain hurtful in itself.'

If there was a drop of hurt still to be extracted, the Headhunter was up to the task.

'The story you told was for an audience of one, Macfarlane. Me and me alone. I simply could not risk it falling into the wrong hands and being shared more widely. The consequences could be disastrous. Committing it to a digital medium would have presented just such a risk.'

I examined the fingers that had hammered out the Wolf's tale. Stiff, aching joints; fingertips left almost without feeling; the pain from the impact on the soft flesh where my fingernails had been. All the result of nothing more than a security measure. We are the playthings of the gods, are we not?

'And that is also why I came so far to observe this experiment myself – to ensure the results were not tainted – all in the vain hope that you would finally be of use to me in these troubled times.'

'What do you mean, *troubled times?*'

'None of that need concern you. In fact, nothing ever need concern you again, beyond these final few hours of the experiment.'

'No, Loker, you've had your fun,' I said, spitting out bloody phlegm for effect. 'I will not be your plaything anymore.'

'Oh, but you will. That is one thing I am sure of. Unless, of course, I have yet again misjudged you. But I think not.'

Holding the manuscript under his arm, the Headhunter walked over to Spurtle, who handed Loker a hunting rifle with a malevolent grin. Only then did I notice the other three men hovering impatiently by the vehicles parked in the background, on the plateau. Big men, out of shape and ruddy-faced, their khaki clothes stained with sweat. They eyed me expectantly.

'Gentlemen,' said Loker, bombastic as he addressed the overfed predators. 'Did I not promise you a prize that has not been offered in three hundred years?'

The largest of the onlookers shuffled forward, his stomach hanging over his belt and straining to escape his long-suffering shirt buttons. He stared at me and the tip of his fat tongue flicked over his lips in anticipation as he stroked the stock of his gun. My revulsion at this creature came only second to my mounting horror as the lie of the land became clear.

'Yes, Macfarlane, you are honoured!' Loker said theatrically, rifle now held in the crook of his arm. 'It has been centuries since man took part in this event.'

'What event?'

'The killing of the last Scottish Wolf.'

Pride hissed at me to say something noble. Defiant. 'Do I get a head start?' I asked. 'It's hardly sport, otherwise, is it?'

I looked at the overfed vultures leaning against their 4x4s and perspiring with wanton abandon. Did they want real prey or a canned hunt? Loker approached me, his mouth curved into a thin, evil smile. My eyes darted from him to the hunters, to Big Yin and Spurtle, and then around the plateau. The old habits were still there, still dying hard. I was doing a sitrep, assessing lines of fire, marking kill zones and charting possible avenues of escape, maybe for one last time.

Pride and Common Sense spoke in unison. *Play up, Mac; play the game. Just one more time.*

Loker jabbed the manuscript at me like a spear. 'I just want you to know, Macfarlane – before you die – that this document marks your final failure. Your final betrayal of everything you held dear. I will so enjoy talking to all those you have named. No! Those you have *shamed*. I will take my time, I promise you. Particularly with Elizabeth . . .'

Anger surged through me. 'Loker,' I whispered, so low he could hardly hear me.

'Yes?' He leaned so close that he was mere inches away – the benevolent general taking the last confession of a man he has just sentenced to be shot.

'I have one last lesson for you. Perhaps this will help you understand.'

'Go on,' Loker murmured, keen to be part of this last confederacy. I could feel his warm breath on my cheek.

'The best advice I ever received and the best advice I can give you . . .' I confided, raising my eyes to meet his.

'What? What is it?'

'At the end of the day, it's a' baws.'

I meant it too, I really did.

His faced wrinkled in surprise – but not half as surprised as when, with a combination of speed and strength that surprised me as much as anyone else, I swung my head forward and to the side, smashing my skull into his temple. Just like Archie had so lovingly taught me, all that time ago. Loker let out a yelp of pain and his knees buckled. I snatched the manuscript from his hands as he dropped and fled over the lip of the plateau, plunging down the steep hill towards the massive lake that spread out so scenically beneath my prison. Sticks and stones tore at my feet as I stumbled on. I slipped, then slid, then fell and rolled downwards, dust swamping me, making me wheeze and cough. The ground grew flat and I was on my feet again, ploughing forward in full flight to God alone knew where.

A scream split the air and the first of the gunshots smashed into a small tree as I passed, sending splinters whipping through the air. The hunt was on.

CHAPTER 15

To Bee, or Not to Bee

I careered across the brief plateau and on down the slope, which was steeper than ever now. The shots drew closer as Loker's hunters found their range. One hit a rock in front of me, ricocheting off and sending razor-sharp shards of stone into the air. I felt a searing pain as something sliced its way up my face. Blood filled my vision, before my right eye went black.

The damage to my sight hardly registered. I was driven by a simple desire to keep moving and never stop. But there was a problem: I had reached the bottom of the hill. In front of me were spiky acacia bushes and mopane trees, the latter lush with their butterfly-wing leaves. I knew that beyond that screen lay the wide-open expanse of basin that held the lake. No matter how fast I went across it, I would be a sitting duck for any half-decent shot. There was no point in hiding in the bushes; they'd find me in no time.

I looked back up the hill, expecting the bone-shattering agony of a bullet to rip through me at any second. Instead, I saw that the final section of the slope and the plateau above it were acting as a false summit, temporarily sheltering me from my pursuers, who were somewhere above the lip. I scanned to my left and right. The vast amphitheatre of the hills curved their way around the pan, encircling the area. To my left the ground became rocky, while to my right were more of the jagged bushes, interspersed with animal trails, leading off down to the water.

As quickly as I could I tore off a piece of my shirt, dabbed some blood from my ruined eye on it for good measure, balled it up, and threw it into the arms of a mean-looking shrub. Then I grabbed a stick off the ground and set off in the opposite direction, walking backwards and arcing the wood across the dust, doing my best to wipe out the tracks. Just as I reached the rocks and leapt behind one of the larger ones, my pursuers laboured their way across the plateau and started making their way down the hillside. I peeked round the side of the rock and watched their slow, sweaty descent. I thanked the Lord, in his infinite wisdom, for giving us the gift of obesity.

Then I saw that amongst the hunters was a man I hadn't seen before. He wore light-green coveralls and stopped at the bottom of the hill, scanning from side to side to find evidence of my tracks. My heart sank. A proper tracker. It took him all of two seconds to stand up, nodding. I darted back behind the rock as he stared directly at my hiding place. He called to Loker, but the Headhunter wasn't interested. He had seen the bloodied rag, letting out a cry of encouragement to his fellow stalkers. I peered back round, terrified the noise had been for show and they were sneaking up on me. The tracker gesticulated in my direction. This evidently infuriated Loker, who barked an order back. Chastened, the tracker led them into the bushes, casting one last look over his shoulder and shaking his head. I took a longing look through a gap in the bush at the shimmering clear water of the lake and fled.

* * *

A word to the wise: the environment is your biggest enemy, should you ever find yourself being hunted for sport through the African bush. Presuming you evade the guns, then it'll be the heat, sun, and lack of cover that kills you long before the animals do. Mad as it sounds, everything is scared of us. Why? Because they're cleverer than we give them credit for, that's why. There is a caveat to this: if you stumble on the wrong one and surprise it, then all bets are off. Chances are you'll get stomped to a pulp or torn to pieces, as is the individual wont of the species. And that's the thing; they're incredibly good at hiding themselves. You can trip over a buffalo – nature's equivalent of a minibus – without even seeing it. You can climb a tree and not notice it's already occupied by a leopard until you try to use it as a pillow. In short, I was much more scared of what I couldn't see than what I could.

As the minutes passed, that fear was replaced by the growing thirst gripping my throat. The heat was building, like a furnace door being opened in my face. I needed to get as far away from my pursuers as possible and find water and cover. Somehow, I also needed to staunch the flow of blood from my face, which continued to drip down my ragged shirt, turning it dark red, the smell of it as good as a formal dinner invitation to hungry animals with big pointy teeth.

After about an hour I came across a large patch of aloes, their spiky arms reaching up into the air like tentacles. After wrestling with a plant and cursing the barbs as they cut my hands, I succeeded in splitting one of its long leaves open. I laid it against my mutilated eye, sighing as the cool, gloopy latex ran over the wound. Then I tied it in place with another shred of my shirt – which now resembled a large handkerchief with holes – and prayed the aloe vera would work its antiseptic and analgesic magic.

The sun continued its inexorable climb until it was high in the sky. The ferocious heat beat down, making my legs feel heavy, and my feet began to drag across the dusty ground. I tried to take comfort from the fact that the heat came from the sun and not burning slugs of lead. Even in the shade of the trees the heat was intense, and I could feel the telltale signs of a dehydration headache forming. My mouth was parched and my tongue started to swell. I attempted to follow animal trails to find water, but I just found myself going in circles. My fears of dying so soon after my escape grew, as did an intense anger at the sheer unfairness of it all – another sure sign the heat was taking its toll.

Then I had some luck (and about bloody time too). A huge steaming pile of fresh elephant dung lay on the trail in front of me. I licked my cracked lips, smiling with relief. In the normal run of things, you might not consider eating animal shit as lucky, but when I saw the pile of fresh droppings on the path I almost cried aloud. I fell to the ground, throwing the manuscript aside (which I had been gripping subconsciously to my breast the whole time). Tearing off what was left of my shirt, I stuffed the faeces into it, straining the water through the fabric and into my waiting mouth. It was warm and sweet and like nectar to my senses. Then I eagerly pulled the poo apart, picking out the undigested seeds and – hallelujah! – marula fruit. On my knees, I closed my eyes and chewed the bounty with undisguised lust.

But the excremental ecstasy could not last. With every minute that passed, the scorching air pressed more closely on me. Now shirt-less, the sun was like hot metal bearing down on my back. I had to find shade or die. Then, amid that infernal heat, I froze. I don't how I knew, but without doubt I was being watched. I turned.

The warthog was staring at me from a raised bank just ahead, tail in the air and little tusks at the ready. For a moment the air shimmered around the creature before it vanished. I stared at the bank, wondering if it had been a mirage or a hallucination, but then it was back.

I leapt to my feet and charged at the pig, which took fright and dashed into the bush. When I reached the mound, I would have wept with happiness, had my desiccated tear ducts been up to the task. There, on the ground, was a large warthog burrow, big enough to slip into and out of the searing heat. In my desperation I didn't even stop to check for bats, parasites or other nibbly crea-tures that might be down in the dark as I crammed myself inside.

I laid my head in the dust and closed my eyes, luxuriating in long, slow breaths of the cool underground air. Perhaps I even smiled as I drifted off to sleep, a vision of Robbie Macfarlane's whisky pits in my mind.

The sun was beginning its slow descent and the furnace door starting to close as I came to, lying groggily in the hole. A voice was crying from far off. Eventually, I recognised it as Common Sense, reminding me that the cooling air and setting sun would soon bring their own troubles. I didn't have long, he reasoned, before dusk, when the predators would start to stir. Perhaps just an hour or two before they cursed their alarm clocks and headed off into the bush for a hard night's slaughter, humming 'The Lion Sleeps Tonight' in a wistful and ironic kind of way.

But I was comfortable and relaxed for the first time in ages, so I waited, unwilling to go back into the heavy embrace of the lingering heat and thence into the night – and the realm of nature's second most effective killers. Only the nasty little teeth of insects and the wafting smell of wild sage carried on the rapidly cooling breeze eventually tempted me out. I monkey-crawled over the still-warm ground to a nearby sage bush and ripped off some leaves, rubbing them as best I could over my exposed skin to keep the wee biters at bay.

Then something made me stop dead, head in the air like a meerkat sentry. All my senses strained to catch the source of whatever subconscious warning now had me on high alert. There was silence. Nothing . . . nothing . . . Then the barest whisper of voices drifting through the stillness, carried on the silken breeze that ruffled the dry, brown grass. The words were indistinct but drawing steadily closer. The hunt was back on. Nature's most effective killers had found me.

I stumbled away from the voices and into the scrub, sticking to the animal trails that criss-crossed between the low bushes and trees, in the vain hope that some passing creature would join the path and destroy any evidence of my existence.

It was just a few minutes before a triumphant yell sailed through the bush – following by subdued but angry admonishment from the tracker. I fled as fast as I could, but my head was light and my thoughts disorderly. I was starving and had to eat soon – or at the very least drink some more – or I'd be in danger of going delirious in the bush. *Bosbefok*, as I've heard folk call it (and not something you're likely to recover from – you'll be lucky if they find your body).

The branch of a tree to my right exploded with an almighty crack. Splinters flew off it, making me turn sharply to the left and scramble onwards in an aimless panic. As I blundered on, I stooped to grab a reassuringly heavy stick of mopane off the ground, happy visions of clubbing Loker's head in dancing before my eyes.

Time was running out. Shots were coming more regularly now, as were the curses of the ill-disciplined marksmen. Everyone wanted to be the one to down the big game, it seemed. It's hell being popular. I was tiring fast, my legs becoming more leaden with every step, my tongue swelling further and starting to poke through my split lips. The bullets were getting closer too as I crashed through the bush, across sharp grass, and between the low, unwelcoming thorns of the acacias. I dared not look back, my head filled with horrid visions of dense lead playing merry hell with my squishy innards.

Ahead was a thick wall of bushes, offering desperate hopes of camouflage and temporary reprieve. The drumbeat of my heart hammered in my ears as I dived into them, ready to burrow deep and wait for the dark to swallow me. Instead, I fell straight out of the other side into a wide-open area – with no cover whatsoever.

The vast sky, now turning all shades of yellow and orange as the sun set, framed a flat and rocky plain. The only landmark was an old baobab tree that stood, ancient and wizened, fifty metres ahead. I made for it, studying the wide trunk as I approached. It had been split in a few places by age and by elephants using it as a scratching post. I threw my club up into the branches above and tucked the manuscript into what was left of my waistband. Then, using the splits as a ladder, I hoisted myself up with the little strength I had left. Brilliant, bright birds scattered from the branches, making for the last vestiges of the sun as it dipped towards the horizon, turning the sky blood red.

Heaving and straining, I pulled myself up to the top of the trunk and was rewarded with the sight of a hollow middle. I grabbed the club, tipped over the top and fell, with a splash, into a small pool of water that the birds had been drinking from. I was trying to dry off the damp manuscript when I heard the hunting party burst through the bushes. Wet and exhausted, I curled up in a ball as the net tightened around me. Above me the night sky was slowly revealing a beautiful panoply of stars.

'He came this way, for sure,' came the voice of the tracker.

'Well, where the hell is he, then?' said a panting American voice. 'Did he go back into the bushes?'

There was a pause.

'There would be broken branches and scattered leaves if he had,' came the tracker's voice.

It seemed bizarre that the tree wasn't being peppered with shot until I remembered the stony ground had almost certainly covered my tracks. Still, it was only a matter of time before my location became obvious and my lone outpost came under siege.

The voices stopped. The silence was sickening; at any moment I expected the wood around my head to explode in an orgy of high-velocity violence. Lying on my side in several inches of water, with my knees up close to my chest and my precious life story clasped to my breast, I twisted my head and looked around for salvation. There must be something I could use. Anything! There wasn't.

The air was warm and still in my little wooden cot as the breeze carried a babble of low voices to me, their words indecipherable. These were secret whispers, laden with overtones of new-found understanding and undertones of clever tricks. The hunters were approaching the tree. This was no longer sport; it was a canned hunt. I tightened my grip on the club and, for the umpteenth time, started making ill-founded promises to myself about dying like a man. (I swear to God, it's terrible for the heart; all this preparing to die will be the death of me.)

A small, darting movement distracted me from my maudlin thoughts. There it was again, appearing out of the corner of my eye. Was I hallucinating? No, I definitely wasn't. There were more. And more. So many more. Bees. Lots and lots of bloody bees. Bees of the angry, swarming kind. They hovered over the water and began landing all over me. They crawled over my chest and, oh God, onto my face. Their furry shoulders were aquiver and their terrible stings stood proud and ready to deliver their poison. I closed my mouth as one made its way across my lips, threatening to crawl inside.

Bees usually sting only in self-defence and I categorically wished them no harm. But how to convince these little monsters of that? I lay motionless, trying not to release the wrong kind of pheromones. The ball was very much in their court. I tried not to whimper as the little feet scuttled over my delicate skin, when the noise of the hunters intruded on my thoughts. I could hear their footsteps now on the rocky ground. The thought of being both shot and stung to death was almost too much to bear. I railed silently at the world, knowing the world was too big and too busy to care one jot.

Then, as another bee landed and began a leisurely perusal of my shoulder, a thought occurred to me: so many bees needed a happy home from which to sally forth, their arses loaded with pain. Slowly, ever so slowly, I turned my head and looked in desperation for the redemption that had so far eluded me. And there it was, just a few feet away: obscured by a small clump of green leaves and dangling from a branch, like a giant teardrop. It seemed to ripple as a mass of bodies flowed over its surface: a thriving, undulating beehive.

With a sluggishness that would have impressed the laziest of snails upon the most precarious of thorns, I raised my club and pushed myself up to peer over the top of the trunk. The bees buzzed around me, alert but unconcerned. I had one shot at this. To fail meant death, scoured with lead and perforated by a thousand poison-bearing barbs.

I peered down at the hunting party. Ruddy, sweat-ridden faces stared back at me, looks of undisguised joy beaming out from features caked with dust.

'Come down, Macfarlane,' sneered Loker.

I shook my head, very slowly indeed.

'Oh, come now, Mac,' he said. 'Cat got your tongue?'

Bees, actually.

'This is your last chance, Macfarlane. Come down and we will give you a fair chance. If you don't then we will, as my colleagues here might say, fill you full of lead.'

They looked at me. Eager. Hungry. That fat tongue of the largest hunter once again flicked over his bulbous lips. They watched as I uncoiled myself from my lair, the slow progress fuelling their sick anticipation. Then the first bee stung me.

I gritted my teeth, the pain like a red-hot needle. The hunters took my twisted face to be a sign of fear and raised their weapons. The big one was panting, taking quick, lascivious breaths in his eagerness to make the kill.

I looked from hive to hunters and back again. They were two or three metres apart, as far as I could judge. All sorts of useless calculations ran through my mind as I tried to gauge how hard to hit the hive so it split on the ground rather than breaking open and releasing its terrible cargo straight into my face.

Now or never.

I swung the wooden club and it connected squarely with the top of the hive, sending it tumbling off the branch. My little cluster bomb crashed to the ground about a metre from the group, who looked in surprise as it split open, releasing a dark cloud of fury. Hundreds – maybe thousands – of bees swamped the shooting party. Screams of pain and fear filled the air as flailing arms thrashed about in a vain attempt to beat off the savage attack. I stood in my tree, mesmerised. Loker and the tracker fled back towards the safety of the bush, their weapons abandoned in the rout. For a brief second I caught the Headhunter's blue eye, now red and swollen with stings, but full of a fury that matched the bees buzzing around him. Then he crashed through the wall of shrubs and was gone. Just behind him came two of the sportsmen who were still crying out anguished oaths and prayers as a thousand poisoned arrows landed in merciless waves. They too barrelled into the bush and were lost from view.

A strange noise filled the air. It was a scream of pain and despair that quickly faded to a gurgle and a whimper. It was a ghastly sound. The final hunter – he of the bloated cheeks and terrible tongue – was paying the price for a lifetime of poor diet and animal cruelty. He had blundered just a few metres from the tree before collapsing on the ground. He lay writhing in agony, covered in a pitiless black blanket. The dark shadow of bees covered almost every inch of him. They darted and scurried and crawled, his immaculate khakis replaced with a thousand-piece suit of pure vengeance. For a second the wave parted and his face appeared, purple and swollen beyond recognition. A rasping sound came from the hole that had once been a mouth, but it was stifled as a stream of scurrying legs, beating wings, and tiny nails of poison poured into the cavity. I watched as the contorting limbs grew limp and the body lay still.

Enjoyable as these last few seconds had been, another red-hot sting on my arm made me realise I was next unless I moved fast. Working on instinct and little more, I lent far out of my waterhole, rammed my club into a cleft in the bark on the far side of the baobab, and let my momentum carry me over the edge. The increasingly ragged story of my life crammed once again into my trousers, I swung on the stick and fell, hitting the ground and rolling forward to ease the impact.

Then I ran as fast as my terrified, emaciated legs would carry me. But the bees were faster. Soon they were all around, closing about me in a black cloud, darting in to pump me full of their venom. I screamed in pain through lips that were clamped shut, the vision of the dying hunter's hellish maw still fresh in my mind. On I went, tearing the manuscript from my waist and trying swat them away.

We mustn't stumble, we must keep going, Common Sense urged. *Bees won't pursue us more than five hundred metres. We must keep going if we want to survive.*

But the pain was growing unbearable, as if red-hot pokers were being indiscriminately pressed all over my body. I dragged one leg after another across the hard ground. Breathing grew harder, my throat constricting as the toxins sent my body into shock.

Then I was pushing my way through spindly branches and out of that damned rock plain. I blundered on a few more paces before falling to my knees onto the soft earth of the bush. Every one of my nerve endings was aflame. Red welts erupted all over me. In a frantic attempt to ease the pain I started pulling every barb I could see out of my skin. I remember counting over thirty, but was delirious with agony and have no idea if that's right.

'Macfarlane!' Loker's shriek carried over the air from somewhere far off. 'I will find you and I will skin you alive! Do you hear me, Macfarlane?'

All I could think was he could have my skin for all I cared. It was giving me nothing but trouble.

We must go on, Common Sense whispered in my ear. *We are not safe; they will come again.*

But I had nothing left. My breath came in gasps. Someone seemed to have strapped lead weights to my legs. I bent over and retched, but nothing came out.

Please, James, keep going, we are almost away. We are almost free. The voice was delicate but insistent.

I ignored it.

Oh, come on, you bloody numpty, roared Pride, unable to hold back any longer. *Get up!*

But I'm so tired.

Nonsense. Why sleep now? You'll be a long time dead. Come on, soldier, one leg up . . . Yes, that's good. Now the other. Better. Now march, soldier. March!

And so I staggered on, lurching and swaying before going down, again and again. Each time I fell that voice came in my ear, demanding I march. So I marched. The air was rapidly cooling and the darkness wrapped around me. The bright moonlight lit the bush with its pale silver beams, but I had no idea where I was or where I was going. Still I marched.

It was only a matter of time until, overcome with poison, dehydration and delirium, I collapsed onto the cool earth. Totally *bosbefok.* I lay there, unmoving, my cheek buried in the earth, my one good eye staring across the ground, through the dust and tenacious clumps of hard grass.

Then, a dull sense of amazement filtered into my fevered mind as I saw the manuscript, lying in the dirt, still bound with its coarse string and prefaced and annotated with Loker's hieroglyphs. I couldn't believe I had clung to it, just as I had somehow clung to life. I idly wondered if it wasn't there at all, a mere figment of my poisoned imagination. Then the hallucinations really started.

Something emerged from the bush. No, wait, *peeled* itself from the bush as if it were an integral part of the surroundings. A pair of bare and ancient feet approached, attached to a pair of thin, sinewy legs that moved with the lightness of a ballet dancer. Then I saw the hallucination had a third leg. It was thin and straight and left a faint small round mark in the earth. The feet stopped next to me and began a leisurely circuit around my prone form. A wizened face dropped into view, right next to mine, a wide grin revealing a handful of yellow teeth. The light-brown skin was furrowed with deep lines, but bright, clear eyes reflected the moon. It studied me and evidently liked what it saw.

Then the hallucination stood up, rearranged the leathery shawl about its shoulders, and prodded me with its third leg, sending waves of pain across my body. I moaned and feebly tried to bat it away, one hand flailing uselessly in the dust. The phantasm seemed content with this reaction. It rose to its full height, lifted its extra appendage up into the air and brought it down hard on my head. Before everything went black, I marvelled that even the illusions in this pitiless place could be quite so unforgiving.

CHAPTER 16

The End of the Beginning

It should speak volumes about my state of mind that I didn't much care when the old bushman sold me into slavery. I was a mere voyeur, lying where I had been dropped on the cold ground, swimming in delirium. He enthusiastically repeated 'White gold! White gold!' amid the stream of unfathomable words and delicate clicks that made up his language. The object of his entrepreneurial zeal was wrapped in vast robes covered in wildly intricate designs. Part man, part carpet, all warlord. Ubaba, as his people call him, and which I understand means 'father', listened and watched patiently as the ancient businessman spoke eagerly, miming how he had dragged me through the bush by means of a rope under the armpits. I have yet to stop marvelling at the strength this must have taken.

'Look, can His Highness not see the rope burns on the white creature's skin?' he (may or may not have) said, poking at me. Then he waved the manuscript in the air. 'And behold: he had this book with him, all filled with mysterious spells, incantations and other *juju*. It surely holds the secret to Your Majesty's immortality, or, at the very least, is certain to keep you safe from minor curses and inconvenient bowel movements.'

Hands splayed, the bushman explained he had done all this at great personal expense, hardship, and risk, no doubt breaking all sorts of trade union rules as he went. All this peril just so Ubaba could benefit from having this white gold for his very own chattel, pet, or – if he might be so bold – dancing girl.

Ubaba stood unmoving, listening to the man's plea before turning his steely gaze and riotous robes in my direction. A strange look passed over his face. If I hadn't been so full of venom, dehydration, and self-pity, I would have sworn it was a look of recognition. Although how he could possibly see anything familiar in the bloated, burned, and dust-caked bundle of bones lying on his stone floor was beyond me. Yet he continued to stare, eyes narrowed. The silence stretched out in the warm air as his shrewd gaze raked over me.

Slowly, Ubaba began to nod, as if satisfied. He said something in a deep voice, causing the bushman to clap and then clasp the huge hands in gratitude.

The deal had been done. Slavery wouldn't be so bad, I thought. At least it would remove the responsibility of decision-making – something for which I had proved so ill-suited.

Some lackeys appeared and led the joyous entrepreneur away. They returned swiftly and, at the command of Ubaba, picked me up and carried me through room after room of an immense building, which I would have called a house had there not been armed men peering furtively from every nook and cranny. This was not a house, it was a compound.

We twisted and we turned down passages, through arches and doorways, until we reached a set of wooden doors, studded with large black nails and flanked by two armed guards. Ubaba pulled a large metal key out his pocket and turned it in the lock. The mechanism responded with the kind of satisfying *clunk* that marked the room out as a repository of Important Things. Gun-toting footmen hauled at the doors, which swung open in a ponderous but well-oiled way. I was carried down a set of stone stairs into the darkness. I was warming to this hospitality – much more civilized than the last time I was forced into a dungeon.

The room was almost pitch black. The light from the open door penetrated only timidly down the stairs, as if pushed back by the murky, cool air. Another low rumble of command saw me laid on the floor, before the room exploded into light. I moaned and tried to cover my eyes, but at a growled command, my hands were politely, but insistently, pulled away.

Ubaba sank to his knees next to me and through screwed-up eyes I watched him study my lumpy face, then look away, then back again. His breath was hot on my cheek and rich with the smell of tobacco. He didn't say a word; he just kept looking from side to side. Most peculiar. His expressions were kaleidoscopic, ranging from bafflement to wonder and back again. He seemed unable to believe . . . something.

Then the big head disappeared and with my eyes now accustomed to the light, I saw what he was looking at and recoiled in surprise and confusion. This made Ubaba laugh out loud, a rich, booming noise that spoke of suspicions confirmed. I whimpered in return. There, standing motionless against the wall, were hundreds of . . . *me*. An army of Macs, dressed to the nines, standing to attention, ready to march. I screwed my eyes tight shut and lay still, praying that when I looked again this insanity would stop.

Eventually, I peeked out. There was to be no respite. There I was – or rather, *they were*: hundreds of smirking Jimmy Macs, smiling down at me sardonically in full military raiment. My mind swam and confusion overwhelmed me. Was this another hallucination? What did this army of grinning doppelgangers portend? Had my mind finally shattered into hundreds of pieces that were now no more than spectators of my long-overdue demise?

'Jimmy Mac!' thundered Ubaba. He seemed delighted at his new acquaintance; little knowing I had no interest in that name whatsoever. It was nothing but trouble. He turned to his colleagues and pointed in my direction, repeating 'Jimmy Mac' over and over while they nodded with the kind of appreciation one must always offer a warlord, whether you have any idea what they are talking about or not.

It was all too much for my addled brain and I sank back into oblivion. After that I slept, safe in the knowledge that nothing could ever surprise me ever again.

* * *

It felt like days later when I woke up and got the surprise of my life. This disbelief soon descended – as my waking periods so often have of late – into terror. There in front of me stood a being I knew I could never see again: my own personal Jacob Marley there to rattle his chains, a denizen of hell sent to mock and punish me for my many and varied sins. Perhaps to finally drag me back from whence it came.

'Hullo, Mr Mac,' said the denizen. 'Yer looken an affy lot better. Ah wiz shocked to see how much ye'd let yersel go.'

I hid under the blankets. This wasn't possible. It was all too much. But wait! I had *blankets*. I was in a bed. A quick appraisal found me clear of mind and cynical of eye, with fear in my heart. I was me again. What the bloody hell was going on?

'Och, he's clearly no' himsel' yet,' the voice continued while I trembled in my makeshift tent. 'He's usually no' so fearty.'

The stress I detected on 'usually' brought years of hard-wired social hierarchy rushing back. I threw back the covers.

'Archie,' I said imperiously, 'what the bloody hell do you mean by *usually*?'

The big man smiled at me and then, all propriety forgotten, I flew towards him to be caught in those giant arms. I held my long-dead friend at arm's length and stared into his great big face. I tried to count his scars, gave up, and totted up his teeth instead, an eminently more feasible task. It was him. No doubt about it. And he was surprisingly, well, *alive*.

'You are quite dead. Please explain this new lease of life.'

You might think this a curt response in the circumstances, but I was deeply suspicious someone was playing silly buggers again.

'Och, nivver you mind,' Archie said. 'Yeh've got tae take a break an' I'll gi'e yeh the whole story when yer ready.'

'I'm afraid we haven't got much more time for rest and recuperation,' came a horribly familiar voice from behind Archie.

Instinctively, I ducked down in front of the big man and, bravely using him as a human shield, peered over his shoulder. 'Archie, don't move a muscle. That bastard Blunt is standing right behind you. He doesn't appear to be armed, so, on my word, you break right, I'll break left, and we'll get him in a pincer movement. Hopefully, he'll go for you, since you seem to have become bulletproof recently.'

'Mr Mac, ah think yeh'd better sit doon, there's a wee bittie catchin' up tae dae.'

Reluctantly, I let him guide me back to my bed where I sat down and eyed both Archie and Blunt warily.

'Mr Blunt pulled me oot o' the river – half-drooned an' covered in fish pish,' Archie began, poking a finger at the insufferable Blunt. 'He smuggled me oot o' Caledon and doon tae England. The Reverend wiz in oan it an' a'.'

I almost interrupted to demand more detail but decided there would be plenty of time to complicate matters later.

'Doon south they patched me up. It wisnae that bad, a few broken ribs frae the bullets and some internal bleedin' – ah've had worse.'

'Just like a successful Saturday night in Inverness, I suppose.'

'Aye, spot on, Mr Mac.'

'England, eh? How did that go?'

Archie had never travelled over the border, and the blood of generations of forebears who still keenly felt English slights dating back hundreds of years ran in his veins. Worse, Blunt had, to all intents and purposes, sold us out and Archie knew it. I couldn't see any way this *entente* could be *cordiale*.

'Aye, it wisnae bad,' he said. I waited vainly for further details until Archie relented, adding, 'They a' talked affy funny like.'

'Is that it?'

'Aye.'

I decided to try and get blood from a different stone. 'OK, park that one for now. But there's one glaring element you've left out – and that is *how are you still alive*? I mean, don't get me wrong, I'm delighted you are, but *why* you are is quite beyond me.'

'Bulletproof vest, obviously,' he said matter-of-factly, looking at me like I was an idiot.

'They could have shot you in the face!' I almost yelled in frustration.

'Och no.' He smiled happily, making one of the guards standing by the doorway shrink back in horror. 'Nae chance o' that. Ah'm way too pretty. It wid be a travesty, would it no'?'

That sense of blissful optimism coloured the whole story of Archie's daring escape, and he related the tale very much in the way you or I might discuss the challenge of boiling an egg. With some effort I discovered the adventure bore many similarities to that of Professor Spring. The big difference was that I hadn't been involved this time, so nothing had been blown up and he'd escaped in roughly one piece. Then came the story of Archie's recovery and recuperation at the hands of the English nurses, who, by all accounts, took great delight in ministering to this romantic and heroic barbarian from the wilds of Caledon. In fact, the looks the nurses were giving him while they were supposed to be looking after me – and the occasional growl he gave them in return – intimated that Archie was working his debonair, jet-setting charm here too.

'So, that gets us here,' I said eventually, 'But one thing you've not told me: where is here, exactly?'

Here, as it turned out, was enjoying the hospitality of a local African warlord, who was ecstatic at his house guest, being a huge fan of both the taste and investment potential of my whisky, as well as the lucrative generosity of the English intelligence services. Apparently, I'd been out for over a week, during which time an enviable chunk of the English intelligence apparatus had set to work to ensure my whereabouts were kept secret from marauding Caledon assassins. Meanwhile, Blunt had hotfooted it out to take care of me and prepare plans that could well see me being taken care of (more of that shortly). When Archie's carers told him I was alive, he threatened ferocious retaliation against the first person that said he couldn't come along. After that, anyone who was asked for permission claimed that it was above their pay grade, or affected not to understand what he was saying. So, in the absence of anyone qualified to say no, the big man was soon in tow.

In that week of heavy and happy sedation, I also suspect that Blunt read the manuscript, as he has asked me surprisingly few questions since our reunion. The revelations within it are sure to cause complications, but we'll cross that smouldering wreck of a bridge when we come to it.

In fact, Blunt just stood silent and impassive, listening as Archie spun his yarn and looking occasionally confused at the Glasgow vernacular. Only when the big man had wrapped up, complaining as he did so about the food on offer (the lack of deep-frying weighed heavily), did Blunt step forward.

'You've been through hell, James,' he started.

'A hell of your creation.'

'Oh, come now, it was a team effort. But let's not quibble. You see, the thing is, old chap – and I don't want you to feel like you're being rushed – you've got to go back.'

'Back where?'

'Caledon.'

I sat bolt upright, appalled. Going back was one of the most lunatic ideas ever put to me – and the competition for that accolade was stiff indeed.

'Oh no I bloody don't. Call the matron: she'll tell you I am excused from all insurgency-based activities. I'll get her to write a note if necessary. I've done my bit for you, for those ungrateful people, for everyone. I'm retired, pensioned off. Or, to use a technical term: go fuck yourself.' I sat back and folded my arms in defiance. I was certain that I – that the Wolf – had gone as far as I could.

'Are you finished?'

'No, as a matter of fact, I am not. For God's sake, what are you thinking? What help have I been to anyone anyway? Because of me, all the good people are either dead or betrayed – by my own hand in some cases – and so the ones who are still breathing are now as good as dead anyway. Loker knows everything, and if the Marischal doesn't already know it too, then he soon will. There is no more I can do. I've buggered this up as comprehensively as anyone possibly could. At best I am an irrelevance. At worst . . . well, that hardly bears thinking about. I am at the end of the road. At rock bottom. There's nowhere left to go.'

But it's just when you think you've hit rock bottom that bastards like Blunt hand you a shiny new shovel and bid you to keep digging.

'But you made a huge difference,' he said calmly. 'You have never been more important.'

'Eh?'

'I watched your execution; it was quite moving.'

'Delighted to hear you enjoyed it.'

'Do you remember the crowd?'

'I remember them trying to attack me.'

'They weren't trying to attack you. They were trying to save you.'

I stared at Blunt for a while, eventually remembering to close my mouth.

'The hubris of the Marischal was quite something. It was bad enough they killed Barclay as a warm-up . . .'

'You mean the publisher? They killed Iain Barclay?'

'Yes.'

'For God's sake, why?'

'He published a self-penned piece asking for your release; railing at the injustice that was being done. Very brave, in the circumstances. He must have known what would happen.'

I was lost for words. I pictured the embittered, gin-soaked hack who I'd last seen trembling as Loker approached Invereiton. The breath caught in my throat as I remembered the handprints on the walls of the O-Tank. All that was left of Iain Barclay; all that was left of his last attempts to speak truth to power. I like to think they gave him a stiff drink first, but I doubt it.

'The crowd was pretty uncomfortable watching him die. The Marischal took his time. Barclay died of heart failure before he could suffocate. After that, you made your stand and then the Farquharsons led their little protest and, well, those straws very nearly broke the camel's back. The event was being live-streamed everywhere. So everyone saw the riot break out in Edinburgh—'

'*The riot?*'

'Oh yes, and a big one by any measure. They even took the castle for a while. Across the country public events set up to celebrate your demise descended into anarchy, one after the other. It was extraordinary to watch. People seemed to have gone mad. They were yelling for Jimmy Mac, howling like wolves, channelling their anger in a way I've never seen before.'

'Then what?'

'The riots went on for four days.'

'Then what?'

'They stopped.'

'Why?'

'Loker had guns.'

He said this as if it was the most obvious thing in the world, but then this was very much his world. I remembered Smith explaining the rules of coups to me as if from an instruction manual. *Revolutions very rarely happen without foreign state intervention.*

'Why didn't your lot get involved, for God's sake?'

'We weren't ready. We couldn't mobilise quick enough. And, I'm ashamed to say, there were a lot of voices who wanted to hedge our bets; to see how it played out.'

'So . . . Then what?'

'The usual.'

'The usual?'

'Oh, you know: mass round-ups, arbitrary detentions, torture, executions. That sort of thing. Somewhere along the way, the Marischal died.'

'When? How?' I stammered. The Marischal . . . gone? It seemed inconceivable; impossible that this titanic and all-encompassing presence, which had watched over us and controlled our daily lives for so long, had gone. I was speechless. The worst bit was, despite my best efforts, I felt sad. Bereft. Lost. No one is immune from the kind of conditioning the Marischal wielded so mercilessly. Anger was building in my chest. I felt a keen injustice at this. Not because my uncle was dead, you understand – rather that if anyone was going to kill my family, it should be me.

'How?'

'We're not sure yet. And I should stress we haven't seen the body. No one has. But it seems very likely it was one of Loker's assassins. We think he had been waiting for his moment to strike for some time. Look at this.'

He handed me a tablet, open on a Caledon Broadcasting Corp news page. I read the story in a trance.

MARISCHAL FINLAY, THE ARCHITECT OF CALEDON, IS DEAD

Caledon grieves, but a united people's nerves are steady.

Today, countless millions in every country in the world are plunged into the deepest grief at the news that the heart of the most outstanding revolutionary leader of all time, DUNCAN FINLAY, has ceased to beat.

The leader of all who love peace, value democracy, treasure their national independence, and desire the banishment of poverty, unemployment, and war for ever, has died.

On and on went the eulogy about ceaseless devotion, self-sacrifice and nobility. Then there were calls for calm and reflection and resolve. Finally, there was a heartfelt plea for the nation to galvanise itself behind, and to pray for . . . Marischal Loker.

'It's a brave new world,' Blunt's voice cut through the silence.

'Bloody hell.'

'Yes, it is rather.'

'What do you plan to do about it?'

'What are *we* going to do about it, you mean?'

I put down the screen and regarded Blunt wearily. 'No, we've already been through this. I'm clearly not equipped for this. For God's sake, you've just said you weren't ready. How the hell am I supposed to be?'

'We weren't ready.'

'Exactly.'

'We are now.'

For a moment, the future spread out in front of me. It bore a striking resemblance to the past; a past that took place far from here in a room that smelled of old books, surrounded by men called Smith. I didn't need a crystal ball. The script went thus: I would refuse to help, Blunt would politely threaten me, I would concede. Those were the rules and I was powerless to change them. Then the rules changed.

'I would threaten you, but there's no need,' said the English spy. 'You see, you've forgotten one other thing.'

'Oh, and what is that?'

'Lizzy.'

He was right. I had completely forgotten Lizzy in all the excitement. A large knot wound itself up in my stomach. 'Where is she?'

'Loker has her,' he replied with a level gaze. 'Our intel says she is locked up in a private suite he keeps in the Tolbooth.'

'But he knows everything. Why is he keeping her alive?'

'We're not exactly sure. Our psychological profilers say it's likely Loker's feelings for her mean he accepted she did it all for her child; we think he *wanted* to believe that. It gave him a reason to save her. Although it's not clear if that's really why *she* did it. We can't rule out the possibility that she planned that story as a fallback cover story. All we can hope, for now, is that Lizzy has it all figured out.'

'Oh, she will have it figured out. Somehow. Trust me.'

'Well, then?'

Blunt's eyes bored into mine, daring me to decline the kind offer of another suicide mission. Daring me to leave Lizzy to her fate. I fancy I even saw his top lip wobble ever so slightly at the thought of it. For a long time, no one spoke. Then a voice, which sounded remarkably similar to mine, broke the impasse.

'What's the plan?' said the voice; a voice with the hollow conviction of someone who had, against his better judgement and in the face of all prior experience, just done one of the most terrifying things in the world: decided to be brave.

* * *

I won't miss Africa. My latest trip has not been a positive experience, although I concede that's not Africa's fault. But the whole thing's been relentless and shows no sign of stopping. Since I was discharged from my makeshift hospital bed and into the hospitality wing of the warlord's fortress, a new set of trials has been sent to test me. I'm heartily sick of all the charts, supply chains, weapon inventories, and poor internet connections that have dominated the last few days. The only thing worse than being part of all those travails is the terrible consequences of them coming to an end. Once again, the clock is ticking. Tomorrow we saddle up to give the whole armed insurrection thing another shot – and not just for me this time. For Lizzy. For Wally. For the Farquharsons. For Caledon. For *auld lang syne*.

For the dead already and for the next to die.

But before we part ways, let me leave you with one last episode, and you can make of it what you will. Less than an hour ago, I came across Archie, alone and silent, staring over the baked clay ramparts of the compound. I sidled up next to him and we stood and gazed out at the countryside beyond. Below us, where the crumbling wall met the dusty, parched earth, the ground dropped away to a wide river. It slid silently past us, a mirror of silver and bronze as the sun began its burning descent towards the horizon of that infinite sky. The temperature was dropping rapidly and the air was close. I took a deep breath and savoured the earthy smell, pulling my coat around me as the cold began to bite.

'Storm's comin',' said Archie.

'Aye.'

'The boys are affy excited aboot it. No rain fer months, apparently.'

'The boys?'

'Mr Ubaba's guard.'

'Of course.'

We lapsed into a silence broken only by the cicadas starting their night shift. I stared out across the plain. Thick clouds gathered far off and towered over the horizon. A stealthy movement at the edge of the bush caught my attention. I looked down as a pair of kudu, their magnificent curled horns held high, slipped out of the treeline and sauntered down to the river's edge. Their dipping heads sent ripples out across the idle flow.

The silence continued, unbroken. Then I noticed Archie's fingers drumming on the top of the wall. Something was playing on the big man's mind. For days the attentions of the nurses, coupled with the appalling savagery promised by our military planning, had kept him in a state of high excitement. But now a frown covered his face.

'What is it, Archie?' I asked quietly.

'Ah wiz jist thinkin' . . .' he said, gazing into the distance, eyes narrowed.

'Go on,' I prompted.

'Aye, ah wiz jist thinkin',' he continued, leaving the words hanging in the air. 'Nothin' stays the same forever, right?'

'I suppose not.'

'So . . . we jist ha'e tae stay alive long enough an' it'll a' be OK?'

'Makes sense. Sort of.'

'An' we're gettin' tae go back hame, eh?'

'Not much choice, really.'

'An' we're gonnae get anither crack at the bastards – this time wi' some real firepower behind us?'

'If you trust Blunt, then yes.'

'An' we're gonnae rescue Lizzy – sorry, ah mean Miss Burke.'

'With any luck.'

'An' get 'em back for whit they did tae Wally?'

'I hope so.'

'So, if that's the case, ah wiz thinking . . .'

Archie stared out over the landscape, trying to marshal thought and word. The kudu ambled back into the trees beyond the river and disappeared from view. Far off, the plaintive cry of a bird carried through the still evening. The air was cold now and the setting sun bathed the land in gold. A bright flash lit up the clouds on the horizon, followed by a rumble of thunder.

'. . . things could still work out OK, no?'

'With a bit of luck.'

'And if that's right, then, yeh ken . . . a' this . . . everythin' till noo . . . it's been shite – *really* shite – at times, aye it has, but if yeh think aboot it, it cannae be *a'* baws, can it?'

'*A'* baws? No, I suppose not.'

'And if it's no' *a'* baws, then it's got tae be *half*-baws at worst. Mebbe even, from now on in, nae baws at a'?'

'Maybe, Archie, maybe.'

'And, Mr Mac, if it's no' *a'* baws, and it's really half-baws or mebbe nae baws at a' . . . d'ye know whit?'

'What's that, Archie?'

He turned to me. His eyes shone and a smile lit up that massive face. 'Ah'd take those odds any bluidy day o' the week.'

I smiled back and patted him on the shoulder. Another bolt of electricity streaked through the distant clouds. A storm was coming.

To find out more about the adventures of Jimmy Mac – and to download your free illustrated digital book, featuring beautiful photography of the places that inspired the world of Caledon – visit www.michaelmillar.info. You can get in touch by emailing hello@michaelmillar.info. Cheery-bye!

A NOTE ON ACCENTS

When it comes to accents and spellings I will fall back on exactly the same threadbare excuses I made in *Hooray for the Next to Die*. To wit: in this story I tried to convey accents and linguistic quirks wherever I could to help bring authenticity and warmth to the characters. I have done everything I can to be faithful to these regional variations, and I write with nothing but respect and affection for the people and places mentioned. Still, spellings and use of particular words and phrases are subjective. On many occasions I also dialled back to make it easier on non-Scots readers. So, if you disagree with my interpretation of different Scots accents, I will apologise and then start making excuses. The easiest excuse is that this story is set in the future and, as language is ever changing, who's to say my usage won't be right in twenty years' time? On the other side of the coin, I've also used some words that have long since disappeared to help reflect the faux-romanticism promoted by the Marischal's regime. But if you want to put me right, please do get in touch at www.michaelmillar.info or hello@michaelmillar.info.

ACKNOWLEDGEMENTS

Originally, the first two books of what is to be the Caledon Trilogy were just one. Then someone pointed out printed copies would be economically ruinous when it came to postage and packing, and my lawyers were horrified at the health and safety implications of someone dropping it on their foot. So, it was with great excitement I decided I had written two books, rather than one. The problem with this is it doesn't lend itself to new and exciting acknowledgements. The same people did the same amazing things. So, just as I copped out with the note on accents above, here I go again with the acknowledgements.

Firstly, to my family: Susanna, Freddie, and Evie, who put up with my obsessing over and writing this story for a long time, often at the strangest times of day or night. Thank you for your support and your tolerance. A similar message goes out to my Scotland and Africa-based families who, in many different ways, afforded me the stories, experiences, and knowledge needed to write this story. Mum, Dad, Clive, Carla, Ali, Laura, J and Phil, and all the wee ones, thanks! Granny and Grampa, I will never forget our times in the Cairngorms.

Special thanks go to Grant Nel, a man with an encyclopaedic knowledge of the African bush and the generosity to share it. Others who have helped me along the way are legion, and I apologise profusely to anyone I forget. This has been a long journey!

To Robbie Knox, who first demanded I pull my finger out and get started. To Adam Sturdy, who lent me a desk in his office so I could pen the first words of this story. To my beta readers, Robbie (again) and Will Paton, for suggesting key changes to the early narrative. To my editors: firstly, Kate Moore, whose work on the original manuscript transformed this story into something worthy of human consumption. Secondly, to Bryony Sutherland, who I cannot thank enough for her amazing eye for detail, as well as plot and character development. Last but not least, on the editorial front, my thanks to the team at whitefox – Chris, Silvia, Sam, Jill and Jack – who finally got me over the line.

To the proprietors of the Hestkuk Arms: Desi Olsen, Tim Lovejoy, Fons Cohen, and Robbie (again!), who made social media truly worthy of the name with their support. To Gustav Pegers, who procured the hut in Devon that broke six months of writer's block. To the Arbuthnott family who, hundreds of years ago, took part in the real murder of Sheriff Melville of Glenbervie that was played out in its own way in *Hooray for the Next to Die* ('sodden and supped in broo!') and who, rather more recently, let me use the text of the real pardon that their ancestors somehow received. Their beautiful home – Arbuthnott House – was the early inspiration for Mac's home Glenlairig House. It is open to visitors. Check out their website (arbuthnott.co.uk).

If I had to choose one whisky company that inspired Glenlairig's products then it has to be Glenlivet. It's my favourite Scotch and their distillery and visitor centre ooze romanticism and adventure. Do visit if you're in those parts. The inspiration for Robbie Macfarlane and his whisky pits was one Robbie MacPherson, whose trail, by coincidence, runs through the glen of Glenlivet. (If you have time to read about the early whisky smugglers, it will not be time wasted.) There's also a decent chunk of Dauvit Ogilvy of Rashiebog in there, that marvellous smuggler, astronomer and philosopher from the braes of Angus.

I made a poorly coded reference to various authors at the start of the book by way of dedication, and they give a flavour of the authors in whose shadow I humbly stand. I must also mention

Anna Funder's *Stasiland*, which provided detail and inspiration for Loker's secret police apparatus. Much of the background that formed the world of Caledon also came from podcasts, including the brilliant *Behind the Bastards*, *Stuff You Should Know* and Dan Carlin's *Hardcore History*. Alex Massie and Chris Deerin were first amongst equals when it came to political commentators whose wry eyes helped shape my view of Caledon's descent into awfulness. The 'Being Scottish' Instagram feed is a riot when it comes to Scots language, idioms, and quirks. Perhaps the most important source of all was the UKBG's *International Guide to Drinks* (1955 edition), which inspired Archie's No. 1 and No. 2 pick-me-ups.

Two final dedications: Firstly to the Cairngorms, a place of unrivalled beauty and happy memories. Secondly, to the original occupants of that horrible concrete prison in which Mac wrote his story. Both the cell and the confessions on the walls (see *Hooray for the Next to Die*) are real; I saw them myself. I can only hope yours was a happy ending and you won't mind me using your words as a reminder of what people are capable of when we look the other way.

ABOUT THE AUTHOR

Michael Millar was an award-winning journalist before taking his pieces of silver and becoming a political lobbyist and corporate spin doctor. Before turning to the dark side, Michael reported from Iraq during the war; was business editor of BBC Radio 4's *Today* programme; and wrote, broadcast and dissembled for all sorts of programmes, websites and publications, some more august than others.

As a non-fiction author, Michael's previous work includes *The Secret Lives of Numbers* (Random House, 2012), which was a best-seller for the publisher and translated into several languages. In this book, Michael began to hone the writing style that drives his latest story. He is also co-author of *The Five-Minute Failure* (Rock-Hill Publishing, 2006).